ABANDONING THE SCRIPT

Linda Rosen

Black Rose Writing | Texas

The author grants the final approval for this literary material.

First printing

This is a work of fiction. Names, characters, businesses, places, events, and incidents are either the products of the author's imagination or used in a fictitious manner.

ISBN: 978-1-68513-723-6
LIBRARY OF CONGRESS CONTROL NUMBER: 2025946461
PUBLISHED BY BLACK ROSE WRITING
www.blackrosewriting.com

Printed in the United States of America
Suggested Retail Price (SRP) $20.95

Abandoning the Script is printed in Book Antiqua

*As a planet-friendly publisher, Black Rose Writing does its best to eliminate unnecessary waste to reduce paper usage and energy costs, while never compromising the reading experience. As a result, the final word count vs. page count may not meet common expectations.

ABANDONING THE SCRIPT

Praise for
Abandoning the Script

"Rich with heart and history, *Abandoning the Script* is a moving, multi-generational story of secrets, and sacrifice. Rosen's remarkable characters convey the resilience of women who are determined to find their own way in a world that wants to confine and define them. From Greenwich Village's trailblazing Heterodoxy Club to the secrets whispered within a family's walls, *Abandoning the Script* is an unforgettable journey into the secrets that can define us, and the courage that might set us free."
–Patti Callahan Henry, *New York Times* Bestselling author of *The Story She Left Behind*

"Linda Rosen's historical novel *Abandoning the Script* tackles the 1920s modern woman...her dreams, her choices, and the fight to see them through. Rosen expertly weaves the line between what women need, and what is best, culminating in a compelling novel rife with secrets, self-discovery, and the power of friendship and family. Engaging and immersive, Rosen delivers a deeply moving plot with a heartfelt conclusion."
–Rochelle Weinstein, bestselling author of *We Are Made of Stars*

"A timeless story of the power of personal choices and the consequences of following your heart wherever it leads you."
–Gail Ward Olmsted, best-selling author of the *Miranda Quinn Legal Twist* trilogy

"A heroine brave enough to make an exit to be true to herself despite the life and love she's abandoning."
–Janis Robinson Daly, bestselling author of *The Path* series

"This extraordinary page-turner, filled with unexpected twists and turns, will lead you to an unforeseen conclusion and questioning whether times have truly changed."
–Jane Loeb Rubin, award winning, bestselling author of the *Gilded City* series: *Threadbare, In the Hands of Women, Over There*

"*Abandoning the Script* is page-turning, historical feminist fiction about a woman ahead of her times. Linda Rosen sets back the clock and gets it all right. A thought provoking, imagination stoking trip back to New York in the 1920s."
–**Marilyn Simon Rothstein, author of *Who Loves You Best* and *Crazy to Leave You***

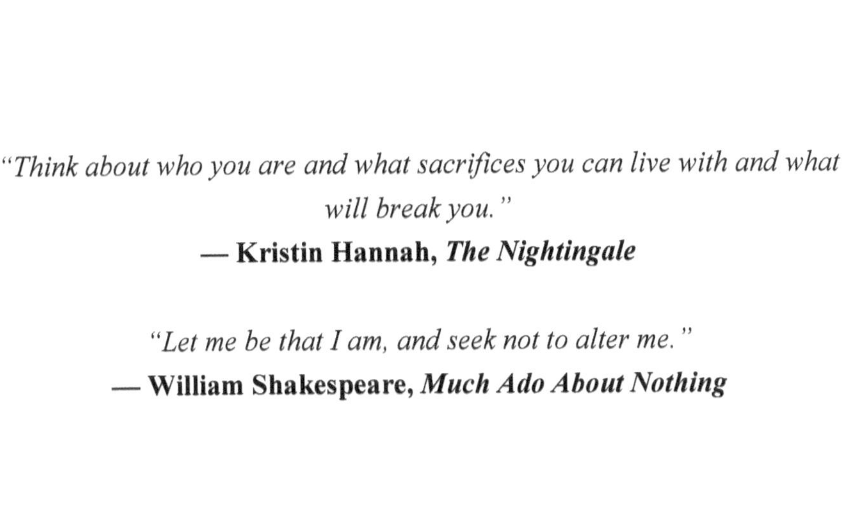

"Think about who you are and what sacrifices you can live with and what will break you."
— **Kristin Hannah, *The Nightingale***

"Let me be that I am, and seek not to alter me."
— **William Shakespeare, *Much Ado About Nothing***

Act One

Chapter 1

Saturday is finally here. I was afraid this day would never come. Wrapped in my wool coat, the raccoon collar warming my neck, I hurry down MacDougal Street, a scruffy block in Greenwich Village so different from mine across Washington Square where the "Manhattan mink brigade" lives. A Model T passes by, rumbling over the cobblestones, its clanking motor adding to the chatter of pedestrians strolling down the sidewalk. Arriving at number 137, I open the townhouse door and descend the stairs to Polly's Restaurant. It's where the Heterodoxy Club meets every other Saturday at 1 p.m.. Though on this particular day, despite the joy of finally being back, the restaurant's sunny yellow walls do not reflect my mood. I can't shake the chill from the day or the silent, never-ending, futile argument with my husband. It seems my jaw is constantly clenched, not to mention my neck and shoulders. The tension is always in the air and deep in the oak floors we tread. Thank goodness he's on rounds at the hospital today. Otherwise, I would never have been able to leave the house.

My mother-in-law, Mama Brandt, or Grandmama as we often call her, is at home with Rosy, our thirteen-month-old daughter. She doesn't realize her son is ignorant of the fact that

I'm out today. She also is unaware of the trouble in our marriage and has no idea of the demands he forces on me. He insists I be home at all times and often grumbles, "Lucy, be the mother you're supposed to be."

Mama Brandt believes I'm simply having lunch with girlfriends. I couldn't tell her I was going to a meeting. That must remain a secret. Mine and the club's. Even though the *New York Tribune* blew the lid off it a few years ago, divulging the names of a few prominent members, only the membership and some guest speakers know what really goes on in the Heterodoxy Club. We don't keep records. As the name suggests, it is a safe place that honors differences of opinion. A place where unorthodox women, artistically minded like myself or politically active, can discuss, doubt, and disagree freely. It's my haven. A place where I truly fit my skin, away from the crying and the diapers and the incessant demands my daughter makes for my attention. Here, at Polly's, I mingle with women of all ages. Bright women. Intelligent. Accomplished. Many the first in their fields. Women with a purpose. For years, they fought to get the vote and finally, last year, the Nineteenth Amendment passed. Today, our purpose, our topic of discussion is one of utmost importance. An option I wish I had. And one I wish my husband had agreed to. Birth control.

"Over here," Crystal calls from across the room, her arm raised, that ever-present bright red metal cigarette holder between her fingers.

Crystal is like a sister to me. We've been best friends since we were in baby carriages. A few years later, when we were skipping rope and playing Double Dutch, the carriages a distant memory, Helen moved into the neighborhood and we became The Inseparable Threesome, as her father calls us. The only time we were apart was for college. I stayed in the City attending Barnard. Crystal and Helen roomed together upstate at Vassar. And now, we're together again, all living in the Village though, unfortunately, I have the title of Mrs. and they retain Miss. My townhouse, on the tony north side of the Square, is a short walk across the park from the rooming house where they live on Thompson Street.

I wave, letting Crystal know I see her, and make my way through the wooden tables crammed close together, stopping to say hello to women I haven't seen in over a year. I reach our table and pull out a chair just as the woman next to me, in a tunic draped over loose pants, says, "We haven't seen you for ages. Have you been in another play? I imagine that keeps you very busy."

I recognize this woman as the socialist who was in my class at Barnard. She's now teaching uptown at Columbia University. Unlike me, who lives with her husband and child in a three-story red brick townhouse on the north side of Washington Square, this buxom woman shares an apartment with her lover. A children's author. They are like so many lesbian couples who feel free to be themselves in the club, in this intimate, safe setting. Some even have children. Kids they wanted. A tired sigh escapes my lips. Or is it a sad one? Or both?

A local artist whose paintings hang on the walls of the restaurant is seated to my left. "Between acting and the baby," she says, "I'm not surprised we haven't seen you. Your little one must be about one by now."

Crystal shoots me a pinched look. My tiny wave back lets her know I am not going to talk about myself. That's not what we do here. My fingers find my gold earring with the three tiny birthstones. Rubbing the amethyst, sapphire, and diamond, I smile at the artist, whose pendulous breasts sway freely in her embroidered caftan, and answer, "Just a month over and quite a bundle of energy. I don't have any time to act, as much as I'd like to."

Enough, I tell myself and drop my hands firmly in my lap. Don't go any further. She doesn't need to know I'm not allowed to act anymore. A sour tang fills my mouth simply thinking of the word allowed. I swallow the bitter taste. Forcing a brighter smile, I tell the artist how happy I am to be back at Polly's and talk about legalizing birth control. "I'm anxious to hear Margaret Sanger today. Don't you agree that birth control will liberate women?"

"Absolutely," she says. "Sanger is correct. Birth control will liberate women in the bedroom and the home."

My shoulders relax. The focus is no longer on me. I can speak on this topic for hours. I would love to be liberated. Before I can utter a word about it, she continues. "Liberate not only in the home but the larger community. Think of all the young women, girls, who should never have had their babies."

My hand goes to my earring again. I need to break this habit, so I grab a glass of water. It doesn't comfort me the way touching the earring does, but I sip the cool drink and think. I am certainly one of those women who shouldn't have had a baby. And suddenly, the night I conceived comes back to me playing like a silent movie. I had just slipped my ankle-length nightgown over my head when Charles came into the bedroom, furiously waving Marie Stopes' book, *Married Love: A New Contribution to the Solution of Sex Difficulties*, in the air.

"Have you read this garbage?" He shouted.

"Yes. But it's not garbage." I tried to keep my voice even.

His head shook. Anger blew from his mouth. I could see the fire in his eyes and how he tightened his shoulders, something he did whenever he needed to tamp it down. Whenever we argued about having children.

"Then you know," he grumbled, "that she suggests waiting two years after marriage before a couple has children. Even though I told you over and over again that I did not want to wait that long. And now," he tossed the book across the room. "We're married almost three years. When will you ever want to be a mother? What's wrong with you?"

I force myself to shake away those thoughts and join the conversation at the table. A contagious buzz flows through the room with Democrats, Republicans, socialists, anarchists, radicals, and liberals all voicing their opinions. Ideas burst forth as they always do in this intimate setting as the women consume plates of goulash, with its smokey paprika, or savory liver and onions. All prepared by Polly's lover, the anarchist Hippolyte Havel. It's simple, inexpensive fare. Food is never the important part of being at Polly's. It's merely to be consumed while we discuss radical ideas, Hippolyte's and others.

"Did you know Sanger went to jail?" one woman says. "All because of her talk about birth control."

"Not all because of her talk," Crystal says. "It was in 1916, only five years ago. I remember it well since it was the year I entered law school. The court in Portland, Oregon, where she was speaking, arrested her and the men who were selling her pamphlets. It was all political. Against the Comstock laws. The judge claimed her talk and written words which described birth control methods, pessaries, condoms, sponges . . ."

"I use the sponge," a woman across the table interrupts.

"Yes," continued Crystal. "Some of us do, but sponges as well as all the other methods, including vaginal tablets that Sanger supports, and douches were all in the pamphlet that sent her to jail. The court claimed her writing was obscene and, can you believe, a danger to the well-being of the nation."

Silverware clinks against dishes. Waiters pour water into cut-glass goblets. Women utter their frustration with the strangling laws prohibiting their personal freedoms. Yet I cannot get the discussions I've had with Charles out of my head.

"It is against the law," he reminded me when I first pleaded he use a sheath or allow me to use a cap. In the same didactic tone, he told me he could lose his medical license. That's a laugh. I doubt he would ever be arrested, as he claims. I can't imagine any officer of the law would actually look into what married couples do in the privacy of their bedrooms. Yet my argument holds no weight with him.

"It was only three months after her arrest," Crystal is saying when I bring myself back to the conversation, "that Sanger opened the first birth control clinic in the US. It was over in Brownsville, in Brooklyn."

Helen, seated next to Crystal, scrunches her nose. The tiny scar on its tip wiggles. It's from a cut she got years ago falling down the banister in the tenement house where, as new immigrants, she and her parents lived. "But that clinic closed," she says. "Then Sanger reopened it and they closed it down again. It went on for a while. She and her husband were arrested several times. One of my early assignments for *The Tribune* was an article on the clinic." She shakes her head and grumbles, "It's that damn Mr. Comstock and his preposterous laws."

A waiter approaches with a pot of coffee. The aromatic scent of chicory perfumes the air around the long wooden table. "You're talking about Mrs. Sanger?" he asks. "I heard she just started something called the American Birth Control League. They're talking about it over at that table." He points across the room.

"That has to help," the Columbia professor says. "Did you know Sanger was a midwife?" I nod. Some mumble "Mmm hmmm." Some look surprised. "That's why she calls this fight for birth control her life's mission," the professor adds. "She's going to talk about that after lunch, and I am one thankful woman to have someone like her lead us in this fight. She's seen so many tragedies from butchered abortions and all those unwanted pregnancies. It's . . . it's . . . just too awful."

A wave of sadness covers me like a shroud. Could my pregnancy have been termed a tragedy? I definitely did not want it, although now I do love my little girl. Yet I'm not like the women Sanger saw. I'm not poor, unwed, or an immigrant. I'm married. Unhappily. And grateful to be well-off. I sit back and cannot control the sigh that escapes my lips. Voices hum around me. I act as if I'm part of the conversation yet thoughts and scenarios play in my mind. One option keeps coming back to me, as frightening as it may be. For so many reasons. Yet it won't leave. I just have to figure out the details and if I really can do it.

Chapter 2

On the sidewalk, looking up at my townhouse, I square my shoulders and climb the white marble stairs. The meeting at Polly's was a welcome relief. It's what I needed to feel myself again. Craving just a few more moments of freedom, I lean against one of the ionic columns flanking the imposing entrance to my house and pull out a Craven "A" from my cigarette case. I flip the top on the sterling silver lighter Mama Brandt gave me for my birthday and watch the flint light the tip to a fiery red. Crimson and gold leaves draw my eyes to the trees lining the street and my mind wanders back to Margaret Sanger's speech from today and the ensuing conversation. I wish I was as strong a woman as she. Taking a deep drag on the ciggie, I wonder if I can ever truly stand up for what I want. What I need. I think about it all the time. Thoughts rattle around my head, my fantasy on how it will play out – and how I will actually feel if it does. Relief, yes. Excitement, certainly. But . . . *one last drag*, I tell myself. I pull the sweet tobacco deep into my lungs, bend my head back, and slowly blow rings of smoke up toward the cloudless sky. Then I put on my Mama face and step inside.

"I'm home," I say. Is my quiet announcement for my mother-in-law or for me, a reminder of who I'm supposed to be? My house key clinks as I drop it in the porcelain dish on the console table. With my gloves stuffed in my coat pocket, I hang it, along with my red cloche, in the foyer closet and walk down the hall to the parlor, my heels clicking on the parquet floor.

Mama Brandt looks so comfortable sitting in the brocade armchair catty-corner to the fireplace, the new Agatha Christie novel in her gently wrinkled hands. "Is Rosy napping?" I ask.

"Yes, finally. She just quieted. She was quite a bundle of energy today."

"Oh, I'm sorry." Though if I'm truly honest, I'm relieved it was Grandmama who had to deal with the baby rather than me. And I'm thankful she's so good with her.

Sitting on the settee opposite her, I wonder again why my acting career – or non-career as it is now – is more important to me than being a mother. While other little girls played with dolls, I dressed up as characters from my favorite books, making believe I was on stage playing the roles. I'd been entranced with acting ever since Nanny took me, at the young age of ten, to see my first Broadway play. For months after, I was Rebecca of Sunnybrook Farm playing the part for Nanny and Helen and Crystal. Often, Helen's mother's kitchen was my stage. I loved that Helen's parents were such an encouraging audience. And heartbroken mine were not. They rarely watched me perform.

I pick up the worn copy of *Mother Goose Nursery Rhymes* from the cherrywood end table. Nanny read it to me when I was a little girl. Running my fingers along the worn cover, I can almost feel her cushiony chest, as if I were snuggled against it, mesmerized by the poetry. Just this morning, I read these same rhymes to my daughter. And it felt wonderful having her nuzzle against me, which surprised me. I would have preferred to have been on stage playing the part of a mother rather than being a real one having to deal with crying and dirty diapers and heating bottles and . . . Staring into the fireplace, watching the flames dance on the logs, I wonder if my child will inherit my love of acting. Or will she be more like her physician father? That would be fine. Women can be anything they want. They just have to know they can be. And have the freedom to be that person.

"Did you have a lovely luncheon with your lady friends?" my mother-in-law asks.

I smile and nod. How I wish I could tell her about Margaret Sanger. I'm positive it would lead to an interesting conversation. Then I could share my aspirations to pursue an acting career, which Charles assumes he squelched. Mama Brandt is modern. How could she not believe in women's rights? In my rights. But being a Heterodite must stay secret. Charles, Mama Brandt's brilliant son, would never approve. There are a few husbands who do approve, who accompany their wives to Polly Holladay's restaurant. Those men are enlightened. Not like Charles who absolutely does not want a comrade, as Max Eastman claimed in his article in *The Times*. The journalist had once written that it was more fun to have a partner who was an equal. Charles laughed at that and tossed the newspaper aside.

"I'm happy for you, dear," my mother-in-law says. "You need to see your friends. Every woman does, and I'm so glad you're feeling better and are able to. You can always depend on me to stay with our precious Rosy Posy."

A rush of love runs through my body, with a bit of frustration sprinkled in. I need my mother-in-law to want to care for the baby, but I wish she understood that I hadn't been ill – that it was Charles who insisted I go to the lake house for all those months. He said it would cure my hysteria. But I wasn't hysterical. I was angry and frustrated, and being there would never cure my need to get back on stage. Charles refuses to accept that acting is what fulfills me. Not being a mother. And he refuses to hear another word about it. The arguing has been so incredibly draining, I finally had to give in. For over a year, I have played the dutiful wife. I'm not sure I can do it anymore.

It's not a role I ever wanted or one I'm cut out to be. I don't know how to be a mother.

A few days later I'm sitting at the kitchen table with *Variety* laid out in front of me. With a lit cigarette in one hand, I turn the page with the other, ignoring the article about Shubert bidding for the new vaudeville show to house at his theater. Instead, I scour the listings of auditions. I can't stop myself, even though, since Rosy's birth, Charles won't allow me to perform in another play. He was never thrilled having a wife in such an unsavory profession, as he calls it. Fortunately for me, the first two years of our marriage he worked nights. The war was going on and the hospital was in dire need of surgeons with most of the doctors overseas. Then, in 1919 the curtain closed for me. I became pregnant. Now the fruit of that pregnancy is in her high chair incessantly banging a spoon on the wooden tray, giving me a pounding headache. And all I want to do is read *Variety*.

Charles walks in. Noticing the magazine, his eyes pinch. "Another cold breakfast?" he grumbles then, without a glance toward me, turns to Rosy with a little triangle of toast in her hand, creamy butter and strawberry jam smeared across her little lips. I don't answer him. I simply get up and go to the icebox. His voice turns sugary sweet when he says, "Good morning, my sweet Rosy Posy." He kisses the top of her head and asks, "Should Daddy have cornflakes today or Muffets Shredded Wheat?"

"Fae fae," she says with a big grin.

Charles shoots me a glance across the room. His hooded eyes suddenly have a rare sparkle. He's a proud father. His little girl is starting to talk. I paste a smile on my face, then pull the bottle of milk from the ice box and lay it on the counter. "Who wants the yummy cream?" I ask, pretending to be the happy housewife. With a spoon, I scrape off the thick white layer on top and hold out the sweet treat. The baby bounces up and down in her chair. Charles laughs and says, "Let Rosy have it." I walk over. Playing my role, I gently slip the spoon into her open mouth. The cream paints a ring around her rosebud lips. It's the shape of those lips that made Charles give her the nickname Rosy just a few hours after she was born. I bristle thinking of how that name has stuck rather than the beautiful one I chose, the one in memory of my nanny. The name on her birth certificate.

Back at the counter, I'm about to pour cereal into a bowl for my husband. My eyes, though, stay on this refined, accomplished tall gentleman who is melting over a baby. Something I cannot do. I'm astounded at the way he dotes on her, wiping her little mouth and cooing and kissing her chubby body. He has never been as loving to me, not even when we were keeping company. Not that I wanted it – or the marriage. My parents insisted on it when Charles came calling, at his own parents' strong suggestion. He was a physician who needed a wife and I – already nineteen, heaven help me – was from a fine family, one they'd known for ages. Our parents met in Newport where they both had cottages on Belleview Avenue and large homes in New York City that came with the precious key to Gramercy Park. A prized possession for the wealthy owners. I swallow a bitter laugh, pouring the milk over his cereal and thinking how our parents, as well as Charles, believed I would give up my absurd, as they called it, ambition of having a life on stage once I was mistress of my own home. And what a home it is. It's on The Row, as Mother explained when she presented it to us as a wedding gift. A townhouse with "luxurious appointments" she said, "and an "elegant rear garden." I truly do not care about the appointments, but the garden is lovely. I'm happy digging in the dirt.

I serve Charles his cereal and coffee and sit opposite, sipping my own, pondering why he is so much more affectionate with Rosy than I am. I try. I just don't know how. It doesn't come naturally. I am simply not a nurturing woman, no matter how much I love my daughter. "What's on your mind?" Charles asks. "You look like you're contemplating the end of the world."

"Oh, nothing as serious as that." I stand and take the empty cereal bowl from his outstretched arm thinking, but you might think it is.

"Well, then you ladies have a lovely day." Charles bends and gives Rosy a loving tap on her tiny nose. "Bye-bye, sweetheart," he says. "Daddy has to go to work now. You eat up all your breakfast and have a fun day with Mama."

He looks at me with raised brows, as if to say, "Will you have a fun day?"

Sensing the sarcasm in his unsaid words, I answer with a casual air. "Oh, yes. We have lots of things planned for today." Then I swallow my thought – if only you knew where we're going.

Chapter 3

Rosy sits bright-eyed in her wicker stroller watching children running and playing, climbing on the rim of the fountain and jumping off. "One day soon you'll be joining them," I say, pushing the stroller across Washington Square, keeping my distance from the automobiles traversing the park. It's one of those autumn days in New York when Mother Nature is confused. Fallen leaves cover the sidewalks and grass, yet all we need is a light jacket. I look at the mothers sitting on benches talking with their friends. I view others, a few feet away from their rambunctious children, ready to grab an arm to prevent them from falling and scraping a knee or elbow. The heady aroma of roasted chestnuts drifts from street vendors' carts. My stomach quivers with the question, is this my future?

We arrive on the south side of the park, walk another block, and turn left onto MacDougal Street. Other than last Saturday, I hadn't been on this shabby narrow road in a very long time. It is one street in this big city that Charles prefers I don't frequent. But here I am. I stop three doors down from Polly's Restaurant, where I hope to go again. A woman in an embroidered silk kimono jacket with a matching headband steps out of The Provincetown Playhouse.

"Lucy," she says, spotting me on the sidewalk, "it's so wonderful to see you." She hurries over and glances in the stroller. "And this little girl is your daughter. How gorgeous."

I'm thrilled to see Susan again, to be here, on the sidewalk, chatting with this fabulous playwright. Instantly, I morph into the actress I'm meant to be, not the mother I am. The actress who once had a role in a Susan Glaspell play. It was right here, in the Playhouse, where I, a recent graduate from Barnard College, had rustled up my confidence and auditioned for her. And it was here I met Edna, who was fresh out of Vassar, the poet friend Helen and Crystal often spoke about. We became fast friends and since then her career has skyrocketed. And I've . . . oh, what's the use going over that again? I look down on my hands, fisted to the stroller so tightly my knuckles are white.

"Are you performing somewhere else?" Susan says. "I haven't seen you in ages."

I shake my head.

"Oh, of course, the baby."

There's a tinge of sadness in Susan's words. Perhaps because she's never given birth? Or is it sarcasm? Susan is a staunch feminist. But so am I, even though I have a baby. Many of us have children. Elizabeth Cady Stanton for one. She's deceased now but what a force she was. Even all those years fighting for women's rights, at the forefront of getting us the vote, she celebrated motherhood, something I don't know how to do.

"You were wonderful in *Women's Honor*," Susan says. "I was very lucky to have you and Edna in my play. Oh, did you know? You must," she says, throwing up her hands excitedly. "Edna is now writing her own plays."

"Yes, I'm happy for her." I lean over Rosy's stroller to adjust the crocheted blanket that doesn't need adjusting. Handing Rosy her favorite baby doll with glass eyes the same green color as hers and mine, I tell Susan I heard Edna will soon be setting up auditions for a full-length play. *Another Edna St. Vincent Millay masterpiece*, I think, fluffing the doll's short bob. The mohair is soft on my fingers. "It'll be here with the Provincetown Players," I say, finally looking up.

"You don't need to wait for that audition," Susan said. "Eugene is holding them now for his new play. It's called *The Hairy* . . ." She looks up squinting as if the sun is in her eyes even though we're completely shaded by a bounteous maple tree. "*The Hairy Ape*. Yes, that's it! Did you see the poster on the door? Auditions start next week. Oh, do come. There are only two female parts. I'm certain you could get one of them. It would be wonderful to have you back here with us." Then she glances at her wristwatch and says, "Sorry. I must run. Please, think about it."

I stand on the sidewalk a few more minutes, staring at the wooden door. This is why I came here, to find out if any auditions are going on. So why am I still out here on the sidewalk? Am I willing to take the risk? Yes. I can't control myself. With a bounce in my step, I push the stroller through the front door.

Chapter 4

The trolley stops at East Twentieth Street. With Rosy on my hip and the wicker stroller collapsed and firm in my left hand, we step off. "Stand right here," I tell Rosy as soon as we reach the sidewalk. "Hold onto my skirt while I open your stroller." This new style carriage truly is a blessing. I was stunned, yet happy, when Charles brought it home last week. After forcing me to stay home for all those months and sending me to the lake house, now he's okay with letting me visit my friends. As long as I take the baby with me. I see a different side of him. He seems to care about my well-being. He said the carriage, being collapsible, would make it easier for me to manage the steps in the rooming house when I visit Helen and Crystal. And it'll be easier to get up and down our own steps. So maybe he will be more amenable to my auditioning.

I push the stroller down the street heading to Helen's mother's home. Mrs. Stokes called yesterday and invited us for tea this afternoon. I could hear her excitement over the wires when I accepted. She adores Rosy. When she was born, Mrs. Stokes asked if she could be called Auntie Mabel. I loved that. I would like to have Rosy call her Gramma though my mother, who insists on being referred to as Grandmother, would not be pleased. Though how would she know? She hardly ever sees the baby. I can think of only two times in the thirteen months since she was born. It was Auntie Mabel who fed her cake at her first birthday party. My mother, Mrs. Stokes's Gramercy Park neighbor and supposed friend, wasn't even in attendance. It was simply too long a trip to make from Newport, where she spends most of her time. Why she keeps the townhouse next to Auntie Mabel's I have no idea.

Strolling along the tree-lined sidewalk across from the park, I remember all the times I played there with Helen and Crystal, running through the shrubbery and flowers. Once we were older, one of their mothers, or sometimes Nanny, would give us the key to go in by ourselves. We felt like such big girls unlocking the wrought-iron gate to our private park. As I gaze through the fencing, I sense a smile creep up my cheeks, something I don't often experience these days. It must be the day, coming to Auntie Mabel's and having been at the theater this morning speaking with Susan and Eugene. It would be wonderful to be in a Eugene O'Neill full-length play, on the stage of that old stable-turned-theater, and I wonder if Charles would be in the audience, sitting on the wooden benches watching. They are the most uncomfortable seats anywhere. Yet is that the only reason he wouldn't attend?

I pull the stroller backward up the stone steps to Auntie Mabel's front door and leave it on the portico. It's probably the only carriage that will ever be here. I doubt Helen will have children. She's determined to have a career as a journalist and often has said children would inhibit that. I agree, though her mother doesn't. Although her work was all volunteer, Mrs. Stokes was always busy with committee work, writing pamphlets arguing for women's right to vote. She may even have been in the Heterodoxy Club early on. She never mentioned it though. Neither have we.

"I wonder what special treat Auntie Mabel has for us today," I say, lifting Rosy from the stroller. There is always something savory or sweet wafting from her oven.

"Yum, yum," says the baby.

"Yes, a yum yum. Let's go see." I tap the big brass knocker against the black-painted door.

"Oh, my little Rosy Posy," Mrs. Stokes says the moment she opens the door. "Come to Auntie." She takes Rosy from my outstretched arms and cuddles her against her big, soft bosom. I follow them into the townhouse, and we settle ourselves around the familiar oak table in the kitchen, my daughter in her very own high chair that Helen's father purchased as soon as Rosy was big enough to sit up. Conversation always flows comfortably in this love-filled kitchen, and I find myself spilling my troubled thoughts and doubts while Rosy plays with her wooden alphabet blocks on the high chair's tray.

"What if he forbids it?" I say after telling Mrs. Stokes about talking to O'Neill this morning, and the upcoming audition.

"Forbid?" she says, cutting us each a piece of freshly baked babka, her special sweet coffee cake. "Lucy, you are a strong woman. You've always known what you want and nothing ever stopped you. Why is this happening now? Are you frightened of Charles?"

"Oh no. He would never do anything to hurt me physically, but . . ." I throw up a palm as if to remind her that he sent me to the lake house for three months. He wanted me away from my friends and the theater and to be alone with the baby. I shudder thinking of those months when Charles would travel back and forth to the city, staying in town most of the time, leaving me alone with Rosy, and occasionally his mother, with only ourselves and the voices on the radio for company. He insisted I needed the time to bond with my daughter, and the lake would calm my nerves. My teeth clench merely thinking about it.

Mrs. Stokes must understand what I mean because she tells me I mustn't give up. "Tell him how you feel," she says, tearing up a piece of the cake and feeding it to Rosy.

"I have!" I slap my hands hard on my thighs. "He doesn't care."

She shoots me a look. I can't tell if there's pity in her expression or frustration. I suppose I deserve both. I should have fought harder. But then he would have confined me to my bed for the "rest cure." He still might, if I bring up acting again.

"Lucy, dear, marriage is not easy. It's a compromise. Sometimes we have to give in to keep our partner happy, even though . . .

"I have. And I'm tired of it."

She sits forward, fingers holding the edge of the table. "I'm not saying you should give in. What I mean is, you should bring this up with Charles." I stare at her with wide-open eyes. "Yes, I know," she says. "You have and it didn't work out well. But think about it this way. Some men want to control their wives. Charles is one, yet the Lucy I know is not the type of woman who will allow that. I don't believe you have ever let anyone control you. So why do you now?"

Yes, why do I?

"Tell Charles," she says, "you'll be a better mother if you feel fulfilled. Unless you can do your art, your passion, you never will be. It's what you've been trained for, as he was trained to be a doctor. Remind him you are not a woman to sit at home and have tea with your lady friends." She laughed and said, "Well, once in a while. But you know what I mean."

I lift my teacup in a toast and we go on with the discussion. Mrs. Stokes reminds me again that marriage is a compromise. "Help Charles understand that a good marriage is based on wanting to make your partner happy. Let him know that you want his happiness, but you need your own too. Be strong dear. I have faith in you. You can do this."

I look at Rosy happily mushing cake crumbs on her high chair tray. Then I look at Auntie Mabel and the china tea cups in front of us. I twirl my earring, contemplating. A plan begins to form in my mind. A lightness grows in my chest.

Chapter 5

The theater door closes behind me. I step out onto MacDougal Street, hurry to the corner, and turn left. Light snow falls as I reach Sixth Avenue, putting everyone in the holiday mood. On the corner, the Salvation Army bell ringer is swinging his hand high in the air, the bell clanging loud and strong. Women in coats with fur collars and men wearing fedoras walk along smiling. We might just have a white Christmas. It all seems perfect.

My day has been perfect. Working in the theater again has lifted my spirits, and I can't wait to tell Crystal about it. I practically skip down the few blocks to the Jefferson Market Court House. We're meeting at one o'clock when she gets out of court. We'll have a quick lunch across the street. I hope Helen can make it. She said she'd try but she's working on a big piece for "The Literary Review" that's supposed to run in tonight's *New York Evening Post*. I'm so happy for her. The editor, Amy Loveman, offered her this spot, and Helen, my friend the avid reader, loves this opportunity. Seems like we both have something to celebrate today though it'll have to be over coffee. Another time we'll have a Manhattan or a Sidecar. *Yes*, I think, waving as I spot Crystal on the courthouse steps. *That's a great idea. We'll go to Club Gallant one night, that speakeasy where O'Neill and lots of actors party.* Then, for a split second, darkness seeps into my chest. I toss that worry away. I'll figure it out. Just like I figured out working in the Playhouse. I'll come up with a plan so Charles doesn't know I'll be going to a speakeasy.

Seated across from Helen and Crystal, I give my soup order to the waitress with a big bust and bright red lipstick. Then I lay my forearms on the wooden table, lean in, and tell them, "I'm back at the theater." Their bright eyes and big smiles let me know they're thrilled. "But this time," I say, leaning back against the booth, "I'm backstage with costumes and whatever help the stagehands need."

"What? Why?" Crystal asks.

"I wasn't right for the part. There are only two women in the play and . . ."

"Are you really okay with that?" Helen says. Her words come out slowly and there's that squint of hers, the one the journalist in her uses when she thinks there's more to the story.

"Yes. I am. Honestly. Of course I was disappointed, but it's an O'Neill play. And Eugene is right. It's not my part." I take a sip of water then continue. "As he says, there will be others. And Susan Glaspell has a new play. She wants me to audition for it. It's more suitable for me than *The Hairy Ape*. That one is a commentary, a statement on the distance between the wealthy upper class and the working class."

Helen chuckles. "Maybe it hits too close to home."

I consider her words. "Could be. Plus, it's very dark and I need something uplifting. Something fun."

"How in the world did you ever get Charles to agree? To let you go back to work?" Crystal asks.

The waitress comes back and sets our lunches on the paper placemats in front of us. Whiffs of savory potatoes and leeks tease my taste buds. I take one spoonful of the delicious soup and smile. A very satisfied one, not only for the soup but for how I dealt with Charles.

"I didn't tell him I was going for the audition," I say, holding Helen's eyes with mine. Her lashes are gorgeous, the longest I've ever seen. "Actually, your mother kept Rosy for me. A few weeks ago when we had tea, she encouraged me and helped me come up with the words I needed to say to him. And they worked." Helen and Crystal both raise their brows. I almost laugh. "Are you wondering what Mrs. Stokes suggested, or are you surprised that whatever I said worked?"

"Both," Crystal says.

"Per her suggestion, I told Charles I could never be a good mother if I wasn't fulfilled, and working in the theater is what does it for me. He wasn't happy when I reminded him that just as he trained to be a doctor, I trained to be an actress and I should be able to use my training as he does. He gave me the money argument, that he makes more than I will ever make and how I am needed at home, that my job is being a mother. I wanted to roar like a trapped animal but knew I had to calm down if I wanted him to agree. The conversation went on practically all night. I think he was so tired of hearing me, and surprised I wasn't giving in or crying, that he finally said it was okay, as long as I was home in the evening."

"How can you be?" Helen says. "The show plays at night."

"Right now, we're in rehearsal. We just started this week and most of the work will be during the day." I shrug. "I'll deal with the night situation when I have to. I'm no longer afraid of Charles. He knows," I say, nodding my head for emphasis, "that I am not hysterical. He cannot play that game with me anymore. No. Not anymore."

Oh, that feels good, I think taking another spoonful of this rich, creamy soup. Simply saying those words aloud cements them deep in my core. *Just let him try.*

Chapter 6

Clasping the crocheted pot holders in my hands, I pull the cranberry pudding from the oven, the deep red fruit bubbling around the edges just like Nanny's used to. The sweet scent of cranberries mixed with brown sugar, a touch of cinnamon, and pinch of nutmeg infuse the air. I place the pudding on the silver tray Mother gave us for our first Christmas as a married couple. She handed it to me in her drawing room, perfectly wrapped in silver paper with a satin bow and said it would bring back wonderful holiday memories of my childhood. Sadly, it doesn't. It's what's on the tray that evokes love, the only real love I ever felt on Christmas. As always, that came from Nanny.

"That smells wonderful, dear," Charles says as I place my surprise dessert in the center of the large dining room table. At his insistence, we are hosting Christmas dinner. Before the baby was born, we had formal holiday dinners in my parents' townhouse in Gramercy Park. Last year, when Rosy was just two months old, we were invited to Helen's parents' home. It didn't matter that Christmas wasn't their holiday. They enjoy having company. And as they say, we are not company – we are family. And family should be together on holidays, no matter whose holiday it is. That's why my mother-in-law was included in the invitation. My own mother was in Newport. Now the same party sits at my table. A genuine smile pulls my cheeks for the first time in months.

"I wondered what you were planning when you refused my help," Mama Brandt said with a little glint in her eye. "The dessert looks as delicious as the entire meal has been. Bravo."

I give my mother-in-law a little wink. She's keeping our secret. Not only did my husband want to host the holiday dinner, he wanted me to prepare the meal. "You can do this," he said the night he announced his plan. "You are a woman. Women cook. And as you once said, you do not want us to employ a cook. Therefore, my dear, the job falls to you. You will have to take some time away from the theater."

That damn haughty expression of his. It makes me want to throw something at him. Anything! Not only because of the theater. Rehearsals were postponed for the holiday. It was because even the casual weeknight dinner is an enormous challenge for me. Though it's true, I don't want to hire a cook. I don't want to be like my mother or her hoity-toity friends. Even though Charles grew up with a cook, his mother dabbled a bit in the kitchen. Over the few years of my marriage, she taught me to make some simple meals – baked pork chops, meatloaf, roast chicken, and Charles's favorite, salmon croquettes. Thankfully, peas, corn, and tomatoes come in metal cans. And now I understand which knife to use to slice bread from the bakery and which to carve a chicken, though I'm grateful Charles takes on that job, as he did this afternoon with my very first roasted turkey. Mama Brandt helped with the chestnut stuffing and minty peas and onions while Charles was at the hospital.

Most girls in the social set I grew up in rarely entered a kitchen unless Cook invited us to taste her freshly baked cookies. Helen is different. She knows her way around a kitchen and admits she enjoys it. That's because there was love emanating from the walls in her mother's kitchen. Her mother didn't grow up privileged, as my mother did. Mrs. Stokes comes from a little village in Russia – a shtetl, she calls it – quite the opposite of my mother who believes she's a Mayflower descendant with all the accoutrements of wealth. It wasn't until Helen was nine that her father became successful and they moved from the crowded tenements on the Lower East Side to our tony neighborhood on Twentieth Street.

We consume the cranberry pudding along with cups of coffee and aromatic tea. Helen, Crystal, and I carry the dirty dishes into the kitchen and stack them in the sink while the older women play with Rosy in the parlor. We leave the Wedgewood soaking in warm soapy water and go to join them.

"It's time to open the presents," I say, passing through the dining room where Charles along with Helen and Crystal's fathers still sit in their suits and ties sipping the brandy Charles collected before prohibition became law.

Charles shoots me a nasty look. Was he still annoyed with my wearing pants? How many times does he have to look at my outfit as if it is the most distasteful he has ever seen? I strut by, enjoying the silky sensation of my harem pants against my thighs and how they flow so freely with each step I take.

In the parlor – the room Mother insisted would be perfect for company – I take a moment to view the formal beadboard and the Persian rug. She had this room, and the rest of the townhouse, decorated for us while we were on our honeymoon on Lake George.

Charles was more affectionate then. He was tender with me on our wedding night. I was so frightened, not knowing what to expect. Petting was not new to me, but the actual sex act was a mystery. Standing in front of him in our hotel room, I couldn't move a muscle as he slipped the negligée off my shoulders. My hands flew across my chest, covering my bare breasts. But Charles gently uncrossed them saying, "You're beautiful. Let me see you." And I let him. Oh how I tingled from the intoxicating touch of his fingers on my skin! And later, he awoke passions in me I could not contain, sensations I never imagined. He taught me the magic of lips and tongue as his kisses traveled from my mouth to my neck down to my small breasts. He ignited a heat between my legs so fierce I could barely control myself. Oh dear, why am I thinking of this now?

I try to push away this picture of us in that soft bed when his tongue slipped from my navel to my mound. I shake the image of me clutching his bottom, pulling him deeper into me. He made me adore sex. I still do. But does that mean I have to love him? Obey him? Yes, he is phenomenal in bed but as a husband . . .? I grab a shiny package tied with a pink bow from under the tree and read the card.

"This pretty package is for Rosy," I say. Charles snatches it from me. I watch him help his daughter rip the paper and open the box.

"Baby," she says, holding her new doll to her little chest.

Charles runs his fingers over the doll's hair. "Blond, just like yours," he tells Rosy who is sitting on his lap. He ruffles her soft curls.

I leave them to play with Rosy's new baby doll, reach for another gift and continue handing out Christmas presents. Helen thanks Charles and me for the linen stationery we gave her, engraved with her initials. Crystal adores the silver filigreed cigarette case. I reach under the Christmas tree and take out my gift to Charles. He smiles as I hand it to him and for a moment I see the man he was at the beginning of our marriage, before talk of pregnancy and avoiding pregnancy became our daily conversation.

"Thank you," he says, lifting the black-and-gold Waterman fountain pen. "This is perfect, dear. Now for my gift to you." His eyes slip to my pants and, once more, I see disgust in his eye. Then he gives me a little peck on the cheek, more for show, and steps back and says, "That's a lovely fragrance you're wearing. I don't recognize it."

"Chanel No. 5," I say. "It's new."

Charles looks at me as if to say, "Who gave it to you?" Could he be jealous? I admit, that gives me a tingle. "I bought it the day before yesterday, in Bloomingdales. A gift to myself."

"Oh, I didn't realize you would have time to go uptown."

Everyone is staring at us. I ignore his sarcasm and give him a coquettish smile. "I had to buy your present, didn't I?" Helen giggles and I look at my guests as if to say, "It's true, isn't it? I had to." My making light of the issue seems to satisfy Charles. I believe he likes that I traveled all the way uptown to his favorite department store. One more plus in the positive column for me. I do keep trying. As Mrs. Stokes says, marriage is a compromise. I will cook a holiday dinner and take time away from the theater to buy him a gift. *Will he keep his promise of compromise*, I wonder as I take my present from him and untie the ribbon.

"Al Jolson." I hold the record album up for everyone to see. "Oh, thank you, Charles. This is from *Bombo*, his new show on Broadway. I'm so anxious to see it." I swallow my question. There's no sense asking it. Most likely I'll go with Helen and Crystal again. As always, it'll be much more fun with them. "And another album," I say, looking at the maroon cover with the words "Second Hand Rose" across the top and, in smaller print, "F. Ziegfeld Jr. Presents," then in a much bolder print, "Ziegfeld Follies of 1921." I wanted so much to see Fanny Brice in *The Follies*, but that's when Charles sent me to the godforsaken lake house for the rest he believed I needed to cure me from the hysteria he claimed I had. I shudder, thinking about that time in a house in the middle of nowhere, without a telephone, where we still lit our lamps with gas and had only recently installed indoor plumbing. He must think my incarceration worked since I'm no longer having screaming fits, as he called them. But that's not why I stopped.

I sit and let Charles continue handing out the rest of the Christmas presents. Helen's mother, seated on the upholstered armchair, turns to me. "How are rehearsals going for *The Hairy Ape*?" she asks. "Is it true the show might move uptown to the Plymouth Theater?"

Charles's hand freezes in midair. A gold-wrapped present dangles from his fingers. He is staring at me with a look as dark as the colors of our burgundy furniture.

"Where did you hear that?" I say.

"In a restaurant a few doors down from the theater. I was there last Thursday," Mrs. Stokes says. "You know, Polly's. I hadn't been there in years. I used to go when you girls were away at college, during the war. Our men were fighting overseas, and we women were here fighting for the vote."

Is she signaling me she was in the Heterodoxy Club? Or still is? I always suspected so, though other than Rose and Anna Strunsky, there have hardly been any Jewish women in the club. I laugh to myself, thinking I'm not surprised. Mrs. Stokes is a force.

"Anyway," she continues, "Susan Glaspell was there and I couldn't help overhearing their conversation. It seems the rehearsals have been contentious – that O'Neill and Cook, his director if I'm not mistaken . . .?"

"That's correct," I say.

"Well, it seems they have some differences of opinion, though I wasn't able to make out everything being said. I didn't want it to look as if I was eavesdropping, even though I was." She winks. "I just hope if it does move uptown it won't stop you from continuing with the show. I know how much this means to you."

My eyes go to Charles. He's handing a gift to Helen's dad. The vein in his throat pulsates. I know he's listening to my conversation with Mrs. Stokes. He isn't even aware her husband is thanking him for the present, and I do not like that angry look in his eyes. The floral-papered walls feel as if they're closing in on me. Compromise, I say to myself. It's his turn now.

Chapter 7

The dishes are done, drying on the drainboard. Before they left, Crystal and Helen stored the leftover food in Pyrex, a brilliant invention. These new glass dishes, which Mrs. Stokes gave me last Christmas, can go from the icebox directly to the oven. Perfect for someone like me who finds cooking every night a chore.

Everyone has gone home and I'm in the nursery putting the baby to bed when I hear Charles's voice. "No," he says, loud enough for it to ricochet up the twelve steps to Rosy's room. I stop, the diaper pin between my lips, Rosy on the table with the cloth covering her privates, waiting to be fastened.

"But she's such a good actress," I hear my mother-in-law say. *Oh, how lovely*, I think, pinning the diaper closed. Her words warm me. Their voices become softer, more conversational. I slip the rubber pants over the diaper then carry Rosy to the open door to hear their words more clearly. Rocking side to side to keep my daughter quiet, I breathe in the floral scent of Johnson's Baby Powder. Her little head drops onto my shoulder and her breath softens.

"You didn't see her in *Hobohemia*," Mama Brandt is saying. "Sinclair Lewis's short story. She practically stole the show."

Charles must be grumbling because Grandmama goes on saying he should not prevent me from pursuing my dream, that I'm talented, and that he should be proud of me. *My goodness, I never knew she felt this way.*

Their voices lower. I realize they must be moving to the parlor so I go into the hall and walk down a few steps. I hear Charles saying, "She should be at home taking care of Rosy, taking care of our home, not on stage like some vamp." I gasp and quickly clamp my lips shut. *Vamp? I am not a vamp. As much as I'd like to be in the movies, I am not Theda Bara. How dare he call me a seductress. Those aren't the parts I play.*

My mother-in-law is calming him down. Her voice is softer, forcing me to go down a few more steps. What I hear makes me smile. "Lucy has many wonderful attributes and she's very talented." I love that she's defending me. She's on my side. Her next words, the ones she says just as emphatically as when she told Charles not to call me a vamp, hit hard. "Lucy is not a loving mama." My pumped-up chest deflates, despite the fact I know she's right. My eyes go to the dark oak floor beneath my feet. I wonder what Charles is thinking. He must have agreed because her next words expound on this thought. "Yes, son," she says. "Lucy does not want to be with her daughter. I'm the one who sits on the floor playing with Rosy, with building blocks or having a make-believe tea party. Sometimes Lucy reads to her but she's never truly engaged. She doesn't show Rosy pictures or ask her questions. She recites the words aloud as if reading a script though not paying any attention to her audience." I hear Charles's voice but can't make out his words, only the grumbling tone, though my mother-in-law's are clear. "You have to face it, son. Lucy is like her mother. There is not an ounce of nurturing in her bones. Allow her to be on stage and do what she loves. She will be a better mother for it. Let me care for Rosy."

~

The silence is soothing. Charles is driving his mother home in our new Sheridan Touring Car and the baby is asleep upstairs. I sit on the settee in the parlor, sliding my hand over the cool silk upholstery, reviewing the conversation I overheard. Mama Brandt is correct. I am not a nurturer, yet hearing those words made me restive and I don't understand this uneasiness in my belly. Perhaps it's best she reminds Charles of the fact that I'm not a good mother so he will be more amenable to my leaving Rosy in her care. And not only for when I'm at the theater.

I reach over to the mahogany end table and pick up my cigarette case, the Fabergé with the yellow-and-gold ribbed cover that Charles gave me last Christmas. A disturbing thought comes to mind. What if Charles is at home Saturday and not in the hospital? I slip a Craven "A" from the case, flick the top on the cigarette lighter, and inhale as the blue-white flame meets the tip. He might be more willing now, after speaking with his mother, to let me have lunch with my girlfriends, which is what I'll tell him. Or maybe I'll say I have a rehearsal. Anything but the truth, which is I'll be going to Polly's for a Heterodoxy Club meeting. "Oh," I sigh. "It'll be so much easier if he's working."

Pushing that thorny scenario out of my mind, I walk over to the phonograph in the corner of the room. Mother added this fancy Silvertone machine to the decor. I open the top and rotate the crank, turning it on. I have a little more time to myself, with him driving his mother home, to enjoy my new Fanny Brice album. As impersonal as it is, I'm happy with Charles's gift. He may not enjoy the theater or want me in it, but at least he's willing to let me listen to its music. Slipping the shellac record from its case, I'm careful to handle it by the edges, as Nanny taught me years ago. I place the album gently on the green felt mat, release the brake, and, to use Nanny's words, get the machine up to speed. Carefully, I place the needle on the running groove and am transported to the stage as Fanny Brice's voice fills the room. Although I prefer playing more serious parts and don't want to be in the Ziegfeld Follies with Miss Brice, I did have a wonderful time singing in the Greenwich Village Follies a few years ago. Charles didn't come to watch. He would never set foot in a theater anywhere near Christopher Street, no matter how much I told him he would enjoy it. The Follies were a parody of life in the Village. There were numbers spoofing the newly ratified Eighteenth Amendment with robust songs about bootlegging, wine, and gin. Being such a stick-in-the-mud, as Crystal describes him, Charles didn't think it would be funny.

"You're enjoying the album," Charles says, entering the parlor. I nod and thank him again then ask how the drive went. "I saw two accidents," he says. "People don't know how to drive." His tone is curt. His strong, square jaw tightens. I sense he's holding something back. I continue smoking, listening to Fanny sing about her man. Charles walks to the liquor cabinet and pours himself a highball. "Want one?" he asks, looking over his shoulder at me. I tell him yes. Not that I believe this will be a cozy moment with my husband, sipping bootlegged gin together in our parlor after all the company has gone home.

"It was a lovely holiday," I say, hoping to soften his demeanor. I continue with words he likes to hear. "I'm glad you wanted me to cook the meal and I enjoyed doing it. It seemed to be a success."

"Yes. It was. And the tree is lovely. You did a good job with that." He turns toward me, his feet planted like a soldier at attention, his drink firmly in his hand. "But your outfit. What were you thinking?"

Swallowing a frustrated sigh that's fighting to escape, I glance down at my jewel-toned harem pants, a bold sapphire-blue and bright-yellow pattern ringed in shiny gold. "It's the style," I say, keeping the irritation out of my voice. "Do you object to the colors? I know they're not the subdued tones you prefer. But Rosy likes them."

"It is not the colors and not even the absurd flouncy style." His hands make big circles in the air. "They are trousers," he says, enunciating each word. "You cannot wear trousers."

I bristle. I will not let him control what I wear.

"They are illegal," he growls with a tightly clenched jaw. Then he takes a swig of his drink and plops down on the chair facing me.

"That's baloney, no one cares. No one's being arrested anymore. Not in the City." I want to tell him not to be ridiculous, though words like that only make him angrier and lead to arguments. And that only leads to me being called hysterical. I cannot let that happen again. Not ever.

Leaning back against the chair, his ankle resting on the opposite knee, he looks like a king, which he thinks he is, giving a decree. "No wife of mine will be seen in trousers," he says. "You will be a proper doctor's wife and wear dresses like Crystal and Helen. They're fashionable women and looked lovely today. They were wearing that new style, that long waist," he says, brushing his hands down from his shirt to his lap as if showing me what a dropped waist looks like. "Not those bizarre pants you have on. I'm taking you shopping. I'll buy you proper clothes and those long ropes of pearls too."

"I have the pearls," I whisper and say no more. Mrs. Stokes's words come back to me. Compromise.

Chapter 8

Sitting on the Windsor rocking chair in the nursery, I stretch out my arms toward Rosy. Her tentative steps and the proud look on her face are adorable. She's been walking for several weeks, ever since New Year's Eve when Charles got so excited I thought he would cancel our dinner reservations at Luchow's simply to watch her do it again and again. It is cute seeing her toddle, though I don't applaud every new thing she does and smother her with kisses. Charles and his mother do that. I can't. It simply isn't automatic for me.

"Grandmama is here," I say, hearing the front door open. My daughter's face lights up. I call out to my mother-in-law, letting her know we're upstairs.

"And how is my sweet little girl?" Grandmama says as she enters the pastel-pink nursery. Rosy flops down on the floor and, as fast as a bunny, crawls to her grandmother. She lifts her little arms, wanting Grandmama to pick her up. I stand and give my mother-in-law the seat.

"Before you go," Mama Brandt says, "I want to talk to you for a moment." Her voice is more serious than usual. I stiffen, wondering what she wants to say, though I keep a nonchalant tone when I answer, "Of course. I'm not in a hurry."

"I'm glad you're going out with your lady friends again," she says. "As I told Charles several weeks ago, I am more than happy to stay with Rosy and let you go to rehearsals and wherever else you want, like last week when you wanted to see the movie with Lillian Gish —"

Cutting her off, I say, "I'm so sorry. I never wanted to get you in the middle of our argument. I didn't know Charles would come home early that day or that he would be angry that you came to mind Rosy." I decide to tell her what I realize she already knows. But I want her to hear it from me. To keep my fury from erupting, I clasp my hands and squeeze them tightly. "It's not that Charles doesn't want you to mind Rosy," I tell her. "It's that he wants *me* to be with her. All the time. He doesn't want me to go out. He thinks he's doing me a favor by *letting* me work in the theater and that *that* should be enough."

"Yes, dear, I know. And I have spoken to him about it. You need to be in the theater and I hope one day you *will* be on stage again. I know it's what you love. And it *is* important for every woman to go out with her friends once in a while. I understand that very well. Sadly, Charles learned from his father. And I do not want to see you stifled, as I was. Times are different now. There are women who have jobs. Careers. Like Helen and Crystal. Although Charles believes they will never marry, or if they do, they will have to give up their jobs."

"That does happen. In teaching, for sure, but I don't think so in the law or . . . ." I could go on and tell her even in her day, though rare, there were women who had careers. There was the actress Mary Shaw, one of the first Heterodoxy members and the writer, Charlotte Perkins Gilman. I shiver thinking of her novella, *The Yellow Wallpaper*. It disturbed me when I read it in college. It still does. The way she depicted a woman's mental deterioration frightens me. It was due to men's oppression – her husband's and the doctors foisted upon her who refused to understand how depressed she was after her baby was born. I shake these thoughts from my mind – they're too close to home – and begin telling my mother-in-law that Crystal has no interest in marrying. She interrupts. I can tell she wants to say more so I slide down onto the soft carpet, adjust my skirts over my knees, and cross my ankles. I can be a little late for today's meeting. Right now, this conversation is more important.

"I have an idea," my mother-in-law says as she places Rosy on the floor and, with a kiss on the cheek, tells her to go play with her blocks. "I'm going to sell my house." My eyes open wide. "Yes. I've given this a great deal of thought. I've already sold the cottage in Newport and , truly, have no need for all the space I have here. The house is too large for one old woman. I don't entertain like I did when Mr. Brandt was alive. I spend more time here in your townhouse than in my own. Therefore it makes sense I move in with you. If you agree, of course."

It doesn't take me long to realize this would be the perfect solution so I assure her I do. "I have already discussed this with Charles. Although he thinks it's a good idea, I actually think he likes that he won't have to drive me all the way uptown after spending a long, exhausting day with patients. I wouldn't move in if you were opposed."

I promise her I'm not and she goes on laying out more reasons, all unnecessary. I'm already sold on the idea.

~

The restaurant is buzzing. I pull out the chair Crystal saved for me and sit. "How come you're late?" she asks.

I tell her about my conversation with my mother-in-law and how I assured her I would love her to move in. "She's aware of how much Charles wants to control me, and she doesn't like it. I even told her about our argument over the harem pants I wore on Christmas."

"What did she say?"

"Well, she did bring up the fact that it's illegal for women to wear trousers and agrees with me it's a non-issue. But she believes it's more about men controlling women. She basically told me that her husband controlled her, and this prohibition against women wearing slacks is a symbol of our broader struggle. Our struggle for the rights we deserve."

"Was Mama Brandt a suffragist?"

"Not that I know. I never heard of her going to any marches. Her husband probably wouldn't have allowed it."

"Well, I like her even more now," Crystal says. "And she's correct. This business about men telling us what we can wear . . . that's just another right we have to fight for." She takes a forkful of goulash then points the empty tines at the room. "Look around. There are several women in trousers here. But don't forget that story I told you about Etta Caulfield, the young woman who was arrested for wearing them."

"That was Halloween night, you said. And the magistrate let her go."

"But he almost didn't. I was in the courtroom when he told her she couldn't dress as a man and he was sending her to be fingerprinted. If it wasn't for the court reporter reminding him that it was Halloween, she probably would have gone to jail, as crazy as it seems."

"Shhh," the woman seated next to Crystal says. "You're absolutely right about the clothing issue, but Elsie is about to speak."

The room quiets as the speaker rises from her chair. My eyes follow anthropologist and sociologist Elsie Clews Parsons to the front of the dining room. She's a sister alum of Barnard, though she graduated in 1896, the year I was born. She's in her late forties and I think looks stronger and healthier than I do at twenty-five. Her complexion has a lovely copper tint, probably due to her being out in the field studying the Pueblo Indians.

"Did you hear that she's been in Mexico and even Peru?" the woman who shushed Crystal whispers to everyone at the table. I'm impressed. All I want to do is go uptown to a theater and her husband doesn't mind her traipsing all over the map, leaving her children at home.

I'm so engrossed in her words, my coffee turns cold. My back straightens when Elsie says, "Like many of you here, the root of my ideas stems from my upbringing, especially conflicts with my mother. I was born in New York, into wealth and privilege, and raised to be a society wife."

Oh, my heavens. That's my story. And she's just a few years younger than my mother. Yet Mother would never own ideas anywhere near Elsie's. Stroking my earring, I glance at Crystal, who I'm sure knows exactly what I'm thinking, then turn back, enraptured by Elsie's story of when she was in her teens and shut herself in her bedroom for two days rather than put on stays.

"My mother insisted I wear that stiff, fully boned garment under my dress," she says. "To have that desired tiny waist. Men's desire, not mine." Elsie uses her hands to show us the triangle women were supposed to have. Bigger bust, narrow waist. "Only I refused," she says. "My mother dismissed it as a silly act of rebellion. But it was more. Those stays were incredibly restricting. We were trapped in that wire cage with no room to breathe and no freedom to move. They not only shaped our bodies, they psychologically tried to shape our lives."

Touching my midriff, I remember the bones of the corset Mother used to insist I wear. Elsie is correct. Maybe corsets are softer than stays, but the bones in them are just as restrictive. I only wore mine when Mother was around. I laugh to myself, picturing the bottom drawer in my armoire where I stuffed them when I left for college. I thought I was finally free.

"Yes," Elsie says. "We got the vote but suffrage was only a small part of women's emancipation. Our liberation is a much larger issue."

Applause resounds. Women are on their feet clapping. Emily waits a moment, then continues and the cheering dies down.

"In my book, in all of my writings, especially *The Family*, which I wrote many years ago under a male pseudonym, I advocated for birth control. As you probably know, I was identified and excoriated in the press for my views."

Over the years, I'd heard about her book. Curious about the concepts, I read it while at Barnard. Elsie didn't only advocate for birth control. She was in favor of trial marriage where a couple could separate if the marriage didn't work out, without suffering public condemnation. But that would only be if there were no offspring. The idea of a trial marriage intrigued me at the time. It might have been a good idea for Charles and me. But then I didn't know how unsuccessful my marriage would be until Rosy was born.

"Marriage and monogamy," Elsie says, "do not have to go hand in hand. Love between adults is private. Couples should be free to end a sexual relationship whenever they please, with no obligation."

Helen, seated on my left, leans over and whispers in my ear. "It's no secret that she and her husband have other lovers. And they have four children."

I raise my brow thinking how unorthodox Elsie is, though I suppose having other lovers is not such an odd thing in this crowd. Or in this day and age. But I can't imagine Charles agreeing to free love. Not with his Victorian ideals. Then I hear Elsie's next words.

"No matter how many other lovers a couple may have and how private an issue it is, when it comes to the welfare of children, *that* is a public matter." I sit up a little straighter. There isn't a sound in the room – no silverware clinking, no murmurs, no waiters' footsteps. Everyone is waiting for what she'll say next. I gasp as she says, "It should be required that when a couple becomes parents they sign a contract with the state. Their responsibilities should be laid out clearly and concisely."

Oh, how Charles would love that.

Chapter 9

In his wool tweed overcoat, Charles leads me through the entrance portico of B. Altman's, his arm firm on my elbow. This magnificent building, a palace as Mother calls it, is one of the department stores she took me to as a young girl. At that time, women shopped downtown on the Ladies Mile, but Mother preferred this posh neighborhood for her shopping forays. Now the center of the fashionable activity in the City is on Thirty-fourth Street, and without the female nomenclature, so Charles has no qualms about accompanying me. In fact, this was his decision. I didn't believe him when he told me he would take me shopping and choose the clothes I wear since he abhorred my sense of style. Especially my trousers. I avoided the dreaded shopping trip for several weeks, always having a rehearsal to attend or to help his mother pack for her move to our townhouse. The second was an excuse he readily accepted. The first made him grumble.

"We'll go straight to ladies' suits," he says as we walk by the perfume counter. A hint of the delicate fragrance of Shalimar, that new French perfume by Guerlain, wafts through the air. The aroma of sandalwood and vanilla reminds me of Helen's mother and I think of her advice to compromise as we make our way to the elevator. Agreeing to shop with Charles is a huge compromise for me.

The stately main floor is quiet. There is one lone woman, wrapped in a long fur coat, admiring a beaded pouchette at the handbag counter. The jewelry department is empty of shoppers but there is a tall young lady at the glove counter slipping on a stunning pair of elbow-length satin gloves. Most women don't shop at 10 a.m. They're home with their children doing whatever mothers are supposed to do. But Charles wanted an early start. And Grandmama is there to do all of those motherly things.

The ornate doors of the elevator open and we step in. Finally, he lets go of my elbow. "Second floor," he tells the elevator operator. I look around this elaborate cage, admiring the carved wood, and give a friendly smile to the man in uniform. Seems like I'm always caged with Charles, though this one I'll exit.

We reach the department and Charles recruits a saleswoman. He tells her to show us some walking suits.

She looks directly at me and asks, "Are you interested in wool jersey or linen?"

Before I have a chance to answer, Charles says, "No matter, as long as it's Chanel."

I want to crawl away. I'm so embarrassed by his haughty attitude. Labels don't matter to me, though what does he care? I wish I could shed this domineering man and shop by myself. I promised Charles when he first brought up this shopping idea and again this morning before we left that I would buy "proper" clothes, as he calls them, so there's no need for him to come with me. Obviously, that didn't work.

The sales clerk invites us to sit on the velvet chairs. "I'll collect a few items the madam will like," she says, dipping her head toward me. Her eyes tell me she understands. She'll focus on what *I* want. Thank goodness she's a modern woman. My shoulders soften.

After trying on several skirts and jackets with blouses to match, I select one in a tan jersey wool. The other, an interesting woven pattern of black and white paired with a striped pleated skirt.

"Not that one," Charles says, pointing to the black-and-white ensemble.

"Why?" I force my jaw not to clench. "This is what I want. It's lovely."

"Since when do stripes and prints go together?" he says, his face scrunched in disgust.

"This is Coco Chanel's latest creation," the saleswoman says and I see Charles's dark eyes turn bright. "It'll be stunning on Madame with her long lithe figure. Layer some strands of beads or ropes of faux pearls, add a simple earring and bracelet and you're all set." She gives me a little wink. "Remember," she adds looking directly at me, "Chanel wants you to have fun with the jewelry. Mix necklaces and beads together, just not too much. When you're about to step out the door, take off one piece and you'll look sensational."

With raised brows and a little tilt of my chin, I thank the saleswoman for her help then follow Charles to the shoe department. "Seriously," I tell him, "I don't need another pair." He doesn't listen and as soon as we enter the carpeted area, he calls for the shoe-fitter.

Standing in front of the Foot-O-Scope, I slide my right foot into the X-ray machine. "This is fascinating," I say, looking up at the silver-haired man measuring my foot.

"This is a recent addition to our shoe fitting," he says. "Look through the fluorescent screen." He points to the little window at the top of the wooden box. "You can see your heel and toes, even your arch and instep."

"Good, good," Charles says. "Just take the measurement and bring us that shoe over there." He points to a patent leather T-strap with a stacked heel.

"I'd rather an oxford," I tell the shoe man.

Charles narrows his eyes. "No!" The shoe fitter jumps back.

My ears and neck turn hot. I'm so embarrassed. To make light of the situation, I use a sweet, soft voice telling the shoe man I have several T-straps already. "It's the style my husband prefers," I say. "But I'd love to try one of those two-toned oxfords." I turn toward Charles and give my shoulders a little shrug. "It's all the fashion now and very sporty."

A little while later we leave the store, packages in hand, and step out onto Fifth Avenue. B. Altman's grand façade harmonizes beautifully with the palatial mansions in this residential neighborhood. I'm pleased with my purchases and glad Charles didn't fight me on the two-tone Oxfords. Whether he didn't want to argue in front of the salesmen or liked the idea of a more modest shoe, I don't know. What I do know is, it was satisfying standing my ground. And now, I'm ready to go home. A deep sigh escapes my lips. All I want is a ciggy with my feet resting on the ottoman in the parlor, warmed by a blazing fire in the fireplace, some jazz playing on the phonograph, and Mama Brandt preparing lunch. Except for Charles to go to the office. Or anywhere. However, that is not to be.

"It's just four blocks to Lord and Taylor," he says, glancing at my feet.

"I can walk eight blocks, even twelve," I say. "That's not the issue. It's that I don't want to shop anymore. I bought what you wanted." His jaw tightens. "But if you want to look at some clothes for yourself, then by all means, let's go to Lord and Taylor." I speak in a conciliatory tone though I know all too well this is not why Charles is practically grinding his teeth.

We walk up the avenue, the winter wind adding to the chill between us. I purposely stroll past the front entrance of Lord and Taylor and head to Thirty-eighth Street. Charles stops and asks where I'm going. "I thought you wanted to go to the Men's Only entrance," I say. This store has a men's door where gentlemen can enter the Manicuring Parlor, purchase whatever items they want from all the men's departments, be shaved and manicured, and never have to pass through departments where women's goods are sold. "I'll walk you there and while you're busy, I'll go up to the Tea Room. They allow women without a male escort, and I'm quite tired of shopping."

Charles stands with his feet wide apart planted on the cement sidewalk. He looks like a piece of cement himself. Hard. Unmovable.

"I do not want a manicure," he says. "And there is nothing I want to buy other than proper clothing for you. Now let's go inside. And if you are so tired, we will go upstairs later and get you a cup of tea."

We go back to the main entrance and enter the eleven story building of brick and limestone. In the ladies' dress department, Charles chooses a beaded chemise in a soft peach. "A little bit modern for my taste," he says, "but it looks lovely on you. Perfect for the hospital's gala."

I admit I do like the straight lines and with my small bust, the silk organza lies perfectly. It's a bit sexy. Oh, what will the other doctors' wives think?

"Now," Charles says, "let's get you a new pair of silk stockings, and you probably could use a new garter belt."

Oh, no, I do not need a garter belt. Not with this dress. I'm going to roll down the stockings to just above my knees and hold them with a fancy knee garter. That will certainly surprise Charles. But . . . I will be wearing the dress he chose.

Chapter 10

Standing behind the stage-left curtain, I peer through the narrow opening watching the women rehearse Scene Two in *The Hairy Ape*. They're lounging on the ocean liner's deck chairs. Mary Blair is brilliant as Mildred, and I realize O'Neill made the right decision giving her the part. Though I would love to play it. I nod as she says her lines because, like the character, I too am a leopard, trapped in an identity with spots I can't scratch off. And Eleanor Hutchinson, I must admit, does justice to the other female part. She's the epitome of a proud, pompous, fat old aunt with a double chin. That would have been fun to play, but I won't complain. I'm thrilled to be a part of this production. Of any play, whether on stage or off, after such a long time. I'm enjoying working in the costume department even though I know every single word of Mildred's part. Hidden behind the curtain, I mouth each one along with her.

"Please do not mock at my attempts to discover how the other half lives," Mildred is saying. "Give me credit for some sort of groping sincerity in that at least. I would like to . . . to, uhh . . ."

There's silence on the stage. Oh my heavens, she doesn't know the line. I whisper it to myself as she shouts, "Line!" No one answers. *Where's the prompter?* I push my head through the curtain and feed her the line.

Mildred picks it up and continues. "I would like to be some use in the world. Is it . . . "

Again, she stumbles and calls for the line, and again, I feed it to her. She glances my way. Gives me a little nod. Picking up my cue, she continues her speech. I stay, watching, ready, just in case. The scene continues without another hitch but when the Second Engineer appears on stage to take Mildred to the stokehole, she puts her hand up motioning to Eugene who's been sitting in the seats watching. "I need a break," she says and walks off stage. I step back as she comes through the curtain.

"Thank you," she says, giving me a hug. "My head is splitting and I . . . I don't know what happened. You're my savior."

Patting her on the back, I let her know I was glad to help. Mary knows I auditioned for the part, but neither of us says a word about it.

"I have to remeasure your waist and hips," I say. "I'm afraid the seamstress isn't able to read my scribble, and I've forgotten what I wrote."

One of my jobs in the costume department is to measure the actors for their costumes and mark down the numbers. I also cut fabric and I'll deal with any costume issues that arise during the production, but my fingers will never touch a needle. That's not my forté. Nanny tried her hardest to teach me to sew, but my seams were always crooked and my buttons fell off. I was never meant to be a homemaker.

Mary unbuckles her belt and slides her wide-legged trousers down a few inches. I wrap the tape measure around her tiny waist and bend to see the number. After repeating the task for her hips, I thank her.

"Oh, no," she says, pulling up her slacks. "I have to thank you. And now I've got to get my headache powder." She hurries away, climbing the steps to her dressing room.

Loud footsteps shake the backstage air. "Where is she?" Eugene shouts. "We have to—"

I cut off his rant. "She has a headache. Give her a few minutes."

His directorial voice booms, calling the characters for Scene Three. "Paddy. Yank. On stage." Then he looks at me. "You fed her the line?" I nod. "Do you know them all?" I nod again. "All right," he says. "You be prompter today. I don't know what the hell happened to him."

My head won't stop shaking. "Sure. Sure. I can do it. I just have to run these measurements to costume. Be right back."

The rehearsal goes smoothly. I have the entire script in my hands, though I don't need it. Mildred is back on stage remembering all of her lines. Paddy, though, stumbles a few times and I don't even need to look at the printed page. I simply fill in the telltale pauses. We finish Scene Four after several re-dos with Eugene wanting a line said more forcefully or more quietly, or any changes he felt were needed.

"Good job," he calls from the third row. "Let's break for lunch."

A huge, satisfied sigh escapes my lip. I make my way backstage past the prop table, heading to costumes. The sewing machines click with needles going up and down, a rhythmic pounding as they fasten stitches to seams and hems. I stop and watch one woman gently push a soft white fabric through the machine, constructing Mildred's costume. Then I grab my bag with my sandwich and a thermos filled with hot coffee. "I'm expected back as prompter in forty-five minutes," I say to all the women. "I'm sorry I can't have lunch with you today."

Eugene curls his head around the open door. "And every day. If you want the job. You were fabulous today, and our prompter is ill. He will not be back."

Oh, this has been a wonderful morning. I want to call Helen and Crystal and tell them all about it. I may not be on stage, but I'm reciting lines.

"Absolutely," I tell Eugene, and my heart sinks. What will Charles say now that I'm needed every day, for every rehearsal?

Chapter 11

I look out my bedroom window across to Washington Square Park. It's a beautiful Sunday. Men wearing their straw boaters and women in their new spring finery stroll along the paved paths lined with purple crocuses. Charles comes up behind me and caresses my shoulder. A warmth flows through me. He's been quite attentive lately, ever since his mother moved in. Is it because he doesn't want her to hear us argue, or has she said something to him? Something to make him realize he hasn't been a loving husband. Whatever the reason, it's been quite pleasant. His goodnight kisses, which had become almost nil, make me feel like a bride again. Maybe he *is* trying to change. He no longer gets angry when I go to rehearsal. He does grumble a bit when I go out the door but never says a word. Perhaps we have come to a compromise. After all, I am only working half the week.

As much as I hated to, I eventually had to tell Eugene I couldn't continue as prompter if he needed me at every rehearsal. At first, I made up fake excuses. It was too humiliating to tell the truth that my husband won't let me work nights. When I said I'm taking acting classes two nights a week, Eugene screamed, "Quit! You're a prompter now," which cut me deep, and when I told him I did charity work at the hospital on Thursday nights, he threw a pen clear across the room shouting "That will have to wait!" Finally, with my chin trembling, I told him the truth. "Damn mothers," he screamed. "Women and children shouldn't be anywhere near a stage!"

I should be thankful he let me stay in the costume and prop departments and work only three nights a week since, as he says, "Those positions are not as pressing." But damn it, they're a comedown from the lead or supporting roles I'm used to. *Let someone else hang costumes and adjust a bow or a belt. I should be on stage!* My jaw tightens. I force it to soften, telling myself things are better at home since I've been working backstage. Perhaps it's worth it. I'm not tied up in knots anymore.

"Let's take Rosy to the park today," Charles says, joining me gazing out the window at the springtime scene. "We'll buy frankfurters from the vendor and have a little picnic."

For some families, this would be normal. But Charles has never joined me for a Sunday stroll. Not with Rosy or by ourselves. Not since we were courting. Often, he's at the hospital and when not, he's reading in the parlor, pipe between his lips, the plummy scent of tobacco seeping into the upholstery.

"That sounds delightful. I'll get Rosy ready," I say and walk out of the bedroom looking forward to what I hope will be a lovely day. The flowers and trees are blooming. Perhaps, like the season, this is a rebirth for our marriage. However, I can't help wondering what got into him to suggest this. He's acting like the affectionate Charles of our honeymoon days. Dare I trust he'll stay this way?

~

Rosy pulls Charles by the hand. Seated on a park bench, I watch her lead him to the display of daffodils at the edge of the flower bed. She bends forward putting her nose practically inside the yellow blooms. He obeys when she motions him to do the same. Not only has Charles been acting differently, he almost doesn't look like himself today. With a collarless button-down shirt and no tie, he has taken the formality down a notch. The day is sunny with a delightful breeze, so the vest and jacket are not cumbersome. But I will never understand why men insist on wearing all those clothes when the temperatures rise and women go about in cap sleeve dresses, some defying old conventions in sleeveless, exposing their bare arms. I wonder how Charles feels about that.

"Come, Mama," Charles calls to me over his shoulder. "Rosy wants you to smell the pretty flowers." With his hooded eyes focused on me, he tousles her wavy hair and says, "Don't you, sweetie?" I rise, walk over, and join my husband and daughter.

After running up and down the paths smelling flowers, petting puppies on leashes, and chasing after squirrels, Rosy's little eighteen-month-old legs tire. She holds onto the edge of her stroller and says, "Uppy." I lift her and settle her in. She runs her pudgy fingers along the sides and giggles at the bumpiness of the woven reeds. Her little laugh, from deep in her belly, always makes me smile.

With me pushing the stroller, Charles and I continue our walk around the perimeter of the park. We walk past several artists with canvases set on easels. I stop for a moment and admire a painting of the marble arch, designed by Stanford White, at the entrance to the square then another water color of an enormous tree.

"That's over there, in the northwest corner," Charles says, pointing to the English Elm. "It's the one we can view from our bedroom window. Some say it was used for hangings in the early nineteenth century, but I've told you that already, haven't I?"

I nod, remembering my horror at the images that story conveyed and how, when we first moved in, Charles teased, saying I might wake up one morning and see bodies hanging from the branches. He tweaked my nose and laughed, saying he would keep the drapes closed so I wouldn't get upset. Then he kissed my forehead, like a papa kissing his little girl. I always feel like a little girl when he tries to control me, whether with the theater, my clothes, or anything. However, recently, his authoritarian manner seems to have abated. I understand men expect to be in control and their wives to be subservient. My father certainly did. And Charles learned it from his father. That's why I listened to what Helen's mother said. Compromise. I'm trying to meet him halfway, as difficult as it is. But in the end, it's worth it. Life is much more pleasant now.

The smoky scent of frankfurters makes my mouth water and I suggest we have our picnic. Charles agrees and heads off to the cart to buy our lunch. Frankfurters and lemonade. It isn't expensive, but thirty cents feels like a splurge when lunch at home is the norm on Charles's day off. Once again it comes to me that my husband is quite different today. A walk in the park, a picnic, his casual attire, even my not having to prepare a midday meal and sit around the table as a family. It's nice. And it's fortunate that rehearsals were canceled today. Otherwise, I would not be here.

With his hands full of our food, Charles comes back. As if he could read my mind, he brings up that very subject. "Your rehearsals should be ending soon, if I'm correct," he says, then casually takes a bite of his frank, his eyes never leaving mine.

"Yes. The show opens next week." Rosy is sitting on my lap with her mouth wide open. I break off a piece of the frankfurter and slip it into her mouth. She looks so cute chewing and smacking her lips.

"Wonderful," he says. "I hope it goes well," he adds then takes a seat next to us.

"Thank you. The Plymouth Theater is gorgeous. I'd love you to come to opening night with me."

"Oh, no," he says. "I won't be going."

I hope that glint in his eye doesn't mean what I think it does. Maybe I can change his mind. His demeanor isn't as off-putting as it usually is when there's talk of the theater so I say, "I know you don't enjoy live theater and, even though we won't be sitting together, I'd love you to be there. It would mean so much to me for you to see what I've been working on. This play is very special to me. Perhaps, just this once, you'll make an exception?"

"No, Lucy. I will not be going to opening night." He takes a bite of his frankfurter, chews and swallows, his eyes on me the entire time. Then in a very serious voice, says, "I won't be going and neither will you."

"What do you mean? Of course I'm going. I *have* to be there." Damn! I am sick and tired of his telling me what I can and cannot do. I am *not* his slave!

He shakes his head. "Your job is done, my dear. Once rehearsals are over, that's it."

I tense. My arms squeeze Rosy's little body and she lets out a cry. "But I'm still working there," I say, keeping my voice quiet.

"No, Lucy! You will be home every night. As a mother should be."

A mixture of shock and anger simmers in my gut. "Charles, please, my job isn't done. The costume crew is needed at every performance. I know how you feel so, as I said, I'll be sharing the work with another person. I'm only working three nights."

He jumps up and punches the air. "Absolutely not!" His voice reverberates through the park. Rosy cries. I hold her tight. He keeps yelling. "You are done! The minute rehearsals end, it's over. I have given in long enough."

"Damn it, Charles. You didn't want to have a nice picnic today. You set this up to tell me this crap. You don't care about being with Rosy and me."

"Watch your language, Lucy!"

"Oh, please, now you're telling me how to talk?"

Jumping to my feet, I shove a crying baby at him, shouting, "Take her. I've . . . I've got to get out of here. I can't talk to you now." Frankfurters tumble. Lemonade spills. I storm off, muscles quivering.

Racing through the park, I scoot around women and men, children and dogs, then sprint across West Fourth Street, my heart pounding, and finally reach the rooming house where Helen and Crystal live. I fling the door open. It slams behind me and I hurry into the parlor. "I'm leaving him," I shout, seeing Crystal sitting in an armchair next to the window. Every cell in my body twitches with anger. I didn't even look to see if we were alone.

"You can't do that," Crystal calmly says. Thankfully no one else is here.

"I can't take it anymore! I . . . I . . . ugh!" My hands are shaking. I want to scream, punch something. I can't stand still. Fists clenching and opening, over and over again, I walk to the window, huff a frustrated breath, turn, walk back.

"Slow down," Crystal says. "Stop pacing. Tell me what happened."

With my hands firmly on my hips, I tell her about the nice day Charles and I were having and how it all changed. "He was furious. Demanding. Shouting. The entire park could hear him. I can't do this anymore. I am done! I want a divorce."

Crystal looks at me, her eyes filled with sorrow. Or is it pity? "Divorce is only allowed for adultery," she explains. "Though there are exceptions made for bigamy or impotence." I look at her with wide-open eyes. "Yes," she says. "And I don't think you fit into any of those categories. Do you?"

"No. Though I wish I did." I plop down on the sofa opposite her and lean forward. My hands grip my thighs. "I cannot stay in this marriage. I thought everything was getting better. And I liked it. But . . . " I throw up my hands, then sit back against the velvet cushion. "Do you remember I told you I overheard his mother one night – it might have been Christmas – and she told him to let me do my acting?" Crystal nods and I continue. "My mother-in-law understands how much it means to me. It's not only my passion, it's what I'm trained for. It's what I've studied. So why can't her son understand?" I let out a big breath and reach for the cigarettes in my handbag. "She even told him I'd be a better mother for it." Flicking the lighter open, I add, "Well, she also told him I didn't have an ounce of nurturing in me, which is true. But he won't listen. And now, he won't even let me work part-time. I tried, Crystal. I can't do it anymore. I won't live with him telling me what I can and can't do, what I can wear – or even what to call my daughter! My gosh, he even changed the name I gave her."

"Well, not legally," she says. "And now we all call her Rosy. I'm sorry, I didn't realize it bothered you so much."

I drop the lighter in my bag and shake her apology away. "It's just that it's one more way of him getting what he wants."

"It's been hard for you, I know. You didn't want to get married. You wanted to live here on Thompson Street with Helen and me. Oh, how you fought your mother! But here you are." She raises her arms like a Sunday preacher. "And you know, married women are expected to devote themselves to running the household, raising children, and . . ." She pauses as if a drum roll would accompany her next phrase. "To bow to their husband's judgment." I shudder and she says, "Yes. It's preposterous. And that is why I will never marry. Plus, employers have the right to fire women after they marry or have children."

"Absurd," I say and let out a long string of smoke. "There are several women in the Heterodoxy Club that are divorced. And others who came before us. Charlotte Perkins Gilman is one. Remember her awful story and how she gave her daughter back to her husband, sending her clear across the country? And there are others. I can't think of their names right now."

"Divorce, other than in the club, is *always* looked upon as shameful," Crystal says. "And I doubt Charles wants that shame thrust upon him."

"True. But what are my options? I understand he's doing what he learned from his own father. Control your wife. Be in charge. Tell her what to think. He expects me to give up all I've worked and studied for to take care of him and Rosy. But I'm not that woman. I want my career too. It's what fulfills me."

Crystal comes and sits next to me. "Oh, Lucy, I'm afraid you're stuck." She takes my hand in hers. "Even when both parties want the divorce – and as I said, I don't see Charles agreeing to it – they have to present their case in court. They have to provide evidence of one partner's infidelity or wrongdoing."

"Well, I can certainly tell a judge about Charles's wrongdoing."

"But, Luce, legally he's done nothing wrong."

I know Crystal is right. She always uses my nickname when she tells me something I don't want to hear.

"Also," she says, "In cases of divorce, women have almost no rights at all, and they have to prove they're of sound mind if they wish to gain custody of their children."

I take a drag on the cigarette and consider her words. Charles would love to prove that I'm not of sound mind. That's why he sent me to the lake for three months. For a rest. To cure me. Why do men think arguing and crying, or depression, mean that women are crazed and need to be treated? Thank goodness it was a lake house for me, not an institution where they send some women. Or . . . oh gosh, I don't want to think about other remedies they used to use, like doctors stimulating a woman's genitals. Can you imagine how humiliating that is? As if anger or depression was due to the uterus and masturbation could take away our hysteria, as it was called. All I know is, I can never again let Charles think I'm hysterical. I inhale another deep drag from the ciggy, then another and another trying to calm my nerves.

Thank goodness Crystal cuts into my disturbing thoughts. "There are other ways to get a divorce," she says. "It's called an at-fault divorce, but I don't think you qualify for any of those either."

I'm desperate so I ask what they are.

"Cruel and inhuman treatment."

Yes, that qualifies, I think. Though Charles would fight me, saying I'm the one with inhuman treatment to our child. He doesn't understand I love my daughter. I'd just rather be in the theater than at home being Mama. My next thought disturbs me, but it's true. I love Rosy, I just love the theater more. A heavy sigh escapes my lips. I look at my feet, see nothing. What kind of person am I? No mother should think this way.

Crystal runs a comforting hand along my arm. She knows me so well. "It's okay," she says. "You don't like who you are right now."

"No. I don't. But this is my truth. I never wanted to be a mother. I don't know how to be. Not a loving, nurturing one. And that's what Rosy deserves."

"That's what every child deserves, and we both know you never had it. So stop beating yourself up. You're a good person, Luce. What you have to understand is, even if Charles agrees to divorce you, you'd never get custody. And you'd probably be penniless."

Her last word sits in my gut. Penniless. Other than the money I've squirreled away from my acting and the allowance my father gave me while at college, I would be. I was very frugal those four years away at school, barely touching the bank account my father set up for me. And when I married, Charles thought he was so benevolent allowing me to keep whatever I made from the theater. He tossed it away as chump change, though it was more than that, saying I should use it for "all those little things you want." I've saved it for, as they say, a rainy day. Now, I'm in a thunderstorm.

Helen steps into the parlor. She's glowing. Even the red highlights in her brunette bob glisten in the sunshine streaming through the window. I imagine she was with her new beau, maybe taking a Sunday stroll in the park, as I'd been just a little while ago. The difference is that she's luminous and I'm distraught. I'm not envious though. I'm happy for her. She wants to get married. Why not? Unlike mine and so many others, her parents have set a good example of how a marriage should work. Her father has always supported his wife's dreams and desires and she supported him.

"You look very cozy," Helen says, looking at Crystal and me sitting close together on the couch. "What are you talking about?"

"Nothing," Crystal says at the exact time I say, "Charles."

Helen's confused expression shoots from Crystal to me. "I just saw him in the park with Rosy," she says. "He was pushing her stroller home, racing down the sidewalk, scowling and mumbling. What's going on? He didn't respond to my greeting. It was as if he didn't see me."

"It's a long story," I say. "Basically, Crystal is telling me why I can't get a divorce."

"A divorce?" Helen plops down on the other end of the sofa and faces us.

"Yes, but I'm drained and I really should get home. Charles is furious. I have to calm things down before he. . . oh . . . before . . . " I jump up and the words rush out. "Before he sends me away again. I've got to go."

"Wait," Helen says. "Obviously something is really wrong. Talk to me. Let me help."

"Thank you, but I better go. Crystal will fill you in."

"All right. How about later?" Helen says. "We're going to see *Blood and Sand* at the Rivoli, the four o'clock show. Meet us there or after. We'll get coffee and talk."

"*Blood and Sand* with Rudolph Valentino? I'd love to. But I'm not sure. I . . . I could certainly use the distraction. And time with both of you. But . . . I don't know. Let me see what happens when I get home." I look at my dear friends, throw them a kiss, and leave.

Out on the sidewalk, I turn left and head to Washington Square. At the corner, I stand, stepping side to side, waiting for a new, swanky Packard to pass. The deep-green interior is stunning against the tan seats, and that cloth roof – oh, how I'd love to be behind the wheel with the top down, touring around the city, or even better, the open country with the wind in my hair. Oh, the freedom! But, alas, that will never happen if I stay in this marriage. It's another one of Charles's dictates. "Women do not drive." The auto's wheels rumbling against the asphalt mimic the rumble in my gut. I've got to calm down and be more conciliatory. He could send me back to the lake if I'm not.

I cross West Fourth Street and head home. Words come to me with each step. Words I will use to try and make Charles understand.

Chapter 12

The door to Charles's study is closed, as always. Having gathered my courage, I tap my knuckles on the solid wood door. His voice has a lilt to it as he says, "Just a minute sweetheart." He must think it's Rosy because, other than his daughter, no one is allowed to intrude in his private space. Plus, he never calls me sweetheart. Positive he'll not be pleased to see me, I cautiously step into the room. He's standing, as if ready to open the door, with a stunned look on his face. "Hello," I say, my voice barely above a whisper.

Charles turns and reclines in his leather club chair. His feet propped on a footstool give off a deceptively peaceful air. The soft glow emanating from the jewel-toned glass shade of the Tiffany lamp adds to the restful scene. It's all quite opposite to the turmoil in my chest.

"I shouldn't have run off," I say. It irks me to add, "I'm sorry," though I do. Humility is the price of this conversation if it has a chance of going my way. I have to be careful to make my point without sounding defensive. I start by saying, "At that moment, when you started . . . " then stop and tell myself not to bring up his shouting. I take a breath and start again. "When you announced that I had to stop going—"

"Lucy, you went crazy! You threw my daughter at me."

Anger crawls up my belly. Instead of blowing up again, I tamp it down and quietly say, "May I sit, Charles? I'd like to talk about this with you."

He points across the room toward the straight-backed chair beside his desk. I carry the cumbersome piece of furniture closer to him. "I understand how you feel," I say, taking my seat. "You aren't used to women working."

With his eyes never leaving the book on his lap, he grumbles. "I don't care if a woman works, as long as it isn't you. You're a mother." His nostrils flare.

I suck in my lips, hard, then continue. "I know that idea is foreign to you and to many men. But there are women who do both. And we're fortunate to have your mother here with us. Rosy adores her. And Grandmama loves Rosy more than anyone ever could."

He shoots up tall, plants his feet wide. "More than you?"

"Oh, Charles, please, try to understand. I love our daughter and I want to be a good mother, but I'm afraid that's not possible if I can't be my true self." I gather my courage and proceed. "Try to think of it this way. If you were forced to stay home, never to go to the hospital again or see any patients, wouldn't you feel you lost yourself?"

He bends his head toward me, his eyes bore into mine. "That's ridiculous. That's never going to happen. I provide for this family. No man stays home and none of my colleagues' wives work." His ferocity makes my shoulders stiffen. He continues, jaw tight. "They may volunteer for charitable organizations but they do nothing as unseemly as the theater. They never consort with those low-brow types. They take care of their home and children. They are available to accompany their husbands to all hospital evening functions."

I pull on my gold earring, then force my hands to my lap. Clasping them like a good schoolgirl, I remind him that I'll only be working part-time. "Half the time I should be. You know I've arranged my hours to be home with you and Rosy. On the other nights, your mother will be here and sometimes you'll be home. She'll be well taken care of. Loved. She won't miss me."

"Hmph."

Does that mean he won't miss me either?

He rises from his cushy seat and strolls across the room. His room. I remain seated in my stiff-backed chair. He remains silent. I want to say more but he's put me on the witness stand and I'm afraid to overstate my case. Perhaps I should ask for permission to continue with the play. I probably should have originally done that and not surprised him with returning to the theater. Though he never would have allowed it. I watch him peruse his bookshelves and wonder what he's thinking. Have my words made any impact?

"No," he says, his face still in the books. Then he turns toward me. Now *his* hands are clasped. So tightly I can almost see the whites of his knuckles. "This is the end," he says. His steel jaw could cut through stone. "No more theater." He walks toward me, grabs the arms of my chair, and leans in. With his nose barely an inch from mine, he growls, "No wife of mine will be on stage. Backstage. Or anywhere near a stage."

I want to run. Throw something. Shout. But I stay seated and just stare at his smug face and temper the fire about to erupt in my belly.

He struts away. At the open doorway, he announces he's going to the office, then says, "I expect to see you here when I get home."

The door slams behind him and I cannot move. My chest heaves up and down with every breath. "Damn him!" As hard as I try, I can't stop the tears. Angry, frustrated, ugly tears pour down my face. Every thought, every emotion I've had to stifle for so long erupts. But I don't want him to hear me. I suck in my lips, trying to stop the deluge. *Damn. What can I do? How do I tell*

O'Neill I won't be at opening night? Or any other night? And the crew? Oh God! How embarrassing to have my husband dictate to me. I grab hold of the chair, clutch the wooden seat to stop my shaking hands. "The hell with him. I don't need him. He can go to the devil. Oh, but . . . oh God, what am I going to do?"

"Lucy, dear," my mother-in-law says from the other side of the closed door. "Are you all right?"

"Yes. I'm . . . I'm okay. I'll be right out." I stand and straighten my skirt, adjust my blouse and run the back of my hand over my wet cheeks, then walk out.

She's waiting on the other side of the door. "Oh, my dear," she says, noticing my tear-stained face and what must be very red eyes. She folds my hands in hers. "How can I help?" I sniff and shake my head. "Nothing." The word barely touches the air. I swallow the hard lump in my throat and ask, "Where's Rosy?" Usually, my daughter would be right at her grandmama's side.

"I left her playing in the parlor. She's having a tea party, jabbering away with her doll and I didn't know who else, so I asked who the dolly was talking to. And, oh my gosh, it made my heart sing. She pointed to me and said, 'Memama.'"

Love, mixed with a tiny bit of jealousy, fills my chest. Rosy chose her grandma, not her mother. And honestly, part of me is relieved. She must feel that strong, unconditional love – a love every child needs, even if it isn't from their mother. When I was a little girl, I rarely played with dolls though whenever I created imaginary characters for a story it was Nanny, not Mother, who got the part. Nanny gave me much more love than my mother ever did.

I stand at the entrance to the parlor with my mother-in-law next to me, watching our little girl sitting on the floor, playing with her doll and tiny tea cups. "May I have some tea?" I say, and Rosy looks up, her eyes as bright as Christmas morning. Is she looking at me or Grandmama?

"How about I make us a real cup of tea?" my mother-in-law says. With a wink, she adds, "I think you could use one."

Sitting on the edge of the sofa with Rosy at my feet, I join in the pretend play, waiting for the real tea which my mother-in-law believes will fortify me. What would truly fortify me, what would feed my soul right now is to go to the movies with Crystal and Helen. I shake that idea from my head. This is not the day to oppose Charles. I don't know how I'm going to get him to change his mind, but I am not giving up. I *must* make him understand. Or . . . Like the pendulum on the clock on the wall, my thoughts swing back and forth. Crystal's explanations come back to me. Tidbits of another idea come to mind. I rub my finger over the stones on my left earring, considering each possibility. No, I tell myself. I can't do it. Trying to erase these thoughts, I pick up the tiny china cup again and go back to playing with my daughter. My chest tightens watching her pudgy hand lift the flowered teapot. Her big round eyes, the same deep green as mine, are serious as she pours the pretend tea. I watch her play and talk to her dolly and wonder if I could possibly do what I was just considering.

Mama Brandt comes in with her bone china tea service on a sterling silver tray. I'm glad for the reprieve from my disturbing thoughts. She sets the tray on the cocktail table, the ornate, Italian, painted-wood one that Mother bought – definitely not my taste – and we sit together on the Chippendale sofa with its ball-and-claw feet, also Mother's taste. It's much more comfortable than the settee she also chose.

Grandmama pours a cup of the sweet, mellow blend and hands it to me. "Lucy, dear," she says, pouring one for herself. "I don't mean to pry, but I heard you . . ." She mouths the word "crying," I assume so Rosy won't hear. My daughter picks up on everything lately. "If there is anything you want to talk about, please understand I'm a good listener."

I shake my head "no" and thank her. We have talked before, yet I don't want to involve her in my marital problems.

"I have a feeling I know what's troubling you. I heard the study door slam. It was so loud it almost shook the walls. Then Charles rushed into the hallway, grabbed his hat and stormed out of the house. I hurried, caught the door before it slammed shut, and stopped him on the steps telling him to wait. To talk to me. All he said was, 'Leave it alone.' I pressed him anyway and he shouted, 'It's that damned theater again.' I tried to get him to say more, but he told me to stay out of it. He had everything under control." She looked at me with wide-open eyes as if to say "Does he?"

Tears pool in my eyes. I blink them away, wishing they would stop, then take a sip of tea.

"Oh, my dear," she says, gently patting my knee. "Couples argue. Give him time. All will be right again. Charles loves you."

I sigh and say, "This is much more than a spat." What I don't say is that I don't care if Charles loves me because I don't love him. I never have. I did try though. Grandmama looks at me, giving me time to go on. Rosy's sweet voice is the background music as I think about when we were first married and how I thought I might grow to love Charles. I hoped I would. Other women did when they were forced to marry. Even today, when he suggested we take Rosy to the park, I thought we might have turned a corner. But no, it's not possible. I take a deep breath and explain to my mother-in-law what transpired.

She listens, not saying a word. When I finish with "I don't know what to do. I can't live with his dictates," her eyes are filled with sorrow. She glances at Rosy on the floor pouring make-believe tea into a cup then turns to me.

"I am so sorry. I'm afraid you won't win this argument. Charles is adamant about you not being in the theater. I have tried to make him understand, but he will not budge. I see where this attitude is coming from. I once told you, he learned his ways from his father. And I understand what you need. It hurts me to see my son so angry and to see you unhappy. Isn't there some way you can make this work? Some way you can stay with the play for only daytime performances?"

I explain there are only two matinees and that I had to plead to only work three nights instead of six. "So two days a week will never work. As much as my love is live theater, I'm going to have to give it up for this marriage to work."

"Of course it will work. We'll find a way."

"I hope so," I say, thinking those are the words she expects, then place my teacup on the cocktail table and turn to my mother-in-law. "While I've been with the play, even though it's behind the curtain, I've felt complete. I desperately need that."

"I understand. It's 1922, and you are what we call the New Woman, like that Gibson Girl." She points to the earrings I'm wearing. I run my index finger over the embossed image. "Yes," she says, "the emancipated woman, educated and independent, pushing the barriers. I agree with all that and I will try to help you any way I can. It wasn't my life, but that does not mean it shouldn't be yours. I envy you, dear. When I was a girl these opportunities were not available."

My mind churns. Charles said I can't be on stage or near one. He never mentioned the screen. I nod, thinking it might be possible. As much as it's not what I truly want, I'll talk to him again. One last try.

~

The light from the Tiffany lamp casts its glow on the pages of *This Side of Paradise,* the novel in my hands. Fiction is the balm I need. It takes me away from my problems. It's so much easier to deal with a character's issues than my own. So I sit here in the parlor in the silence of the night, drapes drawn, Grandmama and Rosy asleep upstairs, trying to focus on Fitzgerald's words while

I wait for my husband to come home. He's been gone for hours since storming out after he laid down his law. A law I cannot abide.

This author I've been hearing so much about, F. Scott Fitzgerald, has created a character I relate to in some ways. The protagonist is a young man around my age living at the same time – the Jazz Age, Fitzgerald calls it. Both the character and I come from monied families and went to fine colleges, though unlike me Amory, the character in the book, is spoiled and lazy and has a wonderful relationship with his mother. At least that's the way he seems at this early point in the story. I wonder how his life will change. I wonder how mine will.

The front door creaks open, then closes with a click. I lift my head from the page and listen, waiting for footsteps to see if Charles will come into the parlor for a nightcap or go straight to bed. It's 10 p.m., so I assume he'll want a sherry. He never goes to bed before eleven, and I'll be right here ready to present my final suggestion. Yet he doesn't come and I haven't heard his feet on the wooden stairs. *Holy moly, how long does it take to hang up a hat?* I wait another minute, bookmark the page and close the book, and walk into the hall. Charles is leaning against the front door, his shirt wrinkled. I step closer to him. He stinks from cheap hooch. "Are you okay?"

He grunts and nods. His head never leaves the solid door, as if it's holding him up. This is not the Charles I know who's used to sipping Scotch in a pressed shirt. Where he gets the bootlegged liquor, I have no idea and am better off not knowing. I've always enjoyed a highball and appreciate whatever maneuvering it takes for him to stock our liquor case during this annoying Prohibition. It's interesting how he views his illegal doings as acceptable, but the ones I want, like birth control, are not.

"How about I make us some coffee?" I'm trying to sound like a caring wife. "We can sit in the kitchen if you'd like."

"No. I have nothing to say to you."

His perfect diction, each word enunciated with disgust, makes me think he's not blotto. I can present my case. "Please Charles, I have an idea I'd like to discuss with you."

He moves an inch from the door and stands with his arms folded across his chest, his feet planted wide. "Okay, I'm listening. What?"

"Can we sit?" The cozy kitchen with its dim light over the table might make him more amenable.

With a swipe of his hand, he pushes away my words, as if they carried a putrid odor. "Just say it. What's your bright idea?"

Playing what might be my most important role, I take a casual stance and lean against the foyer table. I tell him about the movies and how they'd allow me to be home more often. "It'll be daytime work," I say, looking at him with what I hope is love in my eyes. "I'll be home with you and Rosy every night. We'll have dinner together and I'll be able to read her bedtime stories and tuck her in, and after, we'll have quiet time together." I leave out how much I'd be giving up. How much I'd be compromising. Because, other than the silly organ, movies don't have sound and I need to use my voice. The stage is my canvas, my voice the paint that brings the playwright's words to life.

"The studios are right here in the City," I say, trying to keep the plea out of my voice. "Or just across the river in New Jersey. But that's a quick trip."

I force a slight smile onto my face, hoping it looks tender, and wait. Charles remains stone-faced, jaw tight, and as hot and fiery as Mt. Vesuvius spewing rocks and ash and burning hot lava, he erupts. "Not another word! I will not talk about this anymore." He throws his house keys across the hall. Hitting the wall, they clatter. White paint chips freckle the floor, and he storms off.

Fists clenched, I bite back every curse word I know. Damn you, go to hell, or whatever words won't get me anywhere.

Nothing will. Before he stomps up the steps, I try to tamp down my fury and talk to his back.

"I'm sorry, Charles." Foot on the third step, he hesitates. "I can't comply with your demands. This marriage isn't working. We want different things." I wait a moment for him to say something. He turns to me with a scowl, then goes upstairs.

Giving him time to wash and climb into bed – and hopefully, fall asleep – I go back to the parlor. With my heart banging against my chest, I try to read a few more pages. My eyes see the words though they don't register. Other thoughts, characters, scenes play in my head. I shut the book, shut off the light, and, with dread, go up to bed.

Charles is lying face-up on the right side of the mattress, covers pulled to his chest, hands folded over the quilt. I sense he's awake. His breathing is too hard for someone sleeping. I slip under the covers on my side. He turns away and rolls to the edge.

"Goodnight," I say to his bare back, to his sharp and pointy shoulder blades, then turn on my side. Hugging my knees, I wait for sleep to come.

Chapter 13

Someone's pounding on the door, shouting, "Lucy, open up." The words sound like they're coming through a fog. I try lifting my head. It's stuck to the pillow. I call out for the baby nurse, that woman with the beady eyes Charles sent. She doesn't hear me. More banging. More shouting. Pebbles ping the casement window. Smells of lake water mixed with wet grass and mud blow in through the screen. Rosy's howling from somewhere. Outside? Heavens, what's she doing out there in the pitch dark? She's supposed to be next to me, in her crib. Where's the damn nurse? Oh no, Charles is going to be furious. I kick the covers with my right leg. Layers and layers of covers. Quilts, afghans, scratchy wool blankets. I can't get free. Trying with my left foot, I push and shove. My leg's tangled. Twisted. Stuck. "Lucy, it's me, Helen. Open the door." Her voice is loud and clear, then muffled, like there's a hand covering her mouth. I push up on my elbow, grab the layers of blankets. Throw them off my chest. Now to get my legs free. Get to Helen. My sweet Helen. She's come all the way from the city to get me out of here. Damn these covers! Like a heavy brick, they're pressing me down. Pushing me deeper and deeper into the mattress with its black and white stripes. Stripes like on prisoners in jail. The pebbles stop pinging. Thunder rumbles. The leaves on the elm tree rustle. Bang! Flashes of bright orange. Fire in the sky lights up the bedroom. Windows rattle. Walls shake. Petrified, I freeze. The house is crumbling, burying me in wood and cement. Rain slams against the window.

With my heart hammering, I take a few deep breaths. In, out, in, out. Oh my, what a nightmare! But it could be real. He could send me back there after the words I said last night. Back to the lake house with Rosy, away from the theater and all things related. Away from my friends.

Finally, my breaths find a steady rhythm. My chest reclaims its smooth, slow up-and-down movement. I lift my head from the pillow and look around. The right side of the bed is empty. Charles is gone. The brass clock on his nightstand tells me it's eight o'clock. I slide out of the covers and shut the window. The sill is wet from the odd morning thunderstorm.

Morning chatter makes its way up the stairs to my bedroom. I can't make out the words though I picture Charles, Mama Brandt, and Rosy in the kitchen, the Pyrex percolator on the stove, coffee bubbling in the glass pot, my mother-in-law scrambling eggs while her son sits at the oak table. Rosy's highchair is pulled up next to her father and he's singing her favorite nursery rhyme, *Wynken, Blynken, and Nod.* As usual, Grandmama joins in on the second verse, "The old moon laughed and sang a song, As they rocked in the wooden shoe . . ." and Rosy claps. The sweetness of her giggle fills me with bittersweet happiness. As much as I'd like it to be otherwise, I know my daughter will be better off without me. Without a mother who truly would rather be somewhere else. And with a grandmother who adores her.

Fortified by my belief, I wash and dress, ready to put my plan in motion, the one that formed while I tossed and turned all night, the hiss from the coal furnace warming the chill in my bed. The idea came to me as a complete script. This time I have the leading role.

~

The rain has stopped, leaving a damp chill in the air. With my red flannel coat belted and buttoned, I walk east to Third Avenue to catch the elevated train. It's a busy Monday in early May with trolleys carrying shoppers uptown and mothers wheeling babies to grocers and butchers. On the corner of Ninth Street, I climb the steps and deposit my nickel in the slot on the coin machine. The gate opens and I walk to the platform to wait for the El that'll take me to Grand Central Terminal. Today is an exploratory trip to find out the price of a ticket to Los Angeles. I already know the personal price. It's much higher.

A hurricane of emotion roils in my gut as I wait for the train. If I tell Crystal and Helen I'm leaving, I'll be putting them in an awkward position because I am not telling Charles. When he receives the letter I'll send from somewhere along the route, he'll certainly go to them demanding to know where I am. I don't want to force them to lie. Though I wonder, will he want to make me come back? Or will he be as relieved as I am? His mother will be there to take care of him and Rosy. Yet my stomach aches at the thought of being three thousand miles away from my dearest friends, never to have coffee, lunch, or dinner with Helen or Crystal again, to laugh or cry, to share secrets like we've done since we were little girls. *How will I go on without my two sisters? Yes, sisters. That's what they are to me.* I blink back tears. More bubble in the corners of my eyes thinking of Mrs. Stokes. A whiff of perfume coming from the woman to my right reminds me of her. Aside from Nanny, Mrs. Stokes is the only true mother figure I ever had. How many times I went to Helen's apartment and poured my heart out to her mother about so many little girl problems. A dress I hated yet Mother insisted I wear. Having to go to Newport with my parents when all I wanted was to spend summer days playing with Helen and Crystal. When I didn't want to get married, and again, just a few months ago, when I went to her house and she spoke to me about compromising with Charles. Ha! That didn't work.

"Oh," I sigh, a little too loudly. The perfumed woman glances my way. I tap my wristwatch to signal it's about the late train. Really, my deep sigh is because I know Mrs. Stokes will be disappointed in me. And that makes my heart hurt, no matter how strongly I believe I have to do this. As to my own mother, I have no idea what she'll think. Probably that leaving my child is awful, and she'll never realize that, basically, it's what she did to me. All those times she left me with Nanny when she and Papa went to their home in Newport. It was never called "our home." And even when they were in New York, we were barely ever together. I had my meals in the kitchen with Nanny and was presented to them, fresh from my bath, smelling sweetly of soap. That earned me a goodnight peck on the cheek from my parents. Mother didn't tuck me in. Well, maybe once in a while, but she never sat on the floor playing with me. I never cuddled up with her to hear stories. Nanny did all that. Mother did nothing. She's a coldhearted woman.

The morning train rumbles down the track, the sound mimicking the thunder in my belly. Unaware of her part in my scheme, Mother will finally do something for me.

The train pulls to a stop, its wheels screeching. I wait as several people climb on board, then I step in and sit on the woven wicker bench. Looking around at women in belted, mid-thigh cloth coats and cloche hats, some sitting by themselves and others with children on their laps, my stomach tenses wondering what they would think of me if they knew what I was doing. *Yet this is for the best*, I remind myself, digging my nails into my thigh. *It is. It's what I need and, in the end, will be best for Rosy.*

At Forty-second Street, I exit along with throngs of people hurrying in all directions. Back down on street level, I look across at the beaux arts building with the imposing sculptures of

Mercury, Hercules, and Minerva atop the stone façade, representing speed, strength, and intellect. All of which I need to complete my plan. Three triumphal arches surround the entrance, inviting me into Grand Central Terminal. My heels click on the marble floor as I make my way to the ticket counter.

"Can I help you?" says the man standing behind the grated window, his shirt sleeves rolled up exposing hairy forearms.

I smile. "How long is the trip to Los Angeles, California? And how much is a ticket?"

"The 20th Century Limited, our flagship train," he says with pride, "will take you to Chicago where you'll change to the California Limited. Start to finish, four days."

I nod letting him know that's fine. I'm surprised. I thought it was a much longer trip.

The ticket seller continues explaining the first leg of the trip is an overnight. "About twenty hours to Chicago," he says, "and the rest is on the California, another lovely train, with delicious food and all the amenities you'd ever want. Now, the cost . . . well, that depends on whether you reserve a lower or upper berth. Either way, they're both closed off from the aisle by a curtain. Or if you want to pay more, you can have a private compartment." He scans the area around me. "Will you be traveling alone?" he asks.

I tell him I will be, and he suggests I take the private compartment. I hear the prices and calculate the amount I've saved and what I'll need to start while I'm auditioning. There's rent, food, money for the trolley or however I'll get around. Los Angeles is so vast, I doubt I'll be walking to many places. My index finger reaches for my earring. I twirl it around a few times to settle my nerves. *Oh, yes,* I sigh to myself. I'll probably have to get a job, some type of work to keep me going before I land a part. I have a degree, but what am I cut out for? Other than acting.

"Thank you," I say, imagining the citrus aroma of oranges and lemons that will grow from trees in my new backyard. "I'll decide and be back to purchase my ticket in a few days."

The ticket man tells me it's best to buy ahead of time. "To be assured of the sleeping arrangement you want," he says, then wishes me a good day.

With a new lightness in my step, I take myself to the famous Oyster Bar with its vaulted, herringbone tiled ceiling. Seated at the lunch counter among businessmen in suits and fedoras and travelers with luggage at their feet, I order a cup of the restaurant's signature oyster stew. Charles would enjoy this savory meal, though I'll never tell him about it. He won't know I've been to this restaurant or to Grand Central Terminal. Even after he receives my letter. I swallow a spoonful of the briny, smoky stew while firming up the next phase of my plan.

Chapter 14

Crystal places her elbows on the table, folds her hands against her chest, and leans forward. She's ready to divulge a secret. Whether we're here in The Pepper Pot or any restaurant or at Mrs. Stokes's kitchen table when we were little girls, this is the position she always assumes when she has something intriguing to reveal. I lean in to listen, like I've always done. The difference is, this time I, too, have a secret. Though my lips remain silent. As much as I want to tell them about my leaving, I love Crystal and Helen too much to put them in such a difficult position. I'm certain Charles will interrogate them when he receives my letter so they need to be as much in the dark as he. For now.

"The owner of this establishment," Crystal whispers. "Dr. Sherlock. Well, I saw him in court the other day. It seems his landlady, who lives across the street, complained about the music coming from here. She called the jazz 'funny ditties' and claimed the liquor flows despite prohibition."

"Heaven forbid," Helen giggles, pulling a pewter flask from her handbag. "What happened?"

"Nothing. The complainant never showed up." Crystal lifts a cup from the table and winks. "So let's drink."

Helen pours the hooch into coffee cups. The taste of juniper berries sits on my tongue while the gin slides down my throat. Perfect. Just what I need. A potion to help me fib – well, lie – about a sudden trip I'll be taking.

Crystal sits back and rubs her hands along her gray linen skirt. "I'm hungry," she says. "Let's order."

I'm not sure I'll be able to swallow anything more than this bathtub gin, which is surprisingly good. Helen has some advantageous friends at the magazine who keep her liquor cabinet full. When the waitress, dressed in an artist's smock, comes to the table, I choose a toasted cheese sandwich.

"That's all you're having?" Crystal asks after ordering a roast beef au jus with mashed potatoes for herself.

Rather than admitting a queasy stomach, I simply say, "I'm not very hungry."

"But you're the one who planned this evening," Helen says. "You said you wanted to come here because you love their menu."

It's true I chose The Pepper Pot when I telephoned Crystal and Helen about having dinner this evening. I wanted a cozy neighborhood place for our last meal together. This basement restaurant, lit by enormous candles and adorned with bouquets of red peppers hanging from a labyrinth of pipes, has the perfect ambiance for a final dinner with my dearest friends. Rather than explaining that, which I can't, I tell Crystal I love her slacks. "And those high-button shoes are so perfect," I say. "A bit of old with the new." I glance down at my pleated skirt and smile, thinking once I get to California, Charles will no longer be able to command my couture.

The evening goes on with the easy conversation only old friends can have. Helen tells us about the gold ring her father recently designed for her mother, and we laugh, remembering when we were twelve and Helen lost her birthstone ring somewhere in the park's shrubbery. Oh, the trouble she got into!

And Crystal mentions a girl we knew in grade school, the one with the bad teeth and smelly breath, who's expecting her third child already. My finger worries my earlobe. I'm afraid I'll never find this kind of closeness in Los Angeles.

A few actors I performed with in Susan Glaspell's play stop on the way to their table. I introduce them to the girls, and we chat for a bit. I spot a group of musicians I know at a table in the corner, and Helen points out Dorothy Parker, saying she's never seen her here – that she's usually uptown at the Algonquin Hotel. I never met Mrs. Parker though I know of her harsh critiques of theater people, especially the one she wrote a few years ago in *Vanity Fair* about Florenz Ziegfeld. I, too, was offended by her audacious comment stating the Follies were meant to be seen and not heard. How wrong she was, writing there would be no future whatsoever for our musical entertainments once the war was over.

Munching on my gooey cheese sandwich, I drink in the faces of my dearest friends wanting to commit every inch to memory, like a photograph printed on my mind. Crystal's peachy skin and her gorgeous thick, dark eyelashes. The tiny creases around Helen's hazel eyes when she smiles and the spray of freckles across her nose with the faded childhood scar. Listening, I nod or laugh at appropriate times, savoring their words. They may be the last I hear for a very long time, though I pray not forever.

The conversation lulls while we eat. Holding my sandwich between my fingers, as if what I'm about to say doesn't hold much importance, I tell them I'm going up to Newport for a week or so. "Don't be surprised. Mother wrote and asked me to visit." I may be an actress playing a big role here, but I've never lied to my friends. My throat is thick with guilt. I grab the glass of water and take a gulp.

"Is she ill?" Crystal asks, her sweet voice filled with genuine concern.

"Why else would she invite her?" Helen says, throwing up a palm. "It's not as if she misses her granddaughter."

"No, she does not," I say, enunciating each word. "And she isn't ill. Rosy simply is not invited." Their eyes shoot wide open. "That's right. Mother does not want the 'pandemonium and mayhem,' as she calls it, of a child in the house." The clatter of dishes falling off a waiter's tray perfectly punctuates my sentence. These may be the best lines I've ever recited, though there's no joy in Crystal and Helen being my audience.

"Well, then, it's a blessing you have Grandmama," Crystal says, and I think how right she is. Then she adds, "We can help out on the weekend."

Helen nods her agreement, not able to say anything while she's savoring a bite of her chicken and waffles. Warmth radiates through my breast knowing my friends, Rosy's "aunties," will always be there to give her love and guide her to grow into the woman I dream she will become – independent and fulfilled. None of which I would be able to give if I stayed. I can only hope their influence will outweigh Charles's narrow-mindedness.

My friends start planning a weekend adventure for my daughter, taking her to the American Museum of Natural History to see the massive brontosaurus. "Remember how frightened I was," Helen says, "when my parents took us?" We laugh, recalling our first Sunday trip together shortly after Helen moved to Gramercy Park. We were nine years old. The dinosaur exhibit had just opened, and Helen's father was excited to take "his girls." My parents objected at first, not knowing this new family very well. Despite the fact that Helen's dad was a successful jeweler with a beautiful shop downtown, Mother was put off by their being Jewish immigrants who had moved up from the tenements. I sip my coffee and run my finger on my earring – the earring he designed especially for us for our Sweet Sixteens. Can it be ten years already? Since I was given this unique, handmade piece of jewelry, I've worn it often. Helen and

Crystal tease me that I have so many other pieces, I should leave this one in my jewelry box. But it comforts me. Especially tonight.

Dinner is over, our coffee cups empty. It's time. We stand on the sidewalk outside The Pepper Pot, and Helen and Crystal wish me a good trip. "Say hello to your mother for me," Crystal says. Helen adds, "Don't let her rile you," and I grab them both in a big hug, hold tight, and swallow the lump in my throat.

The following morning, I stand in front of the mirror, in our foyer, putting on my felt cloche with the pink silk rose stitched to the side. I tilt it a bit more off-center, giving it a jauntier flair. My mother-in-law, standing in the kitchen doorway across from me, smiles. "You look wonderful," she says. "And I want you to have a fabulous afternoon with your lady friends. Aren't these the women who were in the Susan Glaspell play with you?"

Not able to confirm my lie by uttering yes, I give her a tiny nod and slip on my new spring cape.

"Well, you leave Rosy to me and enjoy yourself." She walks closer and, in a quiet voice, says, "You know, dear, I'd love to see you in another play. I'll try again with Charles."

I turn and wrap her in a hug. "Thanks for trying, but I don't think it'll work." She shakes her head, letting me know she agrees, then steps back. Her eyes fasten on mine. *Is that pity I see? Or sorrow?* Rosy calls from upstairs. Her "Gama, Gama" cuts through the sudden heavy air. Grandmama goes to get her up from her nap. I step out the front door.

Repeating my travels from yesterday, I arrive at Forty-second Street. This time I exit the elevated train and walk down the street to the Bowery Savings Bank. It's my first time at this branch where no one knows me. Or more importantly, knows Charles. I walk through the massive door, dwarfed by the size of the sumptuous room. The giant arches and the marble columns and walls give off an air of wealth, and the wood-beamed ceiling must be fifty or sixty feet high, if not more. But this is not where I'll do my banking business. My eyes scan the large room where male tellers stand behind counters performing financial transactions for men. I walk across the room to the staircase leading to the lower level. To the Ladies Department.

Downstairs, in this well-furnished room created especially for women's banking needs, there are dainty desks with tasteful stationery, pens, and other writing material. I take a seat on one of the upholstered chairs and wait for the woman seated in the corner at a large desk with the title Assistant Cashier pinned to her jacket. She looks very professional in a light-gray, dropped-waist dress and jacket to match.

She seems to be advising a woman who looks a few years younger than me. I'm the only other person here. The room is quiet, so I can't help but overhear bits of their conversation, especially when the banker's voice gets louder offering the lady congratulations on her recent marriage and when the bride repeats "a housewife's budget" and tells the banker she never knew there was such a thing. Neither did I. Charles handles all our money. I suppose the allowance he gives me is my housewife's budget though I've never thought of it that way. Now, I'll have to create a single woman's budget. But that's not why I'm here.

Business completed, the bride, who looked overwhelmed talking with the banker, walks out with a satisfied smile on her face. I'm called over and sit opposite the Assistant Cashier. "I'd like to withdraw all my money," I say after she asks how she can help.

"All of it?" she asks with a straight face. "That would close out your account."

Does she really think I don't know that? I maintain my erect posture, giving off an air of confidence, and tell her it's what I have to do.

With a concerned tilt of her head, she says, "Are you unhappy banking here? Perhaps there's something I can do?"

I don't want to tell this banker I'm moving, yet why not? She doesn't know Charles. He banks downtown. So I let her know I'm moving out of the City.

She nods. "And the Bowery Savings Bank is only here in New York City," she says. "I wish you lots of good luck with your move." She notices the wedding band on my left hand. "You'll need your husband's signature for the withdrawal."

"Oh, no. This is for my *own* account. His name isn't on it."

"Ah." She nods. "Good for you."

With a bank check made out to Lucy Brandt tucked away in my handbag, I walk out of the bank wondering what she meant by those three words. *Good for me that I have my own money? Yes, it is, and more women should.* It's always amazed me that Charles, with his old-fashioned patriarchal views, didn't insist I give him my earnings when he allowed me to perform. Tossing away acting as an unsavory profession, he never could have believed how much I made. Not enough to live his lifestyle. But enough for me, in my new one. As long as I get the parts.

Chapter 15

Charles slams his cup on the cocktail table. There's fire in his eyes, disgust in his voice. "I will never understand your mother. How can she not want to see her only granddaughter?"

It's late in the evening, the dinner dishes are washed and put away, and we're sitting in the parlor, me on the Chesterfield, Charles across on the arm chair. Grandmama is reading in her room. She's just put Rosy to bed. I appreciate her giving us this private time, which she regularly does, though Charles and I do not often sit together over after-dinner coffee. Generally, we go our separate ways. Charles in his study, me by myself reading or writing letters at my desk. Tonight, though, I asked him to join me because I had an invite from my mother I needed to discuss with him.

"How can she be so cold?" he says, staring at me. His eyes narrow. *Is he comparing me to my mother? And oh my gosh, the furor he will have when he realizes I never actually received an invitation. That I never went to Newport. And I'm never coming back.* Charles can't understand that I'm a caged tiger. If I don't escape, there is no way I'll ever be free. I will never be me. And I'm afraid, because of him, I'll grow to resent my daughter even more. That is no way for a girl to grow up. I know that all too well.

"It's better I don't argue with my mother," I say, playing my part. "Grandmama will do a fine job taking care of both you and Rosy.

"Yes, but what about your precious rehearsals?" Ugly sarcasm spews from his lips. "I thought you couldn't possibly miss even one."

I fight the urge to spit back. Instead, knowing he'll like what I have to say, I employ a conciliatory tone. "I've already told O'Neill that I wouldn't be continuing. After all, the show opens in a few weeks." I should have said I couldn't, not I wouldn't, but Charles knows that's what I mean. After all, he's the one who declared I could no longer work on *The Hairy Ape* once it opened.

"Ah, yes," he says. "I'm glad you agree."

Oh yes, I'm a good actress. I give him one of my sweetest smiles and say, "Crystal and Helen offered to take Rosy to the Museum of Natural History on the weekend. It'll give Grandmama a break, and you'll have some time for yourself too."

"That's lovely of them." The shake of his head and downturned mouth tell me he's accepting my story, although he doesn't like it. He asks when I'll leave.

"In a few days. I first want to purchase my ticket, to be assured of a seat. Then I'll have an exact date."

"I'll go to the bank tomorrow," he says, "and take out fifty dollars. That should give you more than enough for the train and steamboat and all your expenses for the week."

I force my jaw not to drop. That's an enormous sum. I never counted on Charles giving me money, but why wouldn't he? He is my husband, and I'm going on a trip to visit my mother. Of course he would pay for it. I thank him profusely, arguing that it's too generous an amount. "I'll never need all of that," I say, knowing full well I will. I press my hand to my heart. A slow smile creeps up my face.

"I'd rather you have more money than you need," he says and with emphasis adds, "I do not want you taking a penny from your mother. And I expect you back here at home one week later."

Knowing how long it'll take me to get to California, and for a letter to reach him, I need to play it safe. He can't have any reason to call my mother wondering why I'm not back yet, so, with a sweet pleading voice, I ask if he minds if I stay longer. "My mother might need me."

"Ten days," he grunts. "Not an hour more."

The following morning, I wake to sunlight dappling through the lace curtains casting strips of bright yellow across my blanket. I dress in a new spring frock with my blue beret jauntily perched on my freshly washed hair. With Rosy in tow, I head up to Grand Central Terminal.

"A one-way ticket on the 20th Century, please," I say to the red-headed man inside the booth. "And I believe I can also purchase the ticket continuing on to Los Angeles at the same time."

"That is correct," he says, adjusting his horn-rimmed glasses. "You know the 20th Century terminates in Chicago. You'll need to change to the California Limited to continue your journey." With pride in his voice, he adds, "Both offer first-class service. Would you like to purchase an upper berth or lower?"

After hearing the price difference, I decide on the lower. I have to keep saving money. It would be foolish to use it all simply to have a single compartment. A bed closed off from the aisle by a curtain is fine for me. I don't need to live as swanky as my parents or my husband. For me, it won't be hard to give up the silks, jewels, and sterling silver.

With my ticket ensconced in my handbag, I push Rosy's stroller through the throngs hurrying every which way through the terminal. She looks wide-eyed at all the people rushing about. The big brass clock atop the information booth shows we have one hour to get to Mrs. Stokes's. When I called her yesterday to say I was going to Newport for the week, she invited Rosy and me to come at noon today for a farewell lunch. I sigh, again, thinking about how much of a goodbye it truly is. The lying twists my gut, but it has to be.

Between the warm, sunny day and the comfortable canvas flats on my feet, I choose to stroll down Park Avenue with its chic residences rather than take the El. It's only a little over a mile to Gramercy Park. Hopefully, I'll work up an appetite for Auntie Mabel's rich cooking. For the past few days, all I've been doing is pushing food around my plate. My leaving is no longer an idea but a reality, and no matter how much I want to do this, the tension is eating away at me.

The avenue is dressed up with purple and red tulips adorning the grassy island that floats down the middle of the street. It makes me think of my own small garden, the one behind our townhouse. Grandmama will be happy to tend it, as she has always helped me trim and feed the roses, which will need to be done soon. Now that Rosy is old enough, she'll be able to help using the little red watering can I bought for her at Woolworth's. My walled garden is the one thing I'll miss from the townhouse. Not the fancy parlor or the Persian rugs. Just the serenity of the enclosed garden amid the brick buildings, an oasis closed off from the bustling city.

We reach Twentieth Street and I wait at the corner twitching my nose from the whiff of gasoline as cars pass by. Finally, there's an opening and I push Rosy's stroller across the street. Heading east, I'm thinking about the West and the flowers I'll grow in California. If I can ever get my own place. First, I'll have to rent a room in a boarding house, one where meals are included since I'll have to save my pennies until I get a part in a play or some type of paying job. I hope I can have a single room but if need be, I'd like a roommate who will become a friend. A lump clogs my throat as I picture Crystal and Helen.

Chapter 16

With pen in hand and a piece of my pale-blue stationery lying on the leather-bound blotter, I'm ready to write. The idea came to me yesterday after saying goodbye to Auntie Mabel and her husband. He was so happy to see that I was still wearing the earrings he'd made for "his girls" as he continues to call Helen, Crystal, and me, even though we're not little ones running in and out of their house anymore, tracking in leaves and mud and all sorts of other stuff. I'm happy with my plan for the earrings, feeling as bright as the sunlight streaming through the window enhancing the luster on my French provincial writing desk. Grandmama and Rosy are out for a late morning walk, Charles is at the hospital, and the house is quiet. Perfect for putting my words on paper.

Dearest Grandmama, These . . .

No, too formal. I crumple the paper, pull out another piece from the top drawer, and start over.

To my dear mother-in-law, Enclosed you will find . . .

I throw down the fountain pen and push away from the desk. The ink sprays all over the paper. *Just write it*, I tell myself. *Don't be formal. Get the words down.* So, I toss that piece into the wastepaper basket and slip another from the drawer, stall for a moment, then write.

Grandmama, please give these earrings

I'm about to write my daughter's name, but stop, pen in midair, and wonder. Should I write the name printed on her birth certificate, the one I gave her the minute I woke from the gas and was told I had a baby girl? Or do I write the nickname Charles gave her, the name everyone calls her, thanks to him? I let Charles win – again. Continuing where I left off, I finish the sentence with:

to Rosy on her sixteenth birthday.

Then, with a lightness in my chest, imagining the gold disks embossed with the image of a Gibson girl and studded with three gems, I continue writing.

They mean a great deal to me and I want my daughter to have something that connects her to me and to her aunties. I'm sure Crystal and Helen will be at whatever celebration you have for Rosy. Please ask Helen to tell her all about how her father made the earrings for us when we turned sixteen. Perhaps you can even have an opal added to represent Rosy's birth month.

I blow out a huge breath and fall back against the chair. Enough. Don't belabor the point. But I can't help myself. I want to say more. I want to tell her not to hate me. To please understand why I have to leave. Instead, I tear up that piece and grab another. This time it's short and to the point.

Grandmama, please give these earrings to Rosy on her sixteenth birthday. They are very precious to me, and I want my daughter to have something of mine, something she can wear that'll connect us to each other.

Yes, that does it. I sign my name then realize I should say thank you. I add the words then carefully press a piece of blotting paper on the wet ink. Once its dry, I slip the note in the envelope.

Upstairs, in Mama Brandt's bedroom, I open the armoire and take down her alligator handbag with the tortoiseshell handle, the one she calls her winter purse. I slip the envelope in along with the earrings, snug in their velvet box, and stash the bag back on the shelf. I'm certain she will find it once I'm in California – after the Thanksgiving turkey has been consumed and the Christmas tree decorated. Not before.

In my bedroom, I pull out lingerie from my dresser, careful not to take everything. After all, I'm only supposed to be going away for ten days. I continue pulling a few skirts, blouses, and dresses from the closet. My fingers caress the delicate fabric of my harem pants. I grab them and several more linen and cotton trousers I haven't been allowed to wear.

Charles's clothes hang in an armoire so I'm comfortable knowing he will never notice my slacks are gone. It would ruin everything if he called me in Newport, angry that I'd disobeyed his order, only to find out I never made it to my mother's cottage. If I do send him a letter from the train, after we leave Chicago, it'll get picked up at one of our stops, possibly New Mexico or Arizona, and take several days to reach New York. If I calculate correctly, it'll reach him while I'm allegedly in Newport. I don't want it to arrive after I should have returned home. That would put everyone in a tizzy wondering where I am, what happened to me, and possibly calling the police. I can't have anyone on my tail checking trains and buses or . . . *Oh, stop*, I tell myself. *All will work out fine.*

I lay the clothes atop the purple satin lining in my leather valise, lock the case, and place it in the corner of the room. In the matching round hat box, I tuck a straw cloche adorned with a wide ribbon tied in a bow, perfect for the warmer southern California weather, along with my toiletries. In two days, Charles will drive me to Grand Central Terminal and let me off in front where a Red Cap will take my bags. I'm positive Charles will not insist on helping me inside.

Chapter 17

Rosy sits on the Persian rug in the parlor playing with her doll, just like it was any other day. I'm sitting up straight on the settee smoking a cigarette, watching, blinking back tears. It's precious how her little brows draw together as she listens to her doll's heartbeat with her toy stethoscope. It's exactly what her father does when he pretends to listen to her heartbeat. Crystal gave Rosy the doctor's kit a few days ago for no other reason than she loves buying things for her Rosy Posy, as she says. It warms my heart to know Crystal will always be around for my daughter. I can count on her to steer Rosy into being a strong, independent woman. Despite Charles.

Poking her head into the parlor, my mother-in-law says, "Your taxi is here. I told him you'd be out in a moment."

Charles didn't find it necessary to take me to Grand Central or even be home to say goodbye. Just as the theater is for me, his work is of utmost importance to him, and after all the care I took in choosing my traveling outfit to appear the proper woman of my station, the woman he expects me to be, it turns out not to have been necessary.

I smash the cigarette out in the ashtray, then go over and scoop up my daughter. "Mama has to go away," I say, hugging her to my breast. "You be a good girl for . . ." My throat tightens. I can't say another word, so as any mother would who is leaving for a week or so, I kiss her goodbye. A peck on the forehead, the cheek, and the top of her soft blond curls. Then I set her back on the floor with her toys and walk into the hall where my luggage sits on the floor, waiting.

"Send my regards to your mother," Mama Brandt says, holding the front door open."And don't worry about us. We'll be fine."

I wrap my arms around her. Her soft, meaty ones encircle my slight frame. I breathe in her lavender dusting powder, holding the memory in my heart. "I know you will be," I say. "You have no idea how much I appreciate your taking care of Rosy." Silently, I pray for my mother-in-law, who's already sixty, to continue living a healthy life for many years to come. My daughter will need her.

Drawing out of the embrace, I remind Mama Brandt that Charles need not call me in Newport. I doubt he would anyway. "I'll be in and out and, if I need anything, I'll wire. The phone rates are too prohibitive to make a call." Then, with a tight grip on my two suitcases, I step out into the balmy spring evening. To my future.

~

"All aboard," the conductor calls in his belting baritone from the platform. Through the large plateglass windows in the observation car, I view porters laden with luggage hurrying latecomers onto the train. Sipping coffee, I'm comfortably seated on a mahogany easy chair upholstered in a velvety-soft tapestry. Electric lights gleam from the ceiling and walls, adding to the elegant decor. Even the spittoon in the corner is of stunning blue and white porcelain. A middle-aged woman dressed similarly to me in a pleated skirt, the hem hitting just below the knee, is tucked into an alcove dressed up with ferns, reading a book. Her legs, like mine, show the full calf adorned in black silk stockings. Another, younger woman sits across from me. Bright red lipstick covers her bow-shaped lips and an ebony spit curl is plastered to her forehead. Between that and the long strands of pearls covering her flat chest, she's the epitome of a flapper. I look down at my chest and laugh to myself. I always wanted larger breasts but at twenty-six years old, I don't think they're going to grow anymore. They barely grew after pregnancy, though I was told they would. Well, at least flat chests are the rage now. They look so much better in a chemise.

Miss Red Lips takes a cigarette from a gold case and reaches her arm out, offering me one. "Oh, thank you," I say and take it from her gloved hand. She slips hers into a long silver holder. My breath catches as I picture Crystal and her ubiquitous cigarette holders. A man with a handlebar mustache and wearing two-tone, brown-and-white wingtips, the new shoe style Charles is not fond of, sits next to the smoking woman. His face is buried in the *New York Tribune*. I notice the announcement on the page facing me. "Mayor Hylan Closes Two Streets in the Bronx to Build Yankee Stadium." It's supposed to be a cathedral for baseball. Early in our marriage, Charles took me to the Polo Grounds to see the Yankees with John "Home Run" Baker. It was the first game I'd ever been to, and I loved it. The excitement on the field, batters running to first base, the noise erupting in the stands when a player slid into home and vendors shouting "Peanuts, popcorn, Cracker Jacks." What fun it was cracking open roasted peanuts, making a blanket of the shells at my feet, and finding the prize in the Cracker Jack box! We went to a few more games until Rosy was born. As Charles said, mothers are supposed to be home with their children, making dinner for their husbands when they return from the stadium. A sour taste fills my mouth at the thought.

The man with a waxy handlebar mustache lowers the newspaper and pulls out his pocket watch. "We should be leaving the station soon," he says "It's almost six."

I look at my wristwatch. "Yes," I say, getting up from my seat. "I think I'll go out and join the people on the rear platform."

On the platform, I find two people sitting in camp chairs, one a man gazing into space smoking a pipe, the other an older woman engrossed in a book. I sit, enjoying the freedom of the open air while the train pulls out of the station. Its steady chugging sound increases while the City recedes. The rocking motion makes my body sway back and forth. Steadying myself, I reach into the leather handbag on my lap. Through my lace glove, I feel the stiffness of a piece of cardboard. I run my finger over its four sides. Clasping an edge, I begin drawing it out then tell myself to let it be. *Leave it in the bag.* Instead, I take out a cigarette. Smoking, I stare at the buildings diminishing in the distance and cock my head to the side, blowing smoke through my lips, watching it slowly twirl in the air. Tears prickle my eyes. My hand slides to my bag again, the tooled design bumpy against my palm. I open the clasp and grasp the hard cardboard. Fingers tight on the edge, I tell myself to leave it alone. To leave it buried in the bag. But then why did I take it? "Oh, stop being so melodramatic," I whisper to myself and pull the photograph out. With the cigarette dangling from my right hand, I focus on Rosy's image in my left. She's in her white lace dress and socks, little Mary Janes on her feet. The picture was taken in a photographer's studio on her first birthday. Holding it against my heart, I think of all the birthdays to come, all I will miss. I try to picture the young woman she will become. Then I look at the image of my baby girl again and let out a long, slow sigh.

An hour later I enter the dining car. I spot the young woman who offered me a cigarette sitting alone at a table for two. A lush crimson carpet mutes my steps as I walk over and ask if I can join her. "Absolutely," she says, and I take a seat opposite on a soft blue-leather chair. The entire car is lined with tables for two or four hugging the sides, some separated by glass partitions offering the ambiance of an elegant restaurant rather than a train car. The tables are dressed in snow-white linen cloths and napkins with fresh flowers. Large plate glass windows allow views of the Hudson River as we travel along the tracks. Helen and Crystal would love this, and what fun it would be if they were sitting here with me. Instead, I look at my dining partner.

"I'm Lucy Perkins," I say. The name rolls off my tongue easily since it's the one I grew up with, the name I wanted to keep when I married. Many women in the Heterodoxy Club kept their maiden names, but Charles and my parents wouldn't hear of it. Now I embrace it. It is who I am and who I will always be.

My dining partner reaches her hand across the table. We shake and she tells me she's Jenny Howe. "I'm going to California," she says. "Are you stopping in Chicago or going all the way?"

I tell Miss Howe I'm going all the way to Los Angeles and her eyes light up. "Wonderful. It'll be nice having someone to talk to and eat with for the next four days. If you don't mind? And please, call me Jenny. I'm not as formal as my mother."

A woman after my own heart. With a lightness in my chest, I tell her to call me Lucy. Although I need time to write my letters, I'm happy for the company and to know someone in Los Angeles when I get there. Possibly a friend. We chat easily about the all-year-round warm temperatures in our new city, the open spaces, beaches, and the fresh oranges and lemons growing on trees in everyone's garden.

"I want to get into the movies," Jenny says. "I know, I could have stayed in New York. Fox Studio is only across the river in Fort Lee. I did have some bit parts with them, and the Selznick Company is there too. But I don't want New Jersey. I want Hollywood. That's really where it's at."

The waiter, in gunmetal gray pants that match the elegant interior of the car, a starched white shirt, and a bow tie, brings us menus. It takes only a moment to choose between lobster and filet mignon with caviar as a starter. Sadly, due to Prohibition, there are no cocktails on the menu. I certainly would enjoy a sidecar right now with its sugared rim. How perfect for a train ride.

A gentleman in a three-piece suit is seated at the table across from us. He's quite dapper with his gold collar pin and white carnation on the lapel of his natty striped suit. He catches my eye and, with a wink, pulls a large pewter flask from his pocket. It's as if he was reading my mind. "Excuse me," he says. "But would you ladies like a drink?"

"Oh, my goodness. Yes," says Jenny. I'm taken aback at how quickly she replied. Though I surely could use one tonight.

"Here you go," he says, extending his arm across the narrow aisle. Jenny reaches out and accepts his offer. "There's some good scotch in there," he says. "We all need a bit of giggle water before a sumptuous meal. Take as much as you want. I've got plenty."

I thank the man with the flower in his lapel, wondering who he is. And why he's so generous with his booze. Could he be one of those gangsters in Al Capone's gang? This train is going to Chicago. Oh, how I wish I could tell Crystal and Helen about this. We'd make up such stories. Crystal would put him on the stand in a pretend court and rip him apart in a cross-examination. Helen would create shocking headlines for the newspaper. I take a sip of scotch, hoping it'll soften the hard lump in my throat.

The murmur of soft voices fills the dining car. Silverware clinks against china, and Jenny and I carry on with easy conversation. Her excitement is infectious so I tell her about my wanting to audition for live theater.

"Why would you go to California," she says, "when you have Broadway right in your backyard?"

Yes, why would I? How do I answer that? I lift a shoulder and in a matter-of-fact tone say, "I need a change." Her drawn eyebrows tell me she's curious. Or is it skeptical? "Like you," I tell her, "I've had parts – some big ones – though in live theater, not movies. The stage is my true love. And it's been quite a while. I'm anxious to get back to it." I won't explain why it's been a long time, and I never will. All I tell her is that I want a fresh start and with a big smile add, "Somewhere new, far from New York," as if this is the most exciting adventure. "A whole new life and Los Angeles has theater, so why not?"

Jenny leans in and whispers, "Sounds to me like there's a man involved – why you're going so far." She cocks her head, though her grin makes it look like she's waiting for some juicy dirt, then takes a sip of her scotch.

"Oh, no," I giggle. "Not really. I mean, of course, I've had some . . ."

"Who hasn't?" she says and we laugh.

The waiter approaches and I'm glad to dig into my juicy steak and think about theater in Los Angeles. I'm intrigued by what I've heard of the Morosco, a playhouse reminiscent of the European playhouses where true drama is performed. That is my true love, not musicals or vaudeville. Though I will audition for any show at any legitimate theater. My pulse quickens thinking of this again with a mixture of excitement and fear. And a pinch of melancholy. But I'll get over that. I have to.

Chapter 18

For our après-dinner coffee, Jenny and I walk to the observation car, holding onto the wall, taking tentative steps, balancing ourselves from the train's rocking and rattling. We step into the club car and pass the barber shop just as the train swerves. Jenny lurches forward. She grabs my shoulder and we burst out laughing. Finally, we get to our destination. I find my footing and let out a breath of relief.

A gentleman, wearing a gold pocket watch, sits by the window staring out at the dark night. Another man in a suit and fedora is absorbed in a book. Two women, appropriately dressed for travel in dark-colored skirts and matching, long-waisted jackets, are seated in the corner, absorbed in hushed conversation. One sports a jaunty red hat. My kind of gal. The quiet atmosphere gives off an air of contemplation. I'm glad to have Jenny keeping me from my thoughts. She's like a breath of cool air on a humid day with her excitement about the movies. Although I don't have any regrets and believe I've done the best for my daughter, I can't help the sadness pressing on my chest, knowing I won't see her grow up. Won't see her go off to school or college or get her first job. I won't see her glowing when she's picked up for her first date or . . . I shake those thoughts from my head. They're not at all productive. And I am truly excited about this trip. About my future.

"We must be coming into a station," I say, hearing the rumble of the wheels get slower and slower. Miss Red Hat throws me a glance then quickly returns to her conversation.

"To take on water," the gentleman with the pocket watch says as we pass by. "That's the way these steam engines run. We'll take it on here in Albany and again in Syracuse and Buffalo, but you'll probably be asleep at that time . . ."

"Probably," I say. The brakes squeal as we come to a stop, but it doesn't stop him. From his seat, he keeps jabbering about track pans and why we're following the water level route. I wish he'd stop bumping his gums. I don't need all these details, and I have no interest in how the train works, only that it gets me to my destination safely. I look over at Jenny who's already comfy in a seat by the window. She's shaking her head and laughing like she thinks I'm nuts for not following her. She's right. What am I still doing here nodding and smiling at the man? Probably because I always had to stand still and listen to Charles. My body shakes, thinking of how I could never cut him off, and now, here on the train with this man giving me a diatribe on steam engines, I'm doing it again. When all I want is to sit, drink my coffee, and gaze out at the moon glistening on the water. With a smirk in her eye, Jenny waves me over. But the man is yammering on, telling me all the stops we'll make. Finally, I get a word in and tell him it's fascinating. I'm so damn polite. I wish him a good evening and take my seat.

Jenny rolls her eyes at me and we share a silent giggle. I may look like a society woman in my linen traveling suit and cloche, but I am far from the stuffy ladies I've seen on this train. Even the one I saw reading earlier, with the shorter hem and black stockings like mine, was adorned in fine jewelry. I reach for my ear and stop. My lobes are bare. A pensive smile pulls my cheeks and I clasp my hands in my lap. Yes, leaving the earrings for

Rosy was the best idea. I hocked my other jewelry to ensure I'd have enough to carry me for several months in case I don't get a part right away. Or some type of job, if I have to.

It's as black as ink outside, but the car glimmers with electric lighting echoing the glow deep inside me. There's a desk in the corner and though I do have to write my letter to Charles, I need tonight to absorb this incredible feeling of independence - despite the unease in my stomach. Every time I play with the words I'll write, my gut tightens. I know Charles will be furious and I will never be able to make him understand, so why try? But I must compose a few words. It's the right thing to do. And I have to think of Rosy. I take a sip of coffee and breathe in the heady scent of hickory, clinging to the belief that Crystal and Helen will, one day, sit down with my daughter and tell her about me and the truth about her parents' marriage. But I'm not kidding myself. I'm well aware my friends will be hurt and probably angry at my leaving this way, yet I have to believe they'll eventually come to terms with it. They're my sisters. They know who I am, who Charles has refused to allow me to be. Leaning back against the soft tapestry on my chair, I force the vinegary thoughts from my mind. Slowly, I nod. Yes. No one should have to compromise her true self. Her soul. It's what I hope my daughter will understand.

"You look quite satisfied about something," Jenny says.

My chest expands with a full breath. "Yes, I am." I hear her prattle on about the lovely evening, the delicious meal, and what she's looking forward to in Los Angeles. I, too, am imagining life in California, free from my cage.

"Do you have somewhere to stay when we get there?" she says. "A friend told me about Mrs. D's in Culver City, near the movie studios. It's a boarding house. I already wrote to her and have a room waiting for me. Maybe she'll have one for you too."

"That would be wonderful. I've been thinking I'd have to stay in a hotel until I could find something. I'd love my own apartment, but I'm not sure I can afford that yet."

"You mean in a women's only building, like they have in New York?"

"I suppose so. Unless Los Angeles allows women to rent in any building. There are some in Greenwich Village that do."

"That's the Village," Jenny says. "It's another world down there."

I laugh. "You're right. I doubt I'll find anything as avant-garde in California." I keep a big smile on my face, though it's sad to think I'll never have the Heterodoxy Club anymore. At least in theater, I'll probably find women with similar views. "Most likely I'll do the same as you," I say. "Does Mrs. D's give you kitchen privileges, or does she supply all the meals?"

"Lunch and dinner are included in the rent during the week. We're on our own on weekends, but we're allowed to use the kitchen. And I think we share bathrooms, maybe two or three girls to one."

I'd love to have my own bathroom, but I don't say that. The Lucy of Washington Square and Gramercy Park is gone. And good riddance to her. I had roommates and shared bathrooms at Barnard and it was fun. I may be older now, but I'm looking forward to this new life, even if it means waiting my turn to bathe. And one day I will have enough money to rent an apartment. Maybe even buy a house, if the law ever changes. Heaven forbid a woman wants to purchase a home in her name, with her own money.

After some more companionable conversation with Jenny and others in the car, I bid them good night. At the tiny sink in the bathroom in the corridor, I brush my teeth. Back in my berth, I close the curtains and slip into my cotton nightgown that brushes my ankles then climb into bed with a book of Emily Dickinson's poems. I turn to my favorite. It begins,

Hope is the thing with feathers
That perches in the soul,
And sings the tune without the words,
And never stops at all,

This stanza sits deep in my soul. I am that bird. My eyelids grow heavy as I continue reading. The soft tchik-tchik of the train traveling down the track lulls me to sleep. And the bird keeps singing.

~

Last night I had my first deliciously restful sleep in a very long time. I stretch my arms overhead. Ah, it feels so good. I'm ready to greet the day and, after breakfast, write my letter to Charles. The words are all in my head; they just need to be put on paper. I rise from the narrow bed and lift the blinds. The glistening sun glimmers on the green water. We've left the Hudson, according to the chatty man last night, and are now traveling the water level route along Lake Erie. In a few hours, we'll arrive in Chicago on Lake Michigan. I never imagined I'd see any of the Great Lakes, their being so far from New York City, and now I'll have seen three. My world is opening up.

After a solo breakfast of poached eggs on toast and hot coffee I walk, swaying with the jerky movement of the train, through the narrow corridors to the club car. With a nod and a good morning smile, I greet passengers along the way. I've always been an early riser and, before I married five long years ago, I cherished the silence as I savored my morning coffee reflecting on the previous night's performance or the upcoming day's rehearsal. I look forward to those quiet times again. And to those same types of reflections.

This morning brings that serenity back, and I'm glad to find myself alone in the car. I sit at the desk in the corner, ignoring the view of the vast lake through the window, and focus on the task ahead of me. With my fountain pen in hand, blotter, and onion-skin stationery in place, I begin.

May 1922

Dear Charles,

From the postmark on the envelope, you'll see I'm not in Newport visiting my mother. Unfortunately, I had to lie to you and everyone else, and I am sorry about that. I'm sorry that I'm not able to be the wife you wanted or the mother Rosy deserves. It's impossible for me to be that woman and still live a life that fulfills me. From the beginning you, as well as my parents, believed I would gladly give up my career in the theater once I was mistress of my own home. You all were sure I would embrace motherhood. That it would make me complete. I'm sorry I couldn't be that woman for you. I wish you all understood me. Your mother is the only person who does. She knows I love Rosy, but that it's not enough, that I'm . . .

My hand stops. That I'm what? What is it I want to say? That I'm not a good mother? I'm not. But I can't write that. It'll feed right into everything Charles believes, and it won't help him understand me. Yet, will he ever? My insides quiver. I thought I had it all figured out, all the words I want to say and now I'm not sure. I have to write this letter. I have to sound strong. I am strong, so why am I having trouble getting the words down? I don't regret what I've done. I am sorry that we couldn't . . . that our marriage didn't work. I tried. And I'm afraid if I had stayed I would come to resent my daughter. As much as I love her, she's the reason Charles won't let me have my career. I threw her at him once, out of anger. What if I did that again? Or worse, heaven forbid. Charles's restrictions on me and his refusal to meet me halfway made my blood boil. I don't want to be that person. That mother. I clench my fists, then tear up the paper and toss it in the garbage. I write again using the same words until I get to "it's not enough." I take a moment then, with assurance, continue.

Your mother once told you I'm not a nurturing mother and you should let me have my life on stage and leave her to care for Rosy. If only you could have listened, could have accepted who I truly am, we might have made our marriage work. But you were unable to compromise. To be able to live my true life, I have to abandon you and my daughter. Yes, that is what I'm doing. It's a harsh reality and a harsh word. People may judge me the same way. I accept that. This is the only way I can see to be free from the cage you've held me in and be allowed to live the life I am meant to. And not resent our daughter.

There, I've said it. I stop. Breathe. Then continue.

The law doesn't give women the right to ask for a divorce, otherwise I would have, though you may not have granted it. Now you can divorce me. You can save face and let it be said you sent me away, if that's what you choose to do. I will not refute it. You need not worry. I will be far away from New York and all of your colleagues. All I ask is that you save the letters I'll send Rosy and give them to her when she's old enough to, hopefully, understand.

I lay the pen on the desk and slump against the chair. My head drops back and I quietly exhale as relief pours over me. With my eyes closed, I think about the last sentence I wrote. Should I keep it? Rosy will probably never understand. What child, no matter how old, could conceive of why her mother abandoned her? And no matter what Charles tells others, as sure as I am of my own name, he will tell Rosy the truth. I deserted her. He'll say I didn't love her enough to stay. It's not that. She deserves a better mother than I could ever be. And I'm sure he'll make her hate me. He won't want his daughter thinking *he* sent me away. No, that would make her angry. She would despise him instead of me, and in his mind, that would never do. It pains me. But I have to accept it. And hope Helen or Crystal will one day help her come to terms with it.

A tight knot of regret mixed with relief sits deep in my belly. Sitting up straight, I place the pen between my fingers and add my signature. A simple, Sincerely, Lucy.

Chapter 19

The train click-clacks along the track carrying me farther from my busy cement city cramped by tall buildings and crowded streets where push-cart sellers hawk their wares and automobiles nudge horses out of the way for their space on the asphalt. The wheels rumble as I gaze out the large plate glass window in the parlor car at the majestic snow-capped mountains in the distance. They soar up to the brilliant blue sky and go on for hundreds of miles. An ethereal, breathtaking scene. It's my second morning on the California Limited, and I feel as sublime as the landscape before me. In only two more days, I'll be in Los Angeles eating oranges freshly picked from trees rather than from wooden crates at the corner market. I'll be breathing in the fresh, salty scent of the Pacific. I'll be breathing in opportunity. Independence. Liberation.

Jenny and I have just finished a lovely breakfast in the dining car. The famous Fred Harvey catering didn't disappoint. The fare was scrumptious and the service elegant, as the literature promised. Over a dish of eggs Benedict with rosemary potatoes and a grapefruit anise salad served in crystal, Jenny told me I needn't worry about finding housing in Los Angeles. When we changed trains in Chicago, she went to the telegraph office in the station and sent Mrs. D a telegram asking her to reserve a room for me. Jenny assumes one will be available. I hope she's right. It would be so much easier than having to live in a hotel and search for a boarding house. And since I must live with other women, Jenny would be a fine housemate. She may look fragile, with those doe eyes and small frame, but she's quite the opposite. Jenny is one determined woman. I have a good feeling about her making it as a screen actress. It would be wonderful if more actresses were living in the boarding house, more women like me rather than telephone operators and shopgirls biding their time until a man comes along to take care of them. I'm well aware there are more of the latter than the women I'm used to being with. I will miss the Heterodoxy Club meetings at Polly's with our heated discussions on birth control and childbirth techniques. And those about socialism and pacifism, education reform, even open marriages. Women everywhere should be talking about this, not only about men. We got the vote. Now let's do something with it. A slight giggle escapes my lips. Yes, I know my people and they are not only actresses. Some might even be clerks or shopgirls. I shouldn't be so judgmental. I vow to find them as the train whistle blows a forlorn call into the mountains.

The letter box is waiting for me. It's time. I took my first step to liberation since getting on the train. Actually, my first step was deciding to leave, to escape the chains called Charles that kept me locked up. Now, there is one last thing that needs to be done. With the envelope addressed to Charles in my right hand, I flip down the hood of the mailbox with my left. Suddenly, a question comes to mind and I drop my hands. *What if I don't post this?* I stand staring at the steel gray box. It sits here on the train waiting for letters to be slipped in, picked up at our next stop – maybe somewhere in New Mexico – and delivered to loved ones back home. Ignoring people entering and leaving the car and the lone man engrossed in a newspaper, I take a moment to contemplate. My eyes never leave the mailbox, though I barely see it anymore. Thoughts tumble in my head. *What if I walked away? Once Charles realizes I never made it to Newport, would he send the police looking for me? Would he worry something untoward had happened? He would never imagine I'd leave him. Though, eventually, after Mother fretting, Grandmama agonizing over where I could possibly be, and Crystal and Helen out of their minds with worry, he'd realize I had.*

"What are you doing staring at a letter box?" Jenny says, interrupting my musings.

"Oh, nothing . . . just . . ." I chuckle. "I was imagining a play I might write." I wasn't but maybe I will try it. It's a good story. An unlikeable lead character, because that's what I am if I'm honest with myself. Yet, hopefully, a sympathetic one. And a controlling antagonist with no redeeming feature. Well . . . maybe one or two. He is a good son. And a good father. Ooh, yes, this could make a good play. It'll have a woman whose soul, whose true inner being roars to be free, and after years of capitulation, she realizes she must do something drastic. She'll trick the man into . . .

"That must be some incredible story," Jenny says, again interrupting my thoughts. "You're smiling then gritting your teeth, and now your eyes are so wide open it looks like you saw a ghost or something."

I was so engrossed in creating my fictitious story that, for a moment, I forgot Jenny was standing next to me. To cover up, I laugh and toss my hand in the air letting her know it was nothing. Then I open the box and slip the letter in. The blue envelope drops down. I slide my arm through my new friend's and say, "Let's go sit in the observation car." We walk away from the cold steel letter box. My final task is done. Whatever happens now is out of my control.

~

Two days later, the taxi cab drops us off in front of a two-story stucco house with light-blue shutters. A wrought iron fence surrounds the front yard that bursts in a kaleidoscope of color. Orange poppies dance in the beds. And there are gorgeous plants I've only seen in florist shops. The elegant birds-of-paradise, with their orange and purple plumage, are growing right from the soil, and I'm stunned by the bright red flowers growing on the tree bordering the neighbor's yard. They look like bottle brushes – the kind I used for cleaning Rosy's baby bottles.

"Oh, how charming!" Jenny says, opening the front gate. I step through, feeling as vibrant and joyous as the brilliantly colored flora. I pray this feeling stays when I meet Mrs. D. I would love to live here and dig my fingers in the garden's soil.

The brrring-brrring of the doorbell is soft and inviting. It takes only a moment for a buxom woman with soft gray curls to open the door.

"Jenny Howe?" she says with a questioning lilt to the name. Her upturned brow scans us both.

"Yes, that's me," Jenny says. Before she has a chance to say another word Mrs. D extends her hand and clasps Jenny's.

"Wonderful. I received your telegram saying you'd be arriving today. And you," she looks at me with a warm smile, "must be Lucy Perkins. Please, come in, ladies. I'm so happy to meet you."

Mrs. D explains the other women are all at work. "You'll see later. The house will be buzzing with laughter and conversation. Now, put your cases down and we'll have a cup of tea. You must be weary from your travels."

Weary is completely opposite of how I feel. After four days and three nights on trains, one might expect to be, yet I am energized. I'm so anxious to dive into my California life. Settle in, get to the theater, be on stage. Oh, I need to take a breath.

Slow down. It all takes time and, now, I have plenty of it. Until my money runs out.

We sit around a kitchen table covered in a white cloth with flowers embroidered along the edge. The mint-green walls, white painted cupboards, and metal cabinet with its gas range remind me of Helen's mother's kitchen, where I always felt loved and supported.

"Lucy, dear," Mrs. D says, carrying a flowered teapot to the table. "I imagine you're wondering if I have a room for you."

I don't say a word, merely look with wide-open eyes at her face. Between her jolly expression, the warm yeasty aroma of freshly baked bread, and the delicate tea service set in front of us I know, deep inside, this is where I want to live. Where I need to live.

"If you're willing to share," she says, pouring the dark, aromatic blend into my cup, "I have a place for you. It's a lovely room and the bed just became vacant." Her smile gets even brighter. With a shoulder shimmy shaking her ample bosom, she says, "One of my girls – oh, such a sweet child – married the most wonderful man. We all went to the wedding last weekend. What a beautiful ceremony." Her hands fold onto her chest. "It makes me so happy when my girls marry. It's what I want for all of you."

I'm sorry I won't be bringing Mrs. D that happiness though all I say is, "Thank you so much. I'd love to rent the room." Jenny, on the other hand, is sitting up straight, eyes so bright, hearing every word Mrs. D says.

We go through a bit of business. Smoking is only permitted outside, alcohol is not allowed anywhere, and men cannot go past the parlor. I can deal with all those rules. Then Mrs. D tells us there are five rooms and, now, with me, they'll all be filled. That's ten women in one house! Oh my gosh. It really is like being back in the dormitory at Barnard. But am I the same woman I was back then? This time, I'll be paying for my board.

I'll be independent. Free from everyone's clutches and demands. I have the rent now and will do my damnedest to have it on the thirtieth of each month.

"Breakfast starts at eight, in the dining room," Mrs. D says. "I place dinner on the buffet at six, though I know sometimes you might not be able to make it. My actresses and dancers are always busy at night, or," she says as she leans in with a glint in her eyes, "a fella might be taking you out."

Jenny giggles. She obviously likes that idea. As for me, I'm glad to hear other actresses live here, but I wish Mrs. D wasn't so anxious to get us all hitched. She waves a hand in the air to erase any concern I might have, which I don't. Other than what my roommate will be like. I hope she's not an early riser. When I'm on stage, I get home very late and need my mornings quiet. And please don't let her be a snorer. Charles was so loud he sounded like the El train barreling down the tracks.

"No worries," Mrs. D says as roommate concerns flood my mind. "I leave the food out for an hour or so. It stays hot and, if you're home late, you can always heat it up in the oven." I nod my thanks. "And," she goes on, "I always have coffee perking and the kettle filled." She pours more tea into our cups. It's as warming and welcoming as she is. "Feel free to keep anything else you might want in the pantry or ice box. Just label it, though all my girls are honest. We have a happy house here and . . ."

I let Mrs. D prattle on with pride about each of her precious girls. She tells me my roommate is a dancer who's at an audition right now. Thank goodness – we'll be keeping the same hours. "Oh," she says, springing up from the chair. "My mouth is running away with me, as my late husband always said. You probably want to get settled. Come, I'll show you your rooms."

Act Two

Chapter 20

May 1922

A few months ago, shortly after I moved in with Charles and Lucy, I confided in a lady friend about how upset I was constantly hearing my son and daughter-in-law arguing. She suggested I bite my tongue and pour my emotions into a diary. I was uncomfortable putting my feelings on paper, yet now, with my heart and thoughts even more a jumble, I must. So here I sit, in the parlor, at what was once Lucy's French provincial desk, writing in the leather-bound journal I bought at Drapkins on Eighth Street yesterday, after learning the shocking truth of what she had done. With Lucy gone who knows where, I, Mama Brandt as she called me, am now the only woman living in this house, and I suppose this carved, kidney-shaped writing desk is now mine. I never expected to claim it as my own – or for Lucy to leave!

Although she has done the unthinkable – what woman leaves her daughter? – I must admit I understand Lucy. Maybe I am even a bit envious of her. Oh, no, not for leaving a child, but for following her dream, her convictions, and I am not angry. I still love her, yet I am filled with sorrow. For Rosy and for myself. I wish I could write her a letter, though that will never be. Charles has decreed we never speak her name or have any contact with her. It is impossible, anyway, since we have no idea where she is. But if I could, I would tell her what happened yesterday when I brought the mail into the house.

Lucy, I would say, I was standing in the foyer when Charles came and took the pile from my hands before I had a chance to sort it. In case something was for me, I waited, watching him leaf through letters and bills. A light blue envelope stood out from all the white ones. He must have held it for a full minute, staring at the handwriting. Curious, I peeked over his shoulder and saw it was your beautiful script. I stared wide-eyed at Charles, watching the lines on his brow grow deeper and deeper as he studied the postmark. It was from some town in Arizona, not from Rhode Island where we believed you to be. My dear, I was completely confused, and even more worried. My stomach was all a-flutter.

Charles ripped the envelope open and pulled out your letter. His nostrils flared and his face turned red reading your words. Fire engine red. Finished, he crumpled the letter. With all his might, he threw it against the wall and stormed out of the house. I grabbed it from the floor and did something I thought I would never do. Read someone else's mail. I had a strange feeling I knew what you had written.

I will admit, I am not surprised though I am saddened for our darling little girl who will never know you as her mother. Charles has forbidden me to tell her about you. I disagree with him, yet I must honor his wishes. It is how I was raised. If I ever tried to oppose my father, I was shut down immediately and told he knew better - that men knew better. It was the same with my husband and, I am sorry to say, I have carried my lack of gumption with me throughout my life. I am glad women today have more backbone than they did in my day. Or most of them. The Suffragists certainly did. I suppose there are still women who smother their dreams and desires. You are not one of them and I am glad of that, though I wish you could have pursued those dreams here in New York. In this house. As Rosy's mama. It is a shame my son takes after his father.

Heavens! The doorbell is ringing and I have so much more I need to write. I must answer it, since it's only Rosy and me at home. But if I wait, maybe they'll go away.

~

Oh, my. It's a good thing I answered, albeit after the bell rang three times. Helen and Crystal were at the door shouting, "He can't keep her from us." It took a minute for me to calm them down and understand why they were so upset.

Helen said Charles burst into their rooming house last night shouting their names. She was petrified something had happened to Rosy or you. (It's odd how I write as if I am actually talking to Lucy, but it makes me feel better.) Charles kept yelling like a madman, she said, insisting they knew, and she had no idea what he was talking about. They invited him to sit, but he refused and stood in the parlor, feet planted, jaw tight, telling them Lucy had left and she was somewhere in the middle of nowhere and never coming back. She never went to Newport. Never went to see her mother. Then Crystal yelled, "How could she do that? How could she not tell us?" As if I had the answer.

I invited them in for a cup of tea and to read your letter and, with that, Helen's eyes opened wide with fear. She told me Charles laid down the law – they could never step into his house again or see Rosy anywhere. They did not accept my invite, afraid to get me in hot water with him. And with the saddest, pleading eyes, Helen begged me to believe neither she nor Crystal had anything to do with your leaving.

I watched your dearest friends walk down the steps. Out of my life. Out of Rosy's.

Chapter 21

Rain patters the windows, odd for Los Angeles in May, I've been told. Like the tears running down my face, the rain drips down the glass. It's 9 a.m. and I'm sitting alone in my room. My roommate left for rehearsal a half hour ago. She's living her dream, dancing in a review at the Music Box Theater. I keep telling myself, "Chin up." It's only four days since I arrived in Los Angeles and three that I've been searching *Playhouse* for an audition. On my first night here, I learned about the local trade paper. It isn't nearly as good as *Variety*, but it'll have to do. I picked it up at the newsie on the avenue first thing the next morning. So far, I haven't seen any Open Calls listed. It's disappointing, but that's not why I have bags under my eyes. Certainly, I'm anxious to audition, but not having any to go to right now isn't what kept me up all night. It's the letter I'm going to write that's causing all the puffiness. Earlier, when I looked in the bathroom mirror, I wasn't surprised. What did I expect after tossing and turning all night composing sentences in my head? Rosy isn't going to read them now. But when she's older and Grandmama gives her the letter, because I decided it's better to send it to my mother-in-law than to Charles, the words need to be honest and heartfelt so she'll understand why I left. At least, I hope she will.

I take the stationery and pen from the top drawer of my nightstand and head downstairs. After a cup of strong coffee with a buttered biscuit, I sit at the roll-top desk in what Mrs. D calls the quiet room. The mint-green walls with pastel-colored wing chairs and sofa on a floral rug bring cheeriness to this dismal day. With pen in hand, I write.

May 1922

To my dear daughter,

It's been eight days since I left you with Grandmama, who loves you very much. At nineteen months old, you aren't able to understand why I had to leave, but when you do read this, at some future time, I hope you'll come to appreciate my reasons. I know it'll be difficult, as you've probably been told that I didn't love you and that's why I left. I can imagine how hurt you've been, living with that lie, and I realize it'll be very hard for you to get past it. But there are always two sides to every story and you need to hear mine.

Sweetheart, please try to understand this was the most difficult decision I ever had to make. I love you so very much. It's because of that love that I know, deep in my bones, it was the right thing to do. I am not a good mother. I'm unable to give you the love you deserve. If I'd stayed and let your father keep me locked up, refusing to let me pursue my career, I'm afraid I would have grown to resent you – and no child should be raised by that kind of mother. You deserve a mother who will put you first, above everything else. I'm so very sorry I'm not able to do that and so thankful Grandmama is.

Your adorable giggle, the one that makes your little shoulders and bottom shake, is with me always. I hope you never lose it, or your sense of adventure. It showed every time you wanted to climb up the tree after the squirrels to see where they lived, or follow the bunnies into the holes they dug under our house. Maybe you got a little of that spirit from me.

There are so many adventures waiting for you. Embrace each one. Live a beautiful life and know that I will always love you.

Leaning back, I inhale a deep cleansing breath and wonder if that's enough. Should I end the letter here, or do I want to say more? Should I write "perhaps one day we'll be able to sit together and I can try to explain a little more"? I rub my hands over my face. Oh gosh! I can't write that. I don't expect to see her again. It wouldn't be fair to her. Charles will divorce me and most likely remarry. That woman, whoever she is, will be Rosy's mother. I only hope she adores my daughter with every cell in her body. And that someday Rosy will know the truth. And accept it. Ha! Who am I kidding? She'll most likely be incredibly hurt and so angry she'll never be able to forgive me. But maybe, with this letter and others I'll send over the years . . .

I stare out the window at the jacaranda tree across the street, bursting with lavender blossoms. The soft hue is calming and uplifting. Spring is such a beautiful time of year in southern California. Flowers dance in the soil. Trees explode with color. A smile spreads across my cheeks. Suddenly I realize, I'm like this season. It's all about rebirth. I get another chance at life. It's my turn to bloom.

With the letter complete, I slide it into the envelope, then write my mother-in-law's address on the front and leave off mine. Next, I dash off a separate note to her. After a short greeting and an apology for having lied, though I had no other way, and a bit more about my faith in her to give my daughter the love she deserves, I write.

Please save this letter and give it to . . .

My pen stops. Give it to whom? Rosy? Again I wonder if I should use her given name. The one I gave her. Not the nickname Charles insisted we use. My hand goes to my earlobe, but the comforting earring is no longer there. I run my fingers around my mouth. My lips are the same shape as my daughter's but Charles never told me they look like rosebuds. No, I will not use the name Rosy any longer. This is my final break from Charles. I put pen to paper again and write. *Please give this to Anna, when the time is right.*

I sit back and reread what I've written. I'm sure curiosity will get the best of my mother-in-law and she'll read the letter. I only hope she doesn't show it to Charles. Then I finish with words of thanks for raising my daughter with the love I am not able to give. A mother's love. Something I never received.

With both pages folded neatly in the sealed envelope, I lick the two-cent stamp and place it in the corner. The rain has stopped. I step out into the bright southern California sun and walk across the street to the letterbox next to the jacaranda tree. I pluck off a flower and bury my nose deep in its petals. There's no scent. No sweet perfume. Yet the blossoms remind me change is coming.

I open the rounded top of the mailbox. But then, I close it with a bang. No. Even though I didn't write a return address on the envelope and I doubt Charles could find me from the location of this mailbox – if he ever looked – I don't want to take any chances. Am I being paranoid? Probably. I shake that off and go back across the street to Mrs. D's and get my pocketbook.

With the letter now tucked inside snuggled next to my depleting coin purse, I head off to catch the streetcar a few blocks away. Washington Boulevard is busy with pedestrians going in and out of shops and automobiles, both gas-powered and horse-drawn, traveling east and west. A luxurious, cobalt-blue Silver Ghost flies by heading toward the ocean and a red Austin Seven almost knocks over the lone bicycle rider. The roads out here are much wider than in New York, and the cars are much classier. Or maybe there simply are more of them. One day I'd love to drive my own. I don't care if it's a Tin Lizzy or a Rolls Royce, as long as I'm behind the wheel with the wind in my hair. Something Charles would never have allowed. "Damn, why am I thinking of him?" A woman in a sleeveless chemise and a beaded cap looks at me with a raised brow. I shrug. I didn't realize I said those words aloud.

The streetcar stops in the middle of the road and the woman in the cap and I step on. After paying my fare, I take a window seat and watch my new city, with the Hollywood Hills in the background, pass by as we travel west. We pass the Arlington movie house where *Robin Hood* with Douglas Fairbanks is playing, and the Goldwyn Picture Studios where Jenny is auditioning today for a new movie. That lucky girl. I hope she gets the part.

At Lincoln Boulevard I step off the streetcar and, right there, on the corner is a rectangular steel letter box attached to a pole. Perfect. I take the envelope from my bag, open the top of the box, and drop it in. In about five days my mother-in-law should receive the letter. I wonder what she'll do. Maybe she won't tell Charles and, instead, contact Helen or Crystal. By now, Charles should have received the letter I mailed from the train. He must be furious, slamming doors, exploding with rage. I can imagine his red-hot neck bulging and steam shooting from his hairy nostrils. All of a sudden, standing here on the corner of Washington and Lincoln, with the California sun warming my shoulders, I grab my earlobe. It's bare. The earring is tucked away in Grandmama's alligator handbag high up on a shelf in her closet. Oh God, my insides are quivering. Helen, Crystal, Grandmama, they're all running around my head. Anna, Auntie Mabel . . . Oh! I grab a cigarette from my bag and with shaky hands flip the lid on my lighter. I need to write to Helen and Crystal. I should have done that first. But no! The flame sears the cigarette tip and I remind myself I couldn't have done that. They had to be in the dark if Charles came to them after he read my letter. But it's been over a week since I left. How could I do this to them? My dearest friends. I take a deep drag letting the sweet tobacco fill my lungs, then toss the butt on the ground and stomp it out with my shoe, squishing it into the cement sidewalk. I've got to get in touch with them immediately. But how? Walking aimlessly down the street, options muddy my mind.

"That's it!" I tell the air, spotting a storefront across the road with Western Union scrolled across the large plate glass window. It's just what I need, as if the universe put it there for me personally. I hurry across the road, skirting around automobiles and side-stepping speeding bicycles. A born and bred New Yorker, I can easily do this and even skip over the horse droppings. Safely on the other side, I open the door to the shop and step inside. Rows of wooden tables face me. There must be a dozen men sitting at them, some sporting newsboy caps, most wearing suspenders or vests, and all in ties over collared shirts, pounding their fingers on telegraph machines. A few women in daytime dresses are scattered through the room, also working the machines. One looks up and asks if she can help me.

"I'd like to send a telegram to New York City."

"Oh, that'll cost ya," says the lady with Lillian Gish's long curls. She could be a screen actress herself with the haughty way she says, "It's a dollar for ten words."

Oh, my word! I didn't expect that, but a phone call is much more and for only one minute. The other night, for fun, Jenny checked with the operator, and boy did we laugh. Who in the world would spend twenty-six dollars simply to say hi? And I need to say a lot more than that. Maybe in my old life, I could have spent that much. Now, I can't even go out for a roll and coffee. Straightening my spine, I look at the Western Union woman and say, "Okay."

"Write your message here," she says, handing me a piece of white paper, then takes a pencil from behind her ear and gives it to me. She steps back and waits with her hands folded across her chest.

I suppose she figures it won't take me long to write a short note, but these are probably the most important ten words I'll ever write. I sit at an empty battered wooden desk near the window and write:

I'm safe.

That's a good way to start. They'll know I'm all right. I continue.

So sorry. Had to do it. I love you both. Will write soon.

I count the words and blow out a big breath. Too many. I cross out "so" and "I" and still have to delete three more. I scribble over all that and start fresh. My chest is pumping hard. Darn it. I'll go over the word limit. I'll pay the two dollars. But that'll really hurt. Jenny and I are going to chip in for eggs and butter for the weekend and that'll be about fifty cents for me. And we need more. Macaroni. Bread. Now my stomach's churning. Stop, I tell myself. It'll all work out. It's only the beginning. It's good for me to be responsible for myself. If others can do it, so can I. Gripping the pencil between my thumb and index finger, I write

Sorry. Had to do it. Love you. Will write soon.

That's ten words. Good. They'll know who it's from. No need to sign my name. Oh, how I wish I could write more. I swallow the lump in my throat and hand the paper to the lady who'll type up the telegram that, later today, will be hand-delivered in its yellow envelope to Helen and Crystal at their rooming house. I hope these ten words will somehow help them understand.

Chapter 22

Sitting on a wooden bench in the backyard enjoying a cigarette, I watch the spray from Mrs. D's Spanish fountain sparkle in the late afternoon sun. Rainbows of color dance in the air. It's been a long day with nothing to do but tend to the flowers in the garden. A deadhead here, a trim there. This isn't what I had in mind coming out to Los Angeles, and I hope things change quickly. I'm aching to be on stage.

Jenny skips into the yard shouting, "I got a callback!" Her big blue eyes are wider than ever. "I have to be at the studio tomorrow and you should come. They're still having auditions."

I jump up and run to her. "Golly! Congratulations!" I grab her in a big hug. She could practically knock me over with her chest pumping so hard and fast.

"This film's perfect for you," she says, stepping back, clapping her hands. "You've gotta audition. Come with me tomorrow. Believe me, it's just what you're looking for."

I'm happy for my friend, but film is not for me and I tell her so.

"Why?" she says, plopping down on the old bench in front of the small fountain. "It's a drama called *The Eternal Three*. And they're going to film some on location. We'll go to Bryce Canyon with its hoodoos and Mexico and . . . Oh, think of all the places we'll go. You've got to do this, Luce."

It feels good hearing her use my nickname, the same one Crystal and Helen called me. I sit and take her hand. "Film isn't for me." I hope she hears the appreciation in my voice. "I'm thrilled for you, but I need to be on stage. Films are silent and I need to use my voice. For the audience to hear it. To hear the emotions pouring from it. And I feed off them, off of their reactions."

"But . . ." her hands circle the air. "The body says so much and you get that on screen."

"Yes. Body language is important and I use it. Directors insist on it. They tell me what to do if I'm not conveying what they're after. But it's the voice, the way I say the words, the way the sentences run together or . . . or . . . . well, you know what I mean. On screen, you only hear organ music. No words. You see them printed, but it's the voice that makes them come alive. And," I shrug, trying to look humble, "it's what I've been praised for." Jenny cocks her head. "Yeah." I give a little embarrassed giggle, not used to tooting my own horn. "My reviews always say I emote and bring the playwright's hard work to life. Plus, I love a live audience. It's intoxicating. It . . . well, it brings out something new in me every time. Every performance. I feel alive."

Jenny's eyes leave mine and stare out at the cacti and succulents bordering the yard. She's contemplating something, moving her head up and down ever so slowly. Then she turns to me. "I know what you're saying. The thing is, I want to be on screen. I want fame. And the movies are where it's all happening now. You need to jump on the bandwagon." She leans in closer, shaking her hands at me, as if pleading. "Everyone's flocking to Hollywood. More movie studios are opening every year. It's why I came out here."

Yes, and I came for other reasons. Though I can't tell her those.

Two days later, I get *my* chance. There's an open call for a drama by the new playwright, Lisa Mont, and it's in the Morosco! Oh, my stars! My heart's pounding.

~

It's only 8 a.m. and already there's a long line in front of the theater. My eyes sweep over all the hopefuls waiting, shifting their weight, shuffling their feet, casting long shadows on the sidewalk. Taking inventory, I see most of the girls are dressed similarly. Some, like me, in wide-legged trousers, some in knickers, others with high-waisted pants topped off by suspenders. Very few dresses.

"This line is ludicrous," a young woman says as I step in line behind her. I chuckle to myself, noticing her harem pants. "It's my first audition ever," she says, collapsing into herself like a turtle. "I'm so nervous."

I give her a sweet smile, remembering those jitters. Hah! I don't only remember it, I have them now. My stomach's been churning ever since I read the notice in *Playhouse*.

"You're not alone," I tell her. "Everyone on this line is nervous, no matter how many plays they've been in."

Oh, how true that is. It doesn't matter that I've been in productions in New York, in Susan Glaspell's plays and so many others, at least a dozen if I count college. Auditioning always makes my stomach roil. Plus I've been out of the game for so long, do I still have it? O'Neill didn't think so. He put me backstage. But Susan encouraged me. I wonder what she'd think about my being out here? Trying out for a play at a theater whose grandeur and size rivals any Broadway house. *Jeez, drop it! Get over it. This is where you need to be,* I silently tell myself. Where I have to be. And I'm damn good. So how come my heart's about to jump out of my chest? I grab a ciggy and join everyone else in line smoking. It's better than chewing my fingernails like the woman in front of me.

An hour later, I'm standing in the wings with the sides in my hands. This is the first time I'm seeing this section or any part of the script. Some guy – the director, stage hand, I don't know who – handed it to me. "This is what you'll read," he said and walked off. I hear the woman on stage reading the lines they gave her a few minutes ago. Damn it, she sounds good. Her voice is full of emotion. How the hell did she get that in just a few minutes? Silently, I read my lines. Gotta get a feel for what this character is saying. Other than she just found out her husband died at the battle of the Somme, I don't know anything about her. *Oh, well,* I think rubbing my earlobe, *that's how it goes sometimes. Auditions aren't meant to be easy.* I swallow hard. *God! I've got to get that dry lump out of my throat or I'll croak these words.*

"Thank you. Next," I hear a soft female voice say, and the last woman who auditioned comes backstage, her double-strapped Mary Janes clicking on the wooden floor. She smiles as she passes by, as if wishing me luck, but I know better. She doesn't want me to get the part. She wants it for herself.

Before stepping out on stage, I take one last glance at the section I'm to read, grappling for the right emotion. Someone calls out "Next" a second time. Quickly, I step out on stage and nod to the three people down in the seats. They tell me to begin. Sucking in a deep breath, I press my shoulders back and embrace the character. I've got this! In less than five minutes, I again hear, "Thank you. Next." With a slight bow, I say my thank you and, keeping my composure, walk offstage, though I'd rather skip. I'm so giddy. It's over! I think it went well. But will I get a callback?

Chapter 23

The tall African marigolds with their large yellow flowers are a perfect backdrop to the purple zinnias in Mrs. D's garden. I'm so grateful she's letting me help take care of these beauties bordering the backyard. If I were to tell anyone, they'd think it odd that, in some way, I see myself in these vibrant flowers. Though I believe Mrs. D, without my saying so, appreciates that. She often says that since I've come here, I've blossomed.

Careful not to disturb the butterfly flitting around the colorful flowers, I bend over and deadhead the spent blooms. Inhaling a hint of their fragrant perfume, I break off a few allowing the plant to continue blooming all summer. This is such a brilliant day. The sun is glorious. The sky is clear. Los Angeles is my kind of climate. Unlike New York with its humidity, the weather here is perfect for sitting outdoors in the middle of July wearing knickerbockers and a short-sleeved blouse. Add the sporty sash tied at my hip and I could be on the cover of *Vogue*. It gives me a sense of confidence which I desperately need to write this long overdue letter.

I sit at the ironwork table in the corner of the yard, under a California Fan Palm. The armchair's seat is cool against my bottom. Digging into my bag, I find my stationery and pen and lay them on the glass-topped table, then pull the chair closer and write.

July 1922
Dear Helen and Crystal,

It's been two months since you received my telegram saying I would write soon. I imagine you're angry with me for taking so long – and furious with me for leaving the way I did. For not confiding in you. If the tables were turned, I would feel the same. Please try to understand I did what I thought best for both of you. I was sure when Charles received my letter saying I'd left him he would go to you, assuming you both knew of my plan. And he'd be fuming. I wanted you to be completely ignorant of it all so he would realize I'd done it on my own. I know how much you love Rosy and believe you'll always be a part of her life, especially now that I've left, and this way he'll let you. I so much want you to be there for her as she grows up. Grandmama will give her the love and nurturing I've never been able to give, and you will give that as well as lead her to become a self-sufficient, independent woman. So please understand, having trusted each other our whole lives, keeping you in the dark on this was very hard for me. I love you both and am incredibly sorry for any worries I caused and any anger you feel.

For a while though, I have to keep my whereabouts a secret. Again, I don't want to put you in an awkward position where you might have to tell Charles my address. I don't want him to know where I am. He can divorce me on grounds of desertion. As I told him in the letter I wrote, it's fine with me whatever story he wants to tell people. I want him to be able to keep his good reputation. I care enough about Charles to let him keep face.

As I lean back against the iron chair, an enormous breath escapes my lips. Whew. I didn't realize how much that would take out of me – like a sinkful of dirty dishwater being sucked down the drain. Writing to Charles on the train was much easier.

With my eyes closed, I rest my head against the back of the chair. My breathing slows to a steady rhythm. I picture Helen sitting in the upholstered Queen Anne chair in the parlor of her rooming house, my letter in her hands. A soft summer breeze blows through the open window behind her, rustling the lace curtains. It's much nicer visualizing her that way rather than sweating from summer's humidity so prevalent in New York. I swipe a knuckle under my eyes, wiping the tears I can't control, and imagine her doing the same as she reads my words. Finished, she'll press the letter to her heart and show it to Crystal later. Helen is usually home first. Crystal often stays late working on a case. Instead of talking about her defendants at the Women's Court, they'll discuss my letter over dinner. I smile, imagining them preparing a meal in the kitchen, Helen at the stove, Crystal setting the dishes on the old oak table. Another woman may be using a different burner or pulling vegetables from the ice box. Meals aren't included where they live as they are in my boarding house. Their rooming house is for single working women who can afford to buy their own food. Or eat in restaurants. The starving artists I live with need our "mother," Mrs. D, to feed us. Cripes, I never knew the difference between boarding houses and rooming houses or ever gave it a thought. Owning my townhouse on The Row, I never had to. Yet, now I live in a boarding house. *Yes, I do*, I think, straightening my spine. An enormous grin pulls on my cheeks. *And I am damn happy!* I pick up my pen, shift my bottom on the hard, latticework iron seat, and am ready to let my friends know. Picking up where I left off, I write:

In the time I've been in California – you'll know that's where I am from the postmark on the envelope, but please don't tell Charles – I've landed a part in a play. I'm on stage again and I couldn't be happier. We opened last week to rave reviews . . .

I stop, wondering if I should tell them more. The name of the show. The theater it's in. The irony that I'm playing a young mother widowed in the Great War who must make a new life for herself and her baby, and all that happens when she remarries and the man adopts her daughter.

A shiver snakes through my skin when I think of the plot. Yet I'm enjoying every moment playing the role, and I know Helen and Crystal would come see me in it if it wasn't three thousand miles away. No! I almost shout it out loud. They can't have any information that'll help Charles find me and then I tell myself to stop it. He's not going to look for me. Why would he? Still, I can't give them my address. I . . . I can't help worrying, even if it's ridiculous. I drop back against the chair. Heat flushes through me. Beads of sweat break on my brow. I reach for my earlobe, then fling my hand away. What if they don't read this letter? What if Helen recognizes my handwriting and tears it up? Or Crystal? Ha! If Crystal gets it first, she probably will toss it in the garbage. What am I thinking? Okay, I'll address it only to Helen. She has a softer heart. But then Crystal will be angry. Oh my God! I look up. "Please," I pray. "Let them open my letter. Let them forgive me." I swallow the hard lump in my throat and finish.

The owner of my boarding house, Mrs. D, is an incredible cook, and I've put on a few pounds. People here don't walk as much as we do in the City. I'm always on a trolley. When I'm not at the theater, I go to the beach. Having my feet in the sand, looking out at the Pacific with a view of the mountains over my right shoulder, is pure heaven. The only thing that would make it better is having the two of you here with me.

I love you,

Lucy

I reread what I've written, then slip it in the envelope and lick the seal. I'll mail it. And never know if they read it.

Chapter 24

July 1922

The oddest thing happened today. Rosy and I were coming home from our morning constitutional when she toddled up the steps to our townhouse pointing at the mailbox saying "letter." It was adorable hearing her pronounce the word, enunciating the "t." Her vocabulary grows daily, and we have to be so careful what we say, with her repeating everything! But that is not what was odd. It was the piece of white envelope peeking through the closed flap of our brass mailbox.

Why would the postman leave a letter hanging out of the box, and why so early, I wondered? I may be getting old, but I know what time the mail comes and it is not by 10 a.m., which showed when I glanced at my lapel watch. When I dressed this morning, I pinned it to the waistband on my day dress rather than to its matching jacket. It is so much easier reading the time from my waist than from straining my head to see the numbers up near my neck. Plus, the day is much too warm to wear the entire ensemble. How silly making watches for lapels! The men are smarter with their pocket watches. But I always wear my lapel watch with its sterling silver bezel and bow, as it was a birthday gift from Lucy last year.

Although I did not recognize the handwriting on the envelope, and wondered why there was no stamp adhered to it, I let curiosity wait until I put Rosy in for her morning nap. I am not sure who needs it more, my granddaughter or me.

We played our game of tag with me chasing after my precious granddaughter while she shouted, "no nap, no nap" as she raced through the upstairs hall past her father's bedroom and the bathroom where she loves to pull the chain and watch the water flush down the toilet. Finally, I scooped her up, which is getting harder and harder to do, and convinced her Dolly, the baby doll with the glass eyes she received last Christmas, needed a nap and wanted Rosy to lie down with her. Finally, a few minutes later, the house was quiet and I went down to the parlor to read the letter, which brings me to why I'm writing in this journal again. I need to speak to Lucy and this is the only way I can. I want to tell her one of the girls left the letter she wrote to them in our mailbox for me to find. When I opened the envelope with my name and address written in beautiful script across the front, I found a folded piece of blue stationery inside with the words, "Read this. Received yesterday" scrawled across the blank side. Whether it was Crystal or Helen who left it for me, I don't know though I suspect it was Helen. She always had the softer heart of the two.

Oh, Lucy, how I wish I could hug you and congratulate you on getting a part in the play you told Crystal and Helen about. I'm thrilled for you and can imagine the joy you feel. I wish I could share it with you, in person. And I wish there was something I could do for your friends, to let them see Rosy. No! I will not call her Rosy anymore. When I write in this journal, I will refer to my granddaughter as Anna, as you did in the note you sent me, where you asked me to give her the letter you wrote explaining why you left. Just as I honor my son's wishes, I will, by golly, honor yours.

If only Lucy could hear my words. I also want to tell her how sorry I am.

Lucy, dear, I did not know how to get in touch with Crystal or Helen when your letter to Anna came without Charles possibly finding out. Your friends want to hear from me whenever I have word from you, but it is too risky and I am not one to take risks. Though, I suppose I am taking a big one keeping this journal and keeping the letter you wrote to Anna tucked inside. Rest assured, I will give it to her. I will do my darndest to save any letters you send to me or Anna, and I will give them to her when she is older. When the time is right. I promise.

Even though Helen knows I cannot invite her in, she came here a second time, without Crystal's knowledge. It was a few weeks ago, on her lunch hour. She was correct in her assumption that Charles was at the hospital, but I still could not bring myself to invite her in. Anna is talking much more now and, like a parrot, repeats everything. I was afraid she would slip about her "auntie" visiting, and I did not want to incur Charles's wrath. I want you to know your friends are not giving up. They want to be in Anna's life. I am sorry, Lucy. I wish I were as strong as you.

Chapter 25

August 1923
Sitting in our pocket garden, in the shade of the dogwood tree, my need to talk to Lucy is even greater than it was a moment ago when I came outside to write. It is a little over a year since she left, yet her presence here is powerful with the tree's pink blossoms perfuming the air, a scent she adored. Every summer Lucy brought branches into the house "to dress up the kitchen," she would say. If only she could see the fruits of her labor now, the profusion of color bursting from the perennials she planted back in 1917 when she and Charles moved into the townhouse after their honeymoon. I pray this little gem, amid the city's brick and concrete, remains as charming as ever, despite the huge change that has recently occurred in our house. I wish I could send Lucy a letter about it, but without an address, it is impossible. Instead, I must be content writing everything I want to say in this journal, seated on an uncomfortable ornate chair made of iron at its matching white table. Mrs. Perkins, Lucy's mother, purchased the set, as she had all the furniture in the

house while Lucy and Charles were on their honeymoon. Lucy used to say she would have preferred a cozier, less formal feel. I wonder what will happen to all the furnishings now, with Charles's new marriage.

If I could tell Lucy about the nuptials, I would say several weeks ago Charles married Florence, a lady he met last summer at the lake house. She is a widow from the Great War, closer to his age than you are and childless. I must admit, Florence is perfect for Charles. Her only ambition is to be a loving wife and mother and to run this household as the wife of a prominent surgeon.

We are keeping the cook Charles hired after you left. To be honest, Lucy, I am glad of that. It is what I was used to. I never understood why you did not want a cook when you were not comfortable in the kitchen. I have a feeling it was not your choice, that it was one of Charles's edicts. His way of forcing you to be the housewife you never wanted to be. And you accepted being the family cook (with my assistance). Was this something you wanted to do, or was it a rebellion against your mother? Your upbringing? Oh, how I wish we could actually have a conversation about that.

No matter how controlling he is and how he acted toward you, I am proud of my son and glad he has found a woman who loves him, as she says, "more than life itself." I know Florence is what Charles needs. What he deserves. But, Lucy, she is not you, even in appearance. Whereas you have a lithe figure, like a ballet dancer, and wavy sandy brown hair with rosebud lips like your daughter's, Florence is full-lipped, a brunette who could use a permanent, with ample bust and hips. She is not college educated or forward-thinking and adores being mistress of the house. She does love Anna, not unlike you. And Anna feels the same about her. I am glad of that and believe it is what you would want. It did not take long for Anna to call her Mama. Charles insisted on it early in their relationship. Florence was always with us, even when Charles was at work, although propriety kept her living in her own home until the wedding. Anna never questioned that. Why would she? She was too young to know other mothers lived with their children.

When we started going to the park together, I steered Anna and Florence to a different section from the one we frequented and all the mothers who met Florence assumed she was Anna's mama. They even referred to her as Mrs. Brandt before she legally had the title. Neither she nor I corrected them. We obeyed Charles.

As you would expect, our little girl is still called Rosy. I suppose she will learn her real name when she goes to school. For now, I am the only one calling her Anna and that is only when I write in my journal.

I wonder, if I actually was able to, would I tell Lucy Anna only asked for her once, several days after she left, and Charles answered she was on a trip? That seemed to suffice, so by the time Florence came into their lives a few months later, Anna simply accepted her as Mama. Or perhaps, the word Mama did not mean anything more to her than a name? No, I would not put that in a letter, and this is ridiculous anyway. I am only writing for myself. But I would like to tell Lucy about her daughter, how she loves her afternoon nap and I am so glad of that. I am getting too old to *be running after her. Thankfully she likes to look at her books when she wakes, which gives me more time to gather my strength. And strength is what I need this month with Charles and Florence on their honeymoon in Europe. They sailed the day after their nuptials in the judge's chambers. I did wonder if they would bump into Crystal in the courthouse. I have not heard from either of Lucy's friends since they dropped her letter in our mailbox a year ago. I do not know if they still live in the rooming house and since I never knew the address – only that it was here in the Village – I do not know where to find them if I ever felt safe to search. What if Charles found out? Anyway, I am not about to go knocking on every rooming house door.*

Putting these thoughts on paper is very satisfying. At times, I feel as if I am sitting with Lucy under this dogwood tree. But am I being honest? I absolutely am glad that Charles found a woman who worships him. And Anna now has an adoring mother who would do anything for her "daughter," as Florence has said many times. So what is it that is niggling at me? That has been sitting on my chest since Charles brought Florence home the first time. Dare I say it? Florence is not Lucy.

Chapter 26

The walnut dining room table is all dressed up with a red linen cloth and matching napkins, perfect for our dinner. Mrs. D sits to the right of me. The gentle scoop neck on her blouse shows off her pearl choker, its luster lighting up her delicately lined face. Jenny, on my left, is exposing a bit of cleavage with her jacquette blouse. She often wears this wrap style with a V-shaped collar. I think she enjoys showing off her perky bosom. The other girls, without family nearby to celebrate with, fill out the rest of the table.

This is my second Christmas in Los Angeles, and what I miss most from past holidays is being with Helen and Crystal. The table feels empty without them. Ever since we were little girls we shared Christmas dinner at either Helen's house or Crystal's, never mine, gobbling up moist turkey and tart cranberry pudding, which always made our lips pucker. Yet . . . I do miss my little girl. Her precious smile and fresh-from-the-bath scent. But I don't miss motherhood. Or the chains it held me in. I stare blankly at the dining room's pale green walls, noticing nothing, remembering everything.

"Are you okay, my dear?" Mrs. D asks. "You look awfully melancholy." She wipes a bit of sweet potato from the corner of her mouth.

I plant a smile on my face. "Oh, no. I'm fine. I'm just looking around the room at how lovely everything is. The beautiful Limoges dinnerware and fine crystal," I say, lifting my etched water goblet. "And the sideboard filled with so many scrumptious-looking desserts. My mouth's been watering, smelling chocolate and cinnamon and . . . mmmm. You must have been baking for days."

Mrs. D buys my fib. Her smile is as bright as the brand-new National Christmas tree President Coolidge lit last night. All 3,000 electric lights! The article in the *Los Angeles Daily News* said it was the start of a new tradition. From now on there will always be a National Christmas tree on the Ellipse. It explained that the park, just south of the White House fence, used to be a military camp for the Union Army during the Civil War. This is a much nicer use of that green space.

"You know I love to bake," Mrs. D says. "And I'm glad if the aromas bring back nice memories of childhood Christmases for you." They don't, but I nod and she goes on. "From your sad expression, I was afraid you might be upset about your roommate. It's a shame, such a beautiful girl. Thank goodness he's marrying her. I can't imagine her being locked up in jail."

"What? Why would that happen?"

"You know, that law – the American Plan or whatever it's called."

'No," Jenny chimes in. "That's for women suspected of having syphilis or gonorrhea. Not for being in the family way. There was a woman several years ago, Nina McCall, who spent three months doing hard labor for a trumped-up charge of having gonorrhea."

"That happened in Michigan where I'm from," Mrs. D says, pouring water from a crystal pitcher into her glass. "It was horrible. She was an innocent young girl sent to jail and subjected to painful, horrendous medical treatments." She mimes quotation marks in the air with the last two words and continues. "I read she escaped and was on the lam for some time, then ultimately sued the government."

"The case went all the way to the Michigan Supreme Court," Jenny says. "She won. But it didn't stop other girls and women for being jailed, whether falsely or not."

"How do you know all this?" I ask, wondering if Jenny was part of the Heterodoxy Club and I'd never seen her there, though she doesn't seem the type. I laugh to myself. Maybe there isn't a type.

"This kind of stuff fascinates me," Jenny says, stabbing a piece of turkey with her fork. "If it wasn't for my dream to be in movies, I might have gone for law. But then I would have had to stay in school. Anyway, I have family in Michigan. They sent me newspaper clippings."

"In Seattle, where I come from," my housemate, a secretary with an hour-glass figure, chimes in. "Women jailed for having VD escaped by tying up guards in sheets and busting through plate glass windows."

Mrs. D shakes her head in dismay. "As I said before, talking about Lucy's roommate, there have been unwed expectant mothers imprisoned. They're thought to be promiscuous and therefore could have syphilis and infect men." She lifts her glass and, before drinking, adds, "This all started during the Great War to protect soldiers and sailors from getting those diseases. And then they took it further."

Stunned by all I'm hearing, I drop my fork. It clatters against the china plate. I wonder why we never talked about this at a Heterodoxy meeting. Unless they did when I wasn't there. I missed a lot of meetings with Charles not letting me out of the house unless I had Rosy with me, and during those three months he sent me away to the lake. I shudder thinking about how he chained me. And for all these unfortunate women. How awful. I can't fathom why anyone would think they deserved to be in jail. My muscles are rigid with anger. When will men stop ruling our lives and our bodies?

Trying to control my frustration, I ask if women are still being imprisoned. "I've heard of all kinds of bizarre laws but I've never heard of this one. It's . . . it's . . ."

"I know," Mrs. D says, her fork, filled with turkey, poised in the air. "It is unbelievable. Back then, they could arrest a woman for merely being with a soldier or eating alone in a restaurant. They'd bring her in and test her for syphilis and the other one, gonor . . . "

"Gonorrhea," Jenny says.

"Right. And if it was positive, they'd lock her up."

"It didn't really have to be positive," Jenny says. "If they wanted to put her in jail, they'd say it was, like with Nina McCall in Michigan."

"Oh my stars." I wish I had better words to describe how horrendous this is.

"I'm pretty sure it's still being enforced today," Mrs. D says. "Though maybe not as stringently."

"But the war's been over for five years," another one of my housemates says. "Certainly the law isn't needed anymore."

This conversation is making me wish even more that Crystal was sitting at the table with us. She'd have answers. I don't remember her ever telling us about a case involving an unwed expectant woman. I shrug. Maybe she never had to defend one. Or maybe the women aren't given a chance to defend themselves. Cripes. What an insane law!

"Anyway," I say. "I'm not upset about my roommate's condition. We didn't talk much. There were so many nights she didn't come home. I guess she was with her boyfriend. But she seems happy getting married. It's such a shame she'll have to give up her dancing."

Mrs. D gives me a sly little smile. "And what about you, Lucy? How's that young man you're seeing?"

I shoot up straight in my seat. "I'm not seeing anyone. Why do you think that?" The squeaky pitch in my voice makes me sound like a child who's been caught with her hand in the cookie jar. But I'm not lying. I have no interest in dating anyone.

"Oh, come now," she says. "Who's that good-looking fella that brings you home from the theater every night?"

I giggle and scoop up a forkful of candied sweet potatoes. "Oh, him. He's in the cast," I say. "He lives a few blocks away, so he drives me home in his spiffy red Model T. It's nothing."

Mrs. D wrinkles her nose, and Jenny's eyes, lifted all the way to her hairline, tell me she doesn't believe me either. "Seriously," I say. "I'm not seeing anyone."

The sweet, creamy potatoes sliding down my throat are more delicious than any man's touch right now. I hope I'll feel differently one day. Now, I twitch, thinking of another man telling me what I can and can't do. Charles did it, and I swear, no other man ever will again. Charles's father treated Mama Brandt that way and my father did the same with my mother.

Yes indeed, my mother. The woman who refused to accept the charges when I called on her birthday last year. I couldn't afford the incredibly expensive phone call so I asked the operator to reverse the charges. I listened as she told her who was on the line. And my mother said "No. I will not accept a call from her." I have no idea what Charles told her after he found out I never went to Newport. It doesn't matter. She'd be on his side anyway.

Damn, why did I call her? I should have known better. When will I stop stepping into deep, poisonous puddles only to get soaked in the putrid water? First, it was trying to fix my marriage by giving up what I wanted, then I go and call my mother thinking she'd want to hear from her daughter. *Okay,* I tell myself. *Stop going down that road. And stop grinding your teeth! This is a holiday. Enjoy it. At least she knows I'm alive. If she cares.*

Chapter 27

May 1925

A few minutes ago, I passed by Charles and Florence's bedroom door. It was odd they should be closeted away behind a closed door in the middle of the day and, though I knew I should move on and let them have their privacy, I stopped. Florence's pleading tone, floating into the hallway, piqued my curiosity. As wrong as it was, I leaned in and listened. What I heard sent me rushing to my room. I grabbed my journal and now, here I sit, at the little iron table in the garden, with pen in hand, pouring my fear onto paper.

It is interesting that I have not written anything in this journal in almost two years. I suppose I never felt the need, although I would have loved to write a real letter to Lucy about Anna and tell her what an adorable little girl she has become. She loves to play "big girl," as she calls it, draping my pearls and beads around her four-year old neck, her dainty feet in my lace-up pumps clomping around the upstairs hall. I would also let her know all has been going smoothly in our townhouse on Washington Square North. We are living a happy, calm life.

Florence is a good mother, a loving mother, and a wonderful daughter-in-law. She has never interfered in my relationship with Anna. We both "mother" her and I believe Anna is flourishing with so much love. But now? I am petrified. What will become of me? Charles is going to sell the townhouse!

I have never minded living on my own, but I do not want to lose Anna. I want… no, I need to see my precious granddaughter every day. When Florence came to live with us, I was already here. This was my home. But when they move, will she want me to continue living with them? She wants to make her own home with Charles. Through their closed door, her words were clear. "For two years," she said, "I've been living in her house. Darling, please, I want my own home."

At first, I was taken aback hearing the word "her" but soon realized she meant Lucy. It was Lucy's parents who bought the townhouse as a wedding gift when Charles married their daughter. And it was Lucy's mother who decorated the house. Regardless of Lucy's less formal tastes. Of course Florence would want her own home. She probably feels Lucy everywhere, even if her name is never mentioned. The Chippendale sofa where she and Charles sit in the evening is Lucy's. The soft bed she sleeps in is Lucy's. Her clothes are in Lucy's wardrobe. Even the Wedgewood china she eats off is Lucy's, an engagement present from her parents' friends.

Then I heard Charles's firm voice. "This is my house," he shouted, emphasizing "my." "It's in my name. Not hers," which is true. Lucy's father put the house in Charles's name. He believed Charles, being fifteen years her senior, would pre-decease Lucy and she would inherit the house. Mr. Perkins kept with the old ways of the man being the sole owner. In so many ways, Lucy's father was like Mr. Brandt. That is why they were friends. Yet her mother and I did not carry on our acquaintance after our husbands passed away. How could we when Mrs. Perkins remained in Newport and I no longer owned our cottage there? Plus she never came to town to see her daughter. Or granddaughter. I do not understand that woman.

Although I have qualms about Charles selling the house and Florence wanting me to continue living with them, I do understand how she feels. Mr. Brandt and I made our houses into homes. We shopped for furnishings and artwork together wherever we traveled. We were fortunate to be able to afford such luxuries, as Charles and Florence are. I only hope when they set up a new home, I will be included. Though, now that I think of it, I never did hear Charles say he would sell the townhouse.

Chapter 28

Sitting at Mrs. D's rolltop desk, staring at the envelope in front of me, I don't understand why I'm hesitating. After tossing pros and cons back and forth like a ping-pong ball, I decided to finally, after three years, write my return address on the envelope. So what's stopping me? Am I still scared? It's a little over three years since I left New York, certainly enough time that if Charles was going to come looking for me, he would have already. Yet he'd have no way of knowing where I am, so why have I been frightened? And as sure as the day is long, I'm positive he told Anna I was a terrible mother. He never believed I loved her. So why would he look for me? Blowing out a huge breath filled with sadness, frustration, and acceptance, I fall back against the desk chair. My stomach settles and I take my pen and write the numbers in the upper left-hand corner of this light blue envelope – 11296 Fletcher Road, Culver City, California. That's it, I say blotting the ink. Now they'll have it and suddenly I feel a big grin spread across my face. We'll be in touch. We'll talk through letters. Oh how I've missed their voices! I lick and press the two-cent stamp to the upper right corner. In my previous life, two cents wouldn't have made a difference, but now every penny is precious. A dozen eggs costs forty-seven cents and the butter to go with it is fifty-two cents a pound, and none of that lasts very long.

Sliding the envelope aside, I wonder if they'll tell Charles where I am. I doubt Helen will, but Crystal? I shrug and lay a clean piece of stationery in front of me. As long as I hear back from them – hear what's been going on in their lives, at the Club, and what they've been doing with Anna and their careers – I don't really care what Charles does.

August 1925

Dear Helen and Crystal,

You'll never believe this! I'm teaching children and loving it. Have no fear, I still am on the stage but acting isn't bringing me enough to live even the simple life I'm enjoying in California. Despite my rent being very affordable, my savings ran out and I needed a job. It didn't come as a shock. I'm glad my money lasted as long as it did and that I've been in several productions already. Presently, I'm playing Mrs. Hale in Susan Glaspell's one-act play, Trifles. It's wonderful being in another of her plays, and this one speaks to me. To all women. Susan is a master at bringing women's concerns to the stage. Trifles is a story of a woman suspected of murdering her husband, though the theme running through says so much more. It's about women's oppression (now you know why it grabbed me). It's about the power of silence, how men silence women and believe women's comments and findings are trifles. If you ever see Susan, please let her know I'm in another of her plays with a local company here in Los Angeles. I know she'll be happy for me.

I learned Trifles was based on a true story that Susan covered when she was working as a journalist. Helen, do you ever get to cover murders? Maybe one of Crystal's cases? That would be fascinating. Wouldn't it be fun if you did and I performed it on stage? I can hear you saying, "I'm not a playwright!" And Crystal reminding us she doesn't handle murders. "I'm lucky to have a job as a lawyer," she'd say.

Oh my gosh, I feel as if I'm sitting with them, laughing and chatting in the parlor in their boarding house or at Polly's or . . . With the pen dangling from my fingers, I travel back to Saturday afternoons in that basement restaurant with the sunny-yellow walls, eating goulash and hearing speakers on controversial topics like birth control. Now, they're probably talking about the ongoing argument for an Equal Rights Amendment with the National Women's Party taking it to the House Judiciary Committee. I read about this amendment in the paper, but would love to hear those speeches and be part of the club's discussions. Shaking that from my mind, I go back to my letter where I feel wrapped in a warm, cuddly blanket "talking" to my two dearest friends. If only on paper.

So, back to my new job. One of the women at rehearsal was talking about Standing Ovations, the acting school where she teaches, and that they're wonderful in working around her schedule. My ears perked up! After hearing more about the school and finding out they were looking for more teachers, I took myself over there last week to fill out an application. Impressed by my background and schooling, the manager hired me on the spot. The children are adorable and so serious about their work, especially a little blond with curls like Anna's. Yes, I call her Anna now that Charles isn't able to insist I use the name he chose. You probably will always refer to her as Rosy, though I hope one day you'll tell her I gave her the name Anna after my Nanny. I hope she'll embrace it.

And not hate me, though I don't write those words.

I'm so anxious to hear from both of you. Now that you have my address, please write. I miss you.
All my love,
Lucy

I wait a moment for the ink to dry, then fold the letter and slip it into the stamped envelope. With a bounce in my step, I walk out into the sunny Sunday morning, cross the street, and slide the envelope into the mailbox on the corner. I'm so anxious to hear back from them. I hope their letter comes soon.

Chapter 29

Jenny is glowing, as all brides should. I look at her holding hands with her handsome guy, the fella who swooped her off her feet last year after they met on the set of *The Age of Innocence*. She's very fortunate. He's a fine young man, also an actor, who is proud of Jenny and in full support of her career. They're the image of happiness standing in front of the judge in his wood-paneled chambers, the groom looking snazzy in white, cuffed trousers, a tan notched-collar vest, and a striped shirt with those fancy French cuffs. Jenny's white satin dress enhances her slim silhouette. Its V-neck exposes a hint of soft cleavage, and the scalloped lace hem and sleeves add a touch of delicacy, as delicate as Jenny herself. Her Juliet cap veil is the total opposite of the voluminous veil I wore at my wedding, with a train that seemed to go on for miles.

I try to push my wedding day out of my mind, but memories swarm like crickets with their irritating chirp. Jenny and her groom are bubbling over with joy. I doubt I had a smile as bright as hers, and she's not fidgeting in her tea-length dress as I was in my gown – a floor-length high-necked, long-sleeved ivory gown enveloped with layers and layers of lace embellished with crystals and pearls. My mother's choice. As was the groom.

It's unfortunate Jenny's mother couldn't afford to come west for her daughter's wedding. Mrs. D and I stepped into that role, taking Jenny shopping for her wedding dress and planning the small reception we'll have in Mrs. D's parlor later today. I treasure this special, big-hearted woman who is so much more than a landlady. With her soft, sympathetic eyes and freshly baked breads and muffins filled with love, she reminds me of my Nanny. And Jenny – she may not be Crystal or Helen – but she's also very dear to me. I'm so glad she and her husband will live only a few miles away in Venice Beach.

Listening to the bride and groom recite their vows, I remember Helen and Crystal as my bridesmaids standing at my side as Charles and I stood in front of the minister stoically saying ours. Sadly, I'll never hear them say their vows. Or I should say Helen, since Crystal always claimed she'd never marry. I wonder if she's changed her mind. I wonder if Helen ever married her beau. Oh, how I wish I'd hear from them. It's been about five weeks since I sent the letter with my return address. Did they not notice it and throw the envelope away when they ripped it open? Or, are they so angry with me that they'll never write back? I swipe my finger across my wet eyelashes. Are these tears of joy for Jenny? I'd like to think so, but . . . I pull my shoulders back and paste a smile on my face. Watching the groom kiss his bride, my smile turns genuine and, once again, my chest fills with joy.

~

"Lucy, dear," Mrs. D says, coming back into the parlor after saying goodbye to the last wedding guest. "I'm going to change into my slippers and housecoat then clean up these dishes."

"I'll help," I say, stacking dirty cake plates one on top of the other. It was a lovely wedding reception with Mrs. D's homemade cakes and cookies. There were about twenty guests, gals from the boarding house and some cast members from *The Age of Innocence*. I'm so happy for Jenny. She's gotten both of her wishes – movie roles and a ring on her fourth finger.

"Thank you," Mrs. D says, looking around at all the dirty cups and saucers and the special glasses she pulled out of the china cabinet for the champagne one of the guests was able to get. He claimed he bought it for medicinal reasons, but we all saw the glint in his eye. "You might first want to read the letter that came for you," she says. My heart jumps. "It was in the mailbox when we got home from the ceremony, but with all the commotion, I'm afraid I forgot to tell you. I know you've been checking the mail every day," she says, raising one eyebrow. "I assumed it was important so I put it in the roll-top desk to keep it safe."

If only I could drop the dishes right here and let them clatter to the floor. Instead, I hurry to the kitchen, place the stack in the sink, then rush to the front room. I open the desk and there it is! The return address is Thompson Street where Helen and Crystal live, but the handwriting is not either of theirs. My fingers grab my earlobe. Feeling the imitation pearl, my shoulders drop. Of course my treasured earring is no longer there. Yet I can't seem to break this habit. It's been quite a while since I've needed the comfort of our birthstones under my fingertips. *No*, I tell myself. *There's nothing to worry about. Helen may have changed her handwriting. She's a journalist. Maybe she's playing with a different style. No, that's silly. She uses a typewriter.*

I grab the letter opener from the desk top, slice the envelope open, and read standing right there, not moving a muscle. It's a short note and I drop into the chair reading the last word. My arms go slack. The letter dangles from my fingers and my head flops back against the chair's cushion. Tears clog my throat. I have no idea how much time has passed with me swallowing the lump, staring into space, when Mrs. D comes into the room.

"Oh, my dear, what happened?" she says, placing a comforting hand on my shoulder. "Was it bad news?"

Barely able to speak, I nod, a tiny up and down movement. Erupting in tears, I slump forward. They pour down my face. Mrs. D bends over, folding me into her warm, cushiony arms. "There, there," she says. "Let it out."

I know she's trying to comfort me, but nothing helps. Eventually, I take some deep breaths. Spent, I look up at her, wiping my wet cheeks and the mucus dripping from my nose. "I don't know where my friends are." The words sound like a little girl whining. "I'll never hear from them again."

Mrs. D takes a tissue from her rolled-up sleeve and hands it to me. "Come," she says. "Let's have a nice cup of tea and you can tell me all about it."

In her cozy kitchen, Mrs. D brings the copper kettle to the table and pours boiling water over the tea bag in my cup. The clear liquid turns a toasty brown. Sitting around this worn oak table with a spray of spring flowers as its centerpiece reminds me of all the loving times I spent in Helen's mother's kitchen, sharing cups of tea with her. Mrs. Stokes brewed real tea leaves in a bone china pot, letting them steep for exactly three minutes, infusing the room with love. No matter the method, the warmth in Mrs. D's compassionate eyes softens the ache in my chest. If it wasn't for her, I'd be in bed buried under the covers, crying my eyes out.

"Now, dear," she says, taking a seat next to me, clasping my hand in hers. "What is it that has you so terribly upset? What do you mean you'll never hear from your friends?"

My eyes bubble with tears. There's so much caring in her voice, so much love in her touch. I can't tell her I abandoned my daughter. What would she think of me? I've lost everyone who ever loved me. Helen, Crystal, Mrs. Stokes, Mama Brandt. Even my nanny who's been gone for so long. I need Mrs. D. I really, truly like her. So I take a deep breath and explain why I'm afraid my friends are lost to me. It takes me a long time to tell the story about Charles and his hold on me and why I had to leave. I never mention my daughter. I can't. I can't tell her Anna is five years old today and I'm not with her to celebrate – that I can only send her a birthday card and hope, someday, when she's older, she'll read it. Tears threaten to pour down my face like a faucet on full. I sniff, wipe my eyes, and swallow hard then finish the abbreviated, altered story of my marriage.

"I understand," Mrs. D says when I finally stop. "Your husband sounds like a lot of men who want complete control over their wives and would be embarrassed to admit they work. I know a few who felt it was a stigma. That it was a sign they couldn't provide. And you say your husband had no reason to feel that way, but that he thinks acting is an unsavory profession." I nod. "It's such a shame it's so difficult for a woman to divorce her husband. That she'd have to prove adultery or abuse or who knows what, and how the man can turn it all around making the woman look like the guilty party."

Hearing the exasperation in her voice, I give my shoulders a little shrug, letting her know I agree. I take a sip of tea then say, "That's why I had to leave. And why I was afraid to let anyone know where I was."

"And now, after three years you told them. And they never received your letter."

"That's right. The letter I received was from their landlady. She said Helen married and moved somewhere uptown. She didn't have the new address. And Crystal also moved about two years ago to an apartment somewhere in the Village. The landlady tried to find her, hoped she'd see her in the neighborhood, but never did."

"Didn't you tell me Crystal was a lawyer? Couldn't she check at the courthouse or somewhere?"

"She wrote she didn't know where Crystal worked, only that she practiced law." Again I shrug. "I suppose she didn't think of that. She said there are so many law firms in the city and she's sorry, but she doesn't have the time to call each one looking for a Crystal Alsop."

"I understand that, but don't you know where your friend works? You could send a letter to her office."

Gazing into my tea cup, I consider her suggestion. I could look up the address of her firm. There might be a New York phone book at the library. All I know is her office is downtown on Broadway in a building across from City Hall. That's if she's still with the same firm. It's been three years, she could have changed jobs. Anyway, I wanted Helen to be the first to read it, to soften Crystal's reaction. I have a feeling she's much angrier with me than Helen.

"No," I say, looking up. "I . . . I appreciate the idea but . . ."

"You're right. It could be awkward getting personal mail at work." There's sorrow in Mrs. D's eyes when she adds, "Don't lose hope, dear. One day you just may hear from them."

Although I don't believe it, I tell her I hope so. Then, as quick as a lightning flash, a solution pops in my head. I'll send them a letter via Mama Brandt and ask my mother-in-law to please give it to Helen. That should work. Though I can't tell Mrs. D my plan. She knows my story. Or part of it. Whether I'll ever tell her the entire story, I'm not so sure.

Chapter 30

September 1926

Lucy's annual birthday card to Anna arrived today. I am tucking it into this journal, as I have all the other cards she has sent, along with the note she enclosed furnishing me with her address. It is comforting knowing where she lives and that she is happy, but I cannot risk sending her letters. It may be nonsensical, but I must do as Charles wishes. I cannot help it. I wish I was stronger.

Earlier this evening, I found myself staring out my bedroom window at the three-quarter moon shining over Washington Square, glistening stars dappling the inky sky, wondering why I save Lucy's correspondence. Sitting at my writing desk now, I realize how foolish it is. What if Charles found them? Yet having them makes me feel she is still part of my life. Our life. Perhaps, in ten years, when Anna turns sixteen and I give her the earrings Lucy asked me to give, I will also hand her all the cards and letters her mother sent. And then she will find out the truth. The lie we have perpetrated her entire life. For certain,

Charles will be furious with me. Will I be brave enough to do it? Oh, why do I let him dictate to me when I am the mother? Am I so afraid of losing him? Several years ago, when my lady friend suggested I write down my feelings, I never imagined talking to a piece of paper would be so comforting. Now, with the house quiet, and Florence and Charles retired to their bedroom, completely spent from an afternoon entertaining five little girls at a birthday party, the pull to reflect is strong, as is my wish to speak to Lucy.

It was very clever of you, I would say to her if I could, to address Anna's birthday card to me. Generally, Florence or I collect the mail, but today Charles brought it in. He asked who I was corresponding with. I looked at the handwriting, which did not look at all like yours, but I knew better. Do you keep changing your handwriting, or has someone else addressed the envelopes for you? Whichever, Charles did not suspect anything. I told him the letter was from a friend of mine from Newport. If he had noticed the postmark, he might have asked about that. I was prepared to say my friend moved to California.

Lucy, if my memory serves me, in a letter you wrote to Charles you acknowledged his being a good father. He is and showed it today when he came home early from work to be with Anna to celebrate her sixth birthday. Not many men would do that. I wonder who he learned from. Certainly not his father. It gives me pause to think – if you were still here, would he have done the same?

At six years old, Anna is quite a big girl now! You should see how beautiful she is with her creamy skin and those big, expressive, green eyes, as beautiful as yours. She is a happy child. Everyone loves her. She is quite the big cheese in school. And quite the belle of the ball. She certainly was today. We had a few of her classmates here for birthday cake and games after school. Oh, the screeching and laughter as they ran through the house, up and down the stairs, in and out of the garden. My heavens, little girls can be quite rowdy. But I am pleased she has so many friends. Why wouldn't she? Everyone is drawn to her. To her engaging big smile and adorable giggle that makes her curls bounce. She is growing more and more to look like you even the way her little rosebud lips open wide when she smiles. I wonder what goes through Charles's mind when he looks at her.

Oh yes, I do wonder, and it would be interesting to ponder this with Lucy. Alas, I cannot. And I am unable to tell her how happy I am that she has been in three plays already. I assume they were short runs since it has only been a little over four years since she left. From what she has written, they sound similar to performances she was in with the Provincetown Players and with those other groups. I do not remember their names though I do remember being awed watching Lucy on stage whether in the Playhouse or in that little theater downtown or wherever she performed. I remember one time I traveled all the way uptown to see her in a college production. I felt like I was going to a foreign country, being so far north in Manhattan. And I felt awful for her that her parents were not there. I am not sure they ever did come to any of her performances. How disappointing that must have been for her.

I hope Lucy will continue sending me notes whether enclosed in cards to Anna or to me alone. I love keeping abreast of her life and want to hear more about her teaching children at Standing Ovation. What a clever name for an acting school. It sounds wonderful. Lucy has a great deal to offer. I am glad she is using her education and talent. The children are lucky to have her as their teacher. But what about Anna? Certainly, she is a happy girl who adores her mother – or who she believes is her mother – and Florence is all a mother should be. It is a shame she is not able to have children of her own.

All in all, I must admit, Lucy's leaving has been for the best. Lucy has what she wanted and Anna has a loving mother who lives her life for her daughter and husband. And Charles seems quite happy with his career and family. Now it is time for me to put this journal back in my night table and go to sleep. Once again, I understand myself better after writing these words on paper.

Chapter 31

May 1927

Last year, when Charles and Florence invited me to move uptown with them to the Dakota, I was relieved yet could not help chuckling about the address. I remembered when, back in 1884, shortly before it opened on Central Park West and Seventy-second Street, my husband took me to see this new luxury building in the hinterlands of Manhattan. Charles was two years old at the time and we were considering making a move. The Dakota was touted to be the tallest structure for miles with views of Central Park to the east and all the way west to the Hudson River. The advertisements said it was a luxury modern residential building, the first to have elevators run by hydraulics. Mr. Brandt was impressed by that. I never understood what it meant, other than it had something to do with water. But once we saw the building, we forgot all about moving. Mr. Brandt called the Dakota a yellow behemoth that looked like it belonged in a German fairytale. The scowl on his face spoke volumes. I was concerned with the neighborhood, or lack thereof. It was surrounded by dirt roads and farms! Now, years later, I see we should not have been bothered. This is a magnificent building, with wonderful appointments, surrounded by a black wrought iron fence with the head of Zeus and other gargoyles incorporated in the elaborate design. The building has its own tennis and croquet courts and Anna is learning to play both. Florence and Charles take her out every weekend, and I take her to Central Park every chance we get. It is what happened yesterday in the park, at Bethesda Fountain, that brings me to my writing desk today.

When we moved uptown, my daughter-in-law suggested I put the French provincial desk from the townhouse's parlor in my new bedroom. Lucy's desk. I was pleased, beyond measure. Though sitting here now, under my bedroom window, with views of Central Park and its winding paths, lakes, and bridges, the same jittery apprehension I felt yesterday at the fountain creeps up my spine. I must tell Lucy what happened. Despite the fact she will never read these words, I am compelled to write them down, as if she will, rather than replaying the scene in my mind. It kept me tossing and turning in bed, not getting a wink of sleep.

Yesterday afternoon, Florence, Anna, and I took a leisurely walk to Bethesda Fountain. Anna was having a wonderful time running her hands through the spray, giggling with the other children, when a little boy in short pants and a sailor blouse took a fancy to her. He was about her age, six or seven, but she wasn't interested. When Florence asked her why she would not play with him, Anna put her hands on her hips and simply stated, "I do not want a boyfriend." I could not help laughing. Florence kept a serious face and tried to explain playing with the little boy did not mean he was her boyfriend. She told Anna, or, as she calls her, Rosy, (which grates on me as does this entire lie we're perpetrating) that she had plenty of time for boyfriends. My adorable granddaughter pursed her lips as if she had swallowed a lemon. Just then, I caught a glimpse of a woman staring at us from across the fountain. Before we could move away, she came hurrying over. I did not know what to do. There I was standing with Florence and Anna with hordes of families around us chatting and laughing. What would I say to her? What could I say? Before I had a chance to come up with some kind of wording, Helen reached out her arms to me.

Yes, Lucy, it was Helen! We had not seen each other in five years. Not since you left. There was that one time she and Crystal came to the townhouse, then one other when she came alone. Helen is persistent when she wants something. I am sure she will be a success as a journalist, as long as she is not trying to get a story out of someone as stubborn as Charles. That time, when she came alone, she and I spoke for a moment. Unfortunately, I had to tell her it was dangerous for me to be seen with her. Not that Charles would do anything drastic, but I did not want to incur his wrath or make a very pleasant home life unpleasant. As I have written before, he refuses to have your name mentioned or for Anna or me to see your friends. Sadly, I am not strong enough to argue with my son.

It must have looked odd when I stepped back avoiding Helen's hug and Anna asked Florence who the woman was. I put on a big smile, covering my nervousness, and introduced everyone. Thank goodness, Helen caught on quickly and played along.

"How lovely," she said when I told her Florence was Charles's wife. I wish you could have seen how surprised she was. Her wide-open eyes told me so, but she covered it well, offering Florence her congratulations then saying, "I didn't know Charles had married. I'm so happy for you. And this must be your daughter," she said, pointing to Anna.

Oh, yes, she played it well. Perhaps she should have pursued acting, like you, instead of journalism. I did not know if I wanted to laugh or cry when she placed a tender hand on Anna's soft cheek and said, "I'll bet you're about seven years old." Anna proudly told her she would be in September. We made the usual conversation women make when running into an old friend and meeting her family.

"Mrs. Brandt used to live near me," Helen explained to Florence. "But I never see her anymore." That's when she learned we had moved to the Upper West Side. I noticed a gold band on her finger, and she told me she married three years ago and they also moved out of the Village. Then she coyly asked if I remembered her friend Crystal.

I pretended to consider that, then said, "Of course. Yes. The lawyer." It was quite a performance, if I do say so myself.

Helen let me know Crystal is now sharing an apartment with two other women on Patchin Place, one an attorney like herself, the other a journalist like Helen. I was surprised. As you know, not many buildings will rent to single women. But that one is in the Village and anything goes in that part of town. I do miss it.

Oh, Lucy, I am so sorry I could not tell Anna about her Auntie Helen and how she was so much a part of her life at one time. If I have the nerve, when Anna reaches sixteen and I give her the earrings you hid away in my alligator bag, which I now have in my bedroom closet in the Dakota and never use anymore, I will also tell her about Helen and Crystal. If I have the strength.

Chapter 32

Seated in the third row of the auditorium, my chest fills with pride watching my young students rehearse the play *Heidi*. The whole staff from Standing Ovations worked so hard with them, meeting every Saturday afternoon plus three evenings a week for the past month. All the children, especially the fair-haired, freckle-faced six-year-old playing Heidi and the young boy with hair the color of straw and just as straight, playing Peter, are wonderful little actors. Their voices project over the rows of hard, wooden folding chairs in the church's basement theater. Despite the uncomfortable seats, the lush velvet stage curtain made by the Women's Club lends the feel of a real theater. I can't help the smile spreading across my cheeks. My work, our work, has come to fruition. Our one-act play is ready for an audience. Though I'd love to be on stage again, in front of the curtain, it's been almost three years since I've landed a part.

"Movies," Jenny keeps repeating, telling me to audition. "Especially now that they're talkies. You can use your voice!"

I know it's true, but I'm thirty-seven. Six years older than Jenny and fifteen years older than that sexy Jean Harlow. Movies don't want women my age. It's hard enough in the theater.

Ah, here comes my cold-hearted hermit, Heidi's grandfather, taking center stage. This plump little boy with a lopsided grin looks adorable as an old man with that long white beard and floppy hat. He scans the audience and his eyes find mine. I shake my head telling him not to look at me. But my chest puffs up hearing him project. It was a struggle getting him to do that. His voice was soft and often cracked. I nod hearing him emote.

Darn it. These kids need my full attention with opening night one week away, yet Claudette Colbert keeps popping into my mind. Maybe it's because Jenny is constantly telling me Colbert is versatile. She's in movie theaters now, starring opposite Fredrick March in *Manslaughter*, and before turning to screen she was on Broadway. I picture Jenny standing, hands on hips, reminding me of that fact. "But I'm older than Colbert," I mumble under my breath, not wanting anyone to hear my thoughts and that I'm not totally focused on the children. I wonder, though, does age truly matter? Or am I using it as an excuse for not getting parts? Shaking that out of my head, I focus on the sheep taking the stage.

I didn't think we'd get kids to put on these costumes and crawl around on all fours, bleating. But they were so excited to get any part. Yes, I know that feeling well. And I'm thrilled for them. The show's going to be a success. I feel it in my bones.

With the rehearsal over and notes given, parents arrive to pick up their children. One woman in high-waisted suspender pants is standing alone watching each child walk out. Something about her – the posture or the tilt of her head – reminds me of someone from college. Judith, an older, very talented girl who lived in my hall. We acted together before she graduated. That must be . . . Let's see, I graduated in 1917. Judith, a year or two before me. So sixteen or seventeen years ago. A long time. So much has happened over the years. Young men we knew died overseas, the Spanish flu took the lives of so many friends – even Mrs. D's husband – women finally got the vote, and now we're in the midst of a depression. Thank goodness for theater. People yearn for entertainment to take their minds off the economic situation and all the people on breadlines.

The children wave goodbye to me as they walk out of rehearsal. Their mothers say "Thank you." I smile and nod, but my thoughts are still in Fiske Hall on 120th Street in New York City with women, including Judith and me, in all states of dress and undress running in and out of each other's rooms borrowing blouses or scarves or getting notes they missed in class.

"Lucy Perkins?" the woman in the suspenders says as I walk past. "Is that you?"

I stop. "Golly. Judith! It *is* you! What are you doing here?"

"Picking up my daughter."

"Oh, of course. How silly of me. I mean, what are you doing in Los Angeles? You're from New York. Upstate if I recall."

"That's amazing. How do you remember that?"

I can't tell her it's because my husband sent me to his lake house for three months when he said I was hysterical and needed time to calm down and bond with our new baby, and I remembered she lived nearby in the Hudson River Valley. I had contemplated trying to find her, but there was no way for me to do that. We didn't have a telephone, and there weren't any trolleys in the area. I was a prisoner in his house. I never thought of that place as mine. Instead, I say, "I remember you spoke about having a long train ride whenever you went home for a holiday, and once you stayed in the city with a girlfriend for Christmas because you didn't want to make the trip. I was impressed. Two young women on their own in the City. What fun that must have been."

We continue reminiscing for a while. Her red-headed daughter, one of the sheep in the play, listens, her head bouncing back and forth when each of us speaks. She lights up when her mother tells me she's now writing.

"Scripts," she says. "In fact, I have a new play. It's called *Earthshaking,* a romance between a fireman and a woman he rescued from a collapsed building during the nineteen-ought-six earthquake in San Francisco. "

She must see the interest in my eyes because she asks if I'm still acting or only teaching. I assure her I'm acting. Though I don't mention how long it's been since I've been on stage.

Judith claps her hands. "Wonderful! I'd love to have you in my play. Auditions are next week." Then she leans in and whispers, "Though I doubt you'll need an audition." She gives me the particulars, where it will be held, and the time. "I'm so glad we ran into each other," she says. "Thank you so much for giving my little girl her first acting role. She loves your class, you know. She talks about you all the time. I had no idea you were the same Miss Perkins I knew at Barnard." She blows me a kiss and is on her way. I place my hand on my chest. It's beating like a drummer in the Macy's Thanksgiving Day Parade.

~

Bursting with excitement, I bounce into the house. The play is going well. We're ready for opening night, and I have an audition! I call out for Mrs. D, anxious to tell her my news, to tell anyone my news, but the house is quiet. My shoulders drop. Two of my housemates, young gals, come bounding down the steps, a third on their tail, and before I know it I'm smiling again. But they rush past me.

"We're going to see *King Kong*," the redhead says, stopping at the front door. "Quick, come with us."

"Ummm, sure. Wait . . . I'll . . ." I can't get my words together. All I want to do is shout out my news. Talk about finding Judith Zell. The audition she's offered me! Not sit in a dark theater watching an ape. "No," I say. "Thanks, but no. You go. Have fun." And my heart shrinks.

My new housemate with the red curls squishes her eyes together. "What's the matter?"

"Nothing. I'm just . . . forget about it."

"Okay," she says and hurries out the door. Another gal calls from the front step, "How'd rehearsal go? How're the sheep?"

I laugh and say, "Great" as the screen door swings shut with a slam.

Walking down the hall toward the kitchen, I notice Mrs. D sitting on the sofa in the parlor staring straight ahead, as if she's watching a movie playing on the wall in front of her. I walk over and sit on the edge of the sofa next to her, my hands on my thighs. Excitement bubbling out of me, I can barely sit still. But before I can utter a word she places her hand over mine and gives it a gentle, tender squeeze.

"What's wrong, Mrs. D?" I ask, sensing something isn't quite right. It's funny my still calling her that after living here eleven years and us being quite close. Though not close enough for her to know the full truth. Families do keep secrets, don't they? And she's absolutely made me feel like family. We're the only family either of us has. Her husband is gone and her little girl died eight years before him, from scarlet fever. She was only five years old. When I heard that story, I understood why we girls in the boarding house are so precious to Mrs. D. Why she treats us as daughters. I suppose that's why I've never moved out.

Mrs. D's mouth turns up a tiny bit into a slight smile, yet there's a tinge of sadness in her eyes. "Nothing's wrong, dear. I was just thinking of my daughter. Today would have been her birthday."

Our eyes meet. I believe she sees the love in mine and my deep sympathy when she unclasps our hands and, with a tiny nod, pats mine. No words are exchanged. They're not needed.

"Enough of that," she says with a slap on her thighs and sits up tall, or as tall as she can get with her five-foot stature. "Now tell me about your day. How's the show going and how's that little boy whose voice keeps cracking?"

The momentary heavy air dissipates. I tell Mrs. D about the rehearsal and Heidi's grandfather and the sheep. Her gentle smile lets me know she's delighted. And when I tell her about meeting Judith Zell and the audition I have tomorrow, that smile goes all the way up to her eyes. Even the little creases around them spread wider.

"This is wonderful," she says. "I'm so happy for you. Tell me more, what's the play about?"

I tell her it's a romance and her brow rises. She gives me a wink.

"Oh, stop. It's only a play." With a little wave of my hand I swipe away her teasing.

"And I'm sure you'll get the part. But, Lucy, dear," she says, her tone turns serious. "You're so wonderful with the children. And time is passing by. Don't you want to remarry and have one of your own?"

My stomach sinks. I wish I could tell her the truth.

Chapter 33

July 1933

Golly, two Negro men just flew an airplane called The Pride of Atlantic City from Atlantic City all the way to California. To where Lucy lives! The article in the New York Sun says it took them two days to fly across the country and land in Glendale, California. Incredible! I wonder if Glendale is near Lucy and if she saw the airplane land – if it flew over her house. That must have been quite a sight. One man was a pilot, but the other was a physician. I cannot imagine Charles ever going up in one of those things. Like Lindbergh, when he flew across the Atlantic in '27, these men did not have parachutes or a radio or lights for landing. I would be petrified. My heavens, the gumption one must have to try such a feat. I do not believe people will ever travel in the air, as they predict. That is just ridiculous. But then, who ever imagined having a home lit by electric lights? What will be next?

Heavens, I hear Anna's footsteps coming down the hall. I must put this journal away – I will be back later . . .

Anna's eyes lit up when she saw the article about the airplane in the newspaper lying on my desk. She said Daddy told her people can pay one dollar for a plane ride at Bader Field, the same airfield the men flew from. In her usual whine, she told me she wants to do it, but Mom thinks it is crazy. Once again, she said, "I don't understand her. She never wants to do anything, and I want to do everything!" Then she kissed my cheek. Now, at nearly thirteen, she no longer needs tucking in, which I miss. Instead, she comes to give me a goodnight kiss. Just before leaving my room, she announced she is going to tell her father she wants to fly in a plane for her birthday.

As always, sitting here, writing at my desk, I picture myself talking to Lucy. You'll get a kick out of this, I would say. Anna has become quite the daredevil and Charles indulges her. Can you imagine that, when he is so controlling over the adult women in his life? Yes, he still is, Lucy. It is his way. But Anna has him wrapped around her little finger. I am quite sure he will grant her this wild birthday wish, and I am also quite sure Florence will disagree. She would like Anna to sit at home like a lady, doing needlework rather than running around Luna Park with her friends eating hot dogs and cotton candy and going on scary rides, much less flying in an airplane. I have accompanied Anna and her girlfriends several times to Luna Park in Coney Island and must say, nothing frightens our girl. She rides that flying machine, the

Circle Swing, and the Cyclone with no fear. My heart is in my mouth watching that roller coaster speed down toward the ground, swerving around sharp curves. I am petrified she is going to fly out of the seat and land in the ocean, yet she squeals with delight.

As I said, Charles gives her whatever she wants, so why not a flight in a hunk of metal with wings? I only hope my heart holds out when she is soaring over the Atlantic, even if it is only for a few minutes. However, I cannot help wondering, what will happen when Anna wants something more from him? When she wants the truth about her birth. Will Charles give her that? She was quite surprised when she entered school and learned her birth name was Anna. She came home that day insisting we all call her Anna, as her teacher and the children in school do. I was hoping we would. It would make me feel that a part of you won. But Charles said, "Never. You are my Rosy and always will be." She pouted and stamped her foot, but it did no good. By now, she is used to being Rosy at home and Anna in school. And always Anna here in my journal, when I feel as if I am talking or writing to you. I doubt she will easily accept the truth about you, Lucy, when I give her the earrings and the facts. She will go to Charles and what will happen then? Will he be honest with her? Or, will he be furiously angry with me and throw me out of the house? And what about Anna and Florence? What will the news do to their relationship?

My stomach cramps thinking about all of this. I was ready to tear up this paper, in fear of someone finding my journal and reading it, knowing I'm "talking" to you, and then I chuckled. How silly of me. I hide the journal in my night table, under papers and other books. No one will ever see it. And, sadly, I will never have any more letters from you, and Anna will no longer receive birthday cards that I hide away in this journal. Perhaps you have written but we have not received anything since your last Christmas card before we moved uptown to the Dakota. I am not surprised. Forwarding mail only lasts a year, I believe, and it is not very efficient when one moves so far from their former neighborhood and mail route, as we have done. I wonder if you put your return address on the envelope. At least then the mail would have come back to you and you would know we had moved. Though what would that matter? I doubt you are ever coming back to see us.

Now I must slip the journal into its hiding place and climb into bed. Despite my exhaustion, I feel lighter, as I always do after getting my thoughts on paper and "talking" to you, keeping you abreast of our girl as she grows up, if only in my own mind. Good night, Lucy.

Chapter 34

The streetcar lets me off in front of the movie house. The marquee, lit up in green and gold, shines on the crowd waiting in line to buy tickets to *It Happened One Night* with the gorgeous, virile Clark Gable, who Jenny claims oozes sex, and Claudette Colbert, who she keeps reminding me started on stage. I finally have a space in my schedule to see it. The film's first reviews weren't great but now it's getting accolades from everyone, including Jenny, who's already seen it twice. Reviewers call the movie a screwball romantic comedy and tout it as an Oscar winner. Colbert has been a huge success in movies. Maybe Jenny is right and I should reconsider. No. It's too late for that. Anyway, Judith's play is still selling seats. Every night, except Mondays, I'm saved from a burning building and fall in love with my handsome fireman with broad shoulders and deep brown eyes. Or my character is. I still don't have much interest in falling in love. Some flirtations, an occasional date, but nothing serious. Nothing, as they say, to write home about. But who would I write to anyway? I don't know Helen or Crystal's addresses anymore, and Grandmama never wrote back after I sent her my address. Charles probably never showed her the letter. That's just like him. Take it from the mailbox, see it's from me, and toss it out. Even Mrs. Stokes never wrote back. I thought she'd get in touch with Helen. She'd certainly know where Helen is and be able to give her my address. But no response from her either. They're probably all angry with me. I blink my watery eyes. *Stop*, I tell myself. It's been twelve years since I left. Nine since I sent them my address. Even if Helen and Crystal never got my letter, my mother-in-law and Mrs. Stokes should have. So why am I going down this road again? It always comes on me out of nowhere, and I've got to stop. They obviously don't want me in their lives anymore. My body tenses. Trying to shake these upsetting thoughts away, I look down the street to see if Jenny or Judith is coming. We're supposed to meet here. I check my watch. Yes, right now. Where in the world are they?

With its bell jingling, a street car comes to a stop directly in front of the theater. "Hey there," Judith calls out with a wave as she steps off. She looks smart in her navy cotton skirt and short-sleeved jacket. The white belt on the jacket shows off her slim waist, accentuating her bust. "Did you get your ticket yet?" she asks.

"No." Just then Jenny appears, looking like the movie star she is with her lightly rouged cheeks and penciled eyebrows. She could be an ad for the Maybelline woman with her perfectly applied facepaint. These two have become very dear to me and I'm so thankful they're in my life. Mrs. D calls us an odd threesome with Jenny married, Judith a mother, and me still single. A chill runs through me every time I hear her say those two words. A mother. It's a secret I'll take to my grave.

Judith throws an arm over each of our shoulders. "Good," she says, leading us to the ticket booth. "Because tonight is my treat."

Thankfully, I can afford the twenty-three cents for the ticket. Theaters everywhere lowered their price when the Depression hit making it easier for me and so many people to spend a few hours being entertained in a dark theater. But if Judith wants to pay, who am I to say no? I do put up a little fuss though and ask why.

"I feel flush tonight." She wiggles her brows. "Plus, I have very exciting news." She looks straight at me, her eyes wide open, then turns to the man behind the ticket booth and asks for three. She gives him a dollar bill, gets her change, and hands us our tickets. I'm bursting to know her news and, if her expression means anything, what it has to do with me. But she says nothing. We walk into the movie house, and the buttery aroma of popcorn makes my mouth water. "I'll get us a bag," I say and head over to wait in line at the new concession stand with all the other patrons.

With the ten-cent bag – big enough for us to share – in my hands, we walk into the orchestra section and find three seats together in a middle row. We squeeze past a young couple holding hands and sit. I take the middle seat, making it easier for my friends to dig in and grab a handful of popcorn. Immediately, Judith reaches over. I grab her wrist before she can get one kernel. "Hold on," I say. "No eating 'til you tell me what's so exciting."

Judith laughs and claps her hands. One big, loud clap with a sharp shake of her head, and she sings out, "We're going on the road!"

My head jerks back. What in the world does she mean?

"Yes! I just got the offer this afternoon. I have a new backer for the play and he has contacts all over."

"Wait. *Earthshaking* is going on the road? Where? When?"

"Once we complete this run, we're heading to San Francisco. We already have the theater. They're giving us a three-month run with an option for more, like we had here, if sales are good."

"That'll be great," Jenny says, dipping her hand into the popcorn. "You sell out practically every night in Los Angeles. Why shouldn't it be the same in San Fran?"

Judith goes on to tell us, if we're successful up north her backer says he can get us Chicago and very possibly New York."

The theater lights dim. The curtain opens. The music plays. The Columbia Pictures icon, a lady holding a sparkling torch, appears on screen. I sit back as the credits role, hoping I can focus on the movie. Though all I can think of is possibly going to New York. I could find Helen and Crystal. Or they would find me. Once they hear I'm in the play, they'd certainly come. They'd know Lucy Perkins is me. It's my maiden name. But what about Charles? And Mama Brandt? I'm sure she'd come. She encouraged my acting. And Anna. A heavy breath escapes my lips. Jenny turns to me with a smile. She thinks I'm settling in, sinking into my seat excited to watch the movie, not that I'm thinking I could meet my thirteen-year-old daughter. So many questions run through my head. They jumble as the movie starts. A yacht appears on screen and I wonder if I will go.

Chapter 35

August 1935

I thought the apartment walls would shake with all the shouting this morning. Never have I heard Anna raise her voice to Florence at such volume or say the things she said. It took the choreography of making a pot of tea to calm my nerves, from minding the faucet as the water flowed into the copper kettle to setting it on the stove to boil to pouring the steaming hot liquid over aromatic tea leaves into a bone china pot and watching the clear liquid turn toasty brown to finally sipping the comforting blend. Now, describing the dance as the sun sinks in the darkening sky, my nerves settle even more. I have so much I need to say. So much to tell Lucy.

The last time I "spoke" to Lucy was shortly before Anna turned thirteen. As expected, Charles granted her wish to fly in an airplane. The four of us – Florence included, though she was not pleased with the idea - took the arduous auto trip to Atlantic City. For a few minutes, our courageous, determined girl soared over the ocean. It was a glorious day and now

Anna has a bigger wish. Lucy, this one is much more important. It is not actually a wish. It is a want. A demand. And Florence has other ideas which would infuriate you.

Although I do not approve of the tone Anna used this morning in their awful row, I do agree with everything she said. Next month, at only fifteen years old, Anna will be entering her last year of high school. I am not sure if I told you that our beautiful girl is very bright and made the accelerated classes, the SPs as we call it, skipping eighth grade. Florence is proud of her yet does not see why a young woman should go to college. It boggles my mind that she has such old-fashioned ideas. It is probably why my son married her. Yet Charles is in favor of Anna's continuing her studies. He says she will make a better partner for her future husband with a classic education. He admires bright women, as long as they do not let careers get in their way of motherhood. Yes, he still feels that way and cannot see a woman having both.

This morning, Anna announced that she wanted to go to Barnard College like two of the older girls in our building. And like you! Though she is unaware of that. She visited the girls at school and loves the idea of being in the City yet living in the dormitory, not at home. I thought Charles would have apoplexy when she named the school. He did not have a chance to say anything because Florence cut Anna off, shouting that girls in her station do not need advanced education. They should live at home until they are married. She said Anna should focus on giving her time and money to charitable organizations, not schools. Red in the face, Anna yelled back, "Who are you? How can you even be my mother?"

Ugly words spewed from Anna's mouth and my heart jumped into my throat. Anna often tells me she is nothing like her mother, that she cannot fathom where she came from and all I say is, "Yes, you are. You do not realize how much. You will when you get older." She looks at me as if I have two heads then shakes her own. She must assume I do not know what I am talking about. I let her think so because I cannot tell her how true my words are.

Anna also told Florence, with much venom in her voice, that she would be charitable because she is going to go to law school after she graduates from Barnard. She will represent women who are wrongfully arrested and wrongfully imprisoned, especially those who "fall prey to that unjust, insane American Plan," to use her words. I did not know what she was referring to and I am positive Florence had no idea either, but I took myself to the Forty-second Street library this afternoon to look it up. I agree with Anna. It is a completely unfair law and shocking it is still on the books. Though Anna's intentions are good, I am afraid she is a bit naïve. Men do run this country. Yet who am I to say? She certainly has gumption. And she is smart, so she just might be one of those women to change things. Our own Elizabeth Cady Stanton. I only hope I am here to see it happen.

There is more that worries me and I am afraid to say anything to Charles. He will hover over me and insist I sit and rest and stay off my feet, which I refuse to do. You know how much I enjoyed my morning constitutionals in Washington Square park. I still do, though now I stroll the paths in Central Park and stop to chat with neighbors at the bench under the chestnut tree instead of at the fountain in the Square. Plus, I enjoy being in the kitchen, standing over the hot stove helping Cook prepare dinner for the family. It makes me feel useful, especially when we bake their favorite cakes.

Lucy, I have been having some shortness of breath and it is worrisome. Thankfully, there are no stairs in this apartment, as we had in the townhouse, so I do not feel this breathlessness often, but when I take the subway and have to climb up the long flights of steps, I realize I do not have the strength I used to. I stop halfway to catch my breath with people rushing past me, almost knocking me over. I know I am getting older. I will be seventy-three on my next birthday so why am I surprised? Several years ago, shortly after you left, I heard through the proverbial grapevine that Mr. Stokes, Helen's father, passed away. It was a sudden heart attack. Her mother, Mabel, whom you adored, moved up to The Bronx to be near her sister. Besides the fact that Charles included Mabel in his dictate of never seeing anyone you were friends with (and I obeyed), I had no way of getting in touch with her to find Helen or to send a message, if I dared. I wonder if Mabel is still alive.

I am afraid darkness has taken a seat in my soul. This is not the woman I want to be.

Act Three

Chapter 36

1951

The art deco clock hanging in the imposing marble lobby of the Manhattan Criminal Court Building shows 3 p.m.. I race past the grand staircase to the elevator and punch the up button. I heard Crystal Alsop, the fierce attorney with more wins for women accused of prostitution than most male attorneys, is giving her closing arguments this afternoon. This one's for a murder trial, and I don't want to miss it. I, reliable, responsible Anna Dodge, skipped out of my office early for it. To learn from the best. In my seven years practicing law, I've never had a murder case. I've handled some burglaries, although not lately. When the GIs came home from fighting Hitler and the Axis powers, women were sent back to the kitchen or demoted to lesser positions. I've been fortunate to keep my job. My firm wants to appear modern, but the returning warriors — men with LLB after their names - appear in front of judges now. That has to change.

Tapping my foot, eyes glued to the elevator, I wait. Finally, with a clanking sound, it reaches the lobby. The doors open. Two men exit, the spicy fragrance of aftershave follows. One woman in a pencil skirt and sweater pushes past me to get inside, then I enter. "Eleven please," I say to the elevator operator. There's silence in the car as we ascend. We reach the eleventh floor, and

I hurry down the hall, heels clicking against the marble floor. Quietly, I open the courtroom door and slip into a seat.

Miss Alsop, in a crisp gray suit, has already begun her summation. She stands straight and tall before the jury saying, "The state has to prove each and every element of the charge beyond a reasonable doubt." She stops and faces the jurors on the right. A second later she looks directly at those seated in the center of the box, then to those on the left, letting each and every one of them believe she's speaking to them directly. Then she continues. "What I am going to talk to you about are facts in evidence. I'm not making these up. These are facts that have been presented to you." She takes her time, enunciating each word. "These are the issues I am asking you to discuss in the jury room. Issues that stem from the evidence in the case. Issues that we believe create the reasonable doubt."

Oh, she's good. I've heard she also graduated from NYU Law, years before me. Rumor has it she's in her mid-fifties though, with her trim figure, she looks younger. It was rare for women to go to law school in her day. In the early 1900s, most weren't accepting females. And, she's one of the few women attorneys who stayed in practice after the war. Or in any job.

She speaks to the jurors as if there's no one else in the room. One man, juror number five, nods his head every now and then, and juror number eight, a woman, leans forward, soaking up every word coming from the lawyer's mouth, as I am. Miss Alsop is brilliant.

I take a moment to scan the audience. I call it that because everyone viewing this summation, those in the wooden seats and those in the jury box, are watching a performance. The courtroom is an attorney's stage, no matter if you're defending or prosecuting the accused. My father never wanted me to be on stage. Not that it was my life's ambition. I acted in a few shows in college and he never came to see me. My mother did. She hoped I'd marry one of the handsome men in the play.

Thinking of my father, I wish he'd lived long enough to see me in front of a courtroom, especially one here at 100 Centre Street. I think he'd be proud of me. His chest was all puffed up at my law school graduation, seeing me accept my diploma and throw my cap in the air, even if he would have preferred watching me walk down the aisle in a wedding gown, a lace veil draped over my happy face. Sadly, due to a massive heart attack, he missed that event last year. I know he would have cried though I'm not sure he would have accepted my being a married woman – finally, at thirty, he would have thought – with a career. Now though, with . . . I shake my head, trying to push those thoughts away. They make my belly quiver. Gently stroking its tiny bump, I focus on the defense attorney's words.

Miss Alsop is reminding the jury of the evidence presented. I'm sitting in this stately courtroom with walls of polished wainscoting and I can't get my father or my situation out of my mind. My finger strokes the three stones on my earring.

Her tone instructive, Miss Alsop brings her summation to a close. "Discuss these issues with your fellow jurors," she says. "Listen to what they say, and ask them to listen to what you say." Then she raises a flat palm and concludes, "But in the end, after examining the evidence in this case – and the lack of evidence – we believe you will find there is a reasonable doubt, and therefore, you must find the defendant not guilty."

The courtroom is silent. Crystal Alsop thanks the jury and returns to her seat at the defense table. The judge excuses the jury for the night reminding them not to speak of the case with anyone, or to read about it in the newspapers. "Court will resume in the morning," he says, "with the prosecution's closing arguments." People rustle in their seats grabbing their belongings, slipping into coats and hats. The lawyers at the defense table gather their papers and folders. I wait for Miss Alsop to leave and follow her out. Only she doesn't go to the elevator, as I hoped. She turns left. I have to go right. But that won't stop me. I must speak to her.

Out on the street, cars honk. Buses belch exhaust fumes. I'm on the courthouse step waiting for Crystal Alsop. Men with briefcases in hand pass by, hurrying to the subway, heading home for the evening. I have a different agenda which is kind of embarrassing, being an attorney myself. I feel like a star-struck fan waiting for Kathryn Hepburn or Vivian Leigh, but this is important to me. I think she can help.

With my shadow growing longer minute by minute, I check my watch. It's already half an hour that I've been standing here with my eyes glued to the large bronze doors. Either I missed her, which I doubt, or Miss Alsop took the rear exit onto Baxter Street. So I give up. On the sidewalk, I turn and take one last look, just in case. "All right, you tried," I mumble under my breath kicking up my pace, heading to the subway. At the corner, waiting for the light to change, I flip ideas in my head. Should I call her in the office or just forget it? Can I do this on my own, or will Miss Alsop have some good suggestions? And there she is, across Canal Street about to descend the subway steps. Her red topper's open, swinging in the spring breeze. Oh, the hell with the cars and traffic lights. I race across the street, skirting around a huge, two-tone-green Buick. A Chevy honks, its driver shouting from the open window, "Idiot, you want to kill yourself?" I skip up the curb and hurry to catch her.

Odors of grease and metal mixed with the acrid smell of cigarette smoke and the occasional whiff of perfume blanket the dank air on the subway platform. Miss Alsop's red coat stands out in the crowd of tweeds and grays. I approach her with a fluttery feeling in my stomach.

"Excuse me, Miss Alsop. I'm Anna Dodge, an attorney with Edward and Elm." I extend my hand.

"The Double E's," she says with a smile and before I can explain why I'm introducing myself, she shakes my hand. "Nice to meet you."

"Thank you. Um, this is a bit awkward, but I'm wondering if you'd let me take you for coffee. I know you have experience being the sole woman in the office and . . . "

"And you'd like to know how I've dealt with it." She chuckles. "It wasn't easy, Anna. It is Anna, isn't it?"

I nod and, raising my voice against the cacophony of trains rattling into the station, their brakes squealing, I explain about my wanting to talk to the partners in my firm in order to get my caseload back.

"So, since the war," she says with raised brows and a cigarette in a gold holder between two fingers. "They're treating you like a clerk. That's simply not acceptable."

"Right. That's why I'd like to take you for coffee, now or another time, to run some ideas by you and hear how you've dealt with the situation. Or maybe you haven't had to."

"Oh, I certainly have" she laughs. "And not just now in this post-World War II world. But I don't— " She stops mid-sentence and gapes at my earrings then quickly shoots her eyes back to mine. "I . . . I don't have time right now." Her voice is odd, like she suddenly can't find the words she wants to say. "Though I really would like to help. Perhaps when my case is finished. Or . . . "

Her eyes keep sliding from my face to my earrings. I touch the gold disk, wondering if it's dirty or dangling and about to fall off. With wheels rumbling, the uptown train pulls into the station.

"Oh, that's my train," she says. The doors open with a chime. She steps forward, then stops. It looks like she's not sure if she wants to go.

"Mine too," I say, scooting next to her. Together, we join the throng scrunched together making our way into the subway car.

She grabs the nearest pole. I hold onto the overhead strap, feet spread apart for balance. The train jerks forward, jostling us. Her shoulder bag bangs my hip.

"I might have time to meet while the jury is out," she says over the rattle of the subway. "How about I call you in your office?"

"That would be great." We smile and nod at each other, then stand swaying, staring out the window into the blackness of Manhattan's underground as the train rolls along the track. It's creepy. It feels like she's examining my profile.

Darkness turns to light as we pull into the Astor Place station. The train stops with a jolt, pushing me forward and back. Passengers hurry to the doors. "This is where I get off," she says. "We'll meet soon."

Chapter 37

A cold blast of March wind flies through the coffee shop as the door opens. I look up from my seat in the red-vinyl booth. Spotting Miss Alsop walking in, I wave. She lifts a gloved hand and responds with a big grin, as if she's thrilled to see me. My hands tingle. I'm happy she doesn't think of me as a nuisance asking for her help.

"I'm so glad I caught you," she says as she stuffs the leather gloves in the pocket of her long wrap coat then hangs it on the hook at the side of the booth. She slides in and tosses her pocketbook and briefcase on the bench next to her. "I debated calling in the middle of the day, in case you were in court."

With a chuckle, I tell her I'm rarely there.

"Right. Of course. That's why you want to talk to me." With her elbows on the table and chin resting on her clasped hands, she leans in. "So, I've been thinking about your situation and . . . "

The waitress comes over. We order two coffees and wave away her suggestion of a piece of cherry pie, no matter how fresh and yummy it is. Speaking over Guy Mitchell singing "My Heart Cries For You" from the jukebox in the booth behind us, I take the opportunity to congratulate Miss Alsop on her win.

"The jury came back fast," she says, sitting back, expelling a big breath. "A day and a half and they acquitted her on all counts." She waves her hand in the air, as if erasing a chalkboard in school, and says, "But we're here to talk about you. And please, call me Crystal."

She's old enough to be my mother and I've never called any of *her* friends by their first names. But being colleagues, I suppose that makes it all right. Again, I thank Crystal for being willing to meet me, as I did when she called my office a few hours ago asking if coffee at four o'clock would work. "With this win," I say, "and all the others you've had . . . "

"And losses," she interrupts, pointing her index finger in the air. "I've had plenty of those."

I laugh. "Yes, I'm sure. But when you were younger, just starting out in practice, it couldn't have been easy. Not many women were lawyers back then." I shrug. "Not that there are so many now. When I graduated from law school in '43 women only made up about two and a half percent of all lawyers in the US."

"Now it's a little more," she says, slipping a Chesterfield from its soft pack. "The bar association claims we're about three and a half percent. Not a huge jump in eight years. And you're correct. It wasn't easy. I had to prove myself, as you've had to do. The problem now is figuring out how you can get your caseload back."

The bouquet of freshly brewed coffee mixed with the woody scent of tobacco drifts across the booth as the waitress arrives and pours the steamy joe into our white ceramic cups. She leaves and Crystal continues reminding me that I had the chops when I started in the office and I still have them now. "Probably even more so," she says. "Don't let Edward and Elm intimidate you. They hired you. True, we were at war and there was a dearth of male attorneys, but they gave you a spot. They gave you cases. Some big ones you said."

"Some paying clients, though mostly pro bono cases, and now I don't even get those. They give them to the returning vets and men just out of law school."

The look on her face is pure disgust. "It makes my blood boil when some men think they're above defending indigent clients. Oh, no, they won't dirty their white collars with burglaries or robberies or, heaven forbid, rape. They have no idea how exhilarating the challenge is to find that one reasonable doubt that'll bring an acquittal." With a frustrated shake of the head she adds, "The firm has to fulfill a quota and somebody's got to do the job. You go and show them how it's done."

Sipping my coffee, I listen to her pumping me up. She's right. I simply need to get my confidence up again, yet . . .

"Don't go in demanding. That'll never work," she says. She points to the gold band on my left ring finger. "I'll bet you know how to get what you want from your husband." Her brow goes up, accompanied by jesting, wide-open eyes. "Use the same tactics. They're only men, dear."

Oh yes, husband, I think stroking my belly. Quiet conversation hums from other tables and booths. Silverware clatters, chilly air blows through the door as it opens for more patrons wanting hot coffee, a donut, or a piece of cherry pie for a late afternoon snack. "Do you have children?" I ask.

"No. That hasn't been an issue for me in my career. Neither has marriage." She lifts her hands and wiggles her bare fingers. "But I do know married women who have careers. A few even have children. Yet there are those who had to make hard choices."

"I'm afraid I might have to also." Her brows draw together. With a tiny shoulder lift I add, "It's a conundrum. I don't know what to do."

She leans across the white Formica table top with squiggly silver lines. In barely a whisper, she asks if I'm expecting. I nod.

She drops back against the hard vinyl seat. "That's a whole different story."

We sit staring at each other. The waitress comes and tops off our coffee. All I hear is the hot liquid sloshing in our cups.

"But it doesn't have to be," she says, sitting up straight. "You've shown what you can do. Remind them of that. Remind them of your record. It's a good one, isn't it?"

"I'm proud of it."

"And don't say a word about the pregnancy. How far along are you?"

"Not sure. I have a doctor's appointment tomorrow."

She shoves a hand through the air, like shoving away something distasteful, something so unnecessary it doesn't deserve even thinking about. "Then you might not be. Don't worry yet."

Ha! That's easy for her to say. I shake my head and let her know I've missed two periods. What I don't say, because this is a conversation between two professionals – she's not a close friend or a cousin or an aunt – is that my breasts are so hot and sore I can't even let my husband touch them.

"You're tiny," she says. "You probably won't show for several months. I had a friend a long time ago who looked like you." She swallows hard. "I mean she had your type of body – like a ballerina's, graceful, slender – and when she was expecting, it wasn't obvious until she was much farther along. So there's no need to rock the boat now."

"Was your friend working?"

Crystal's chest fills with a deep breath, then quickly deflates. "That's a story for another time. I'm just making the comparison. You get some cases and show those men what you can do. Be the tiger you are. You had to be one to get the job. Now go out there. Be fierce. They'll see how important you are to the firm. Then, when you have to tell them you're having a baby, they won't want to lose you."

"That's when they'll most likely let me go. How many pregnant women do you see in court? And I don't mean defendants."

"Make a deal with them. Say you won't go to court the last few months, that you'll go back to doing the office work you do now. And get them to agree, in writing, that you'll be back at work two weeks after you deliver."

"That's not very long."

"No, but you want the job. Nobody's giving new mommies any time off." She puts the cup down hard. "Though there should be a law giving new mothers some leave."

"And," I say, pointing my cup at her, "preventing employers from denying women jobs while they're pregnant."

Coffee and discussion finished, I insist on paying the bill. "Please, it's the least I can do," I say when she argues. "I owe you much more than a thirty-cent cup of coffee. How about I take you for a real drink when I get my caseload back?"

"That would be lovely. I look forward to it," she says. "Go get 'em tiger."

I slide an arm into my swing coat and shrug it on, then wrap the pink scarf my mother knitted around my neck. Crystal buttons up her camel hair coat and slips on her gloves. Together, we walk out onto lower Broadway. The March wind hits us in the face. This day is so different from the warm tease of spring we had two days ago when I first met Crystal.

"I've got to go back to the office," she says, turning left. "Next time we meet, and we definitely will, you've got to tell me about those gorgeous earrings you wore the other day. They're not the usual ones we see in jewelry shops."

Chapter 38

Carrying two cups of hot coffee, I walk into the living room and notice colorful pamphlets laid out on our coffee table. My husband, in khaki pants and V-neck sweater, his casual weekend outfit, is standing to the side of it with a glint in his eye.

"What are these," I say, placing each cup on a coaster, protecting the polished teak table. We've just completed decorating our two-bedroom apartment in Stuyvesant Town. It was exciting going furniture shopping together, especially choosing our bedroom set. Not wanting to be the entitled girl I grew up as, I chose a modestly priced one in walnut. But Will wanted the more expensive Henry Link French provincial set. "After all," he said, when we stood in Sloan's that sunny afternoon, "we'll be cuddled up in this bed together when our false teeth float in a glass of water on the night table. It has to last." The intricate floral carvings and ornate hardware reminded me of Grandmama's writing desk, so I happily agreed.

Seated on our new turquoise couch with the wide upholstered arms, I lift a shiny pamphlet with the Eiffel Tower pictured against a blue sky. Opening it, I find a street map of Paris with red lines leading to the tower. Another pamphlet with the Arc de Triomphe on the cover lies on the table next to a

Michelin Guidebook. "What's this all about?" I look up at my husband. I love the way his golden-brown eyes crinkle at the side when he smiles.

"I want to take my special gal to the City of Love," he says then sits down next to me and clasps my hand. "Now's the time. After the baby comes, we won't be able to take trips like this." He brings my hand to his lips. The soft kiss is as delicious as a flaky croissant fresh from the oven.

"How can I ask for time off, when soon I have to tell them I'm expecting?"

Will looks down at my tiny belly bump, then up at me and shakes his head. "You're twelve weeks and barely show. There's plenty of time before you have to tell them. Plus, you have vacation time accrued."

My handsome husband, with a chiseled jaw and dimple in his chin that I love to kiss, is behind me all the way. Some of my friends are not as fortunate. My roommate in college, who became a second-grade teacher, told me her husband said when their kids are in school full time she could substitute a few days a month, but not have her own class anymore. That's not going to happen anytime soon with her having three kids under the age of five. There are others I grew up with, played hopscotch and dolls with, who never wanted to work, only wanted to continue playing house with a real husband and child. And all those classmates I had in college who abandoned school or jobs to marry and attach themselves to aprons, *The Joy of Cooking*, and washing machines. I can't imagine myself in any of those scenarios and, luckily, I don't have to.

"Of course, you're going to keep working," Will said the evening I told him we were having a baby. It was four weeks ago. I came home from the doctor and told him I was pregnant and worried I'd have to give up my career. He was in his office, which will soon be the baby's room. As the words tumbled from my mouth, words *he* hoped and prayed I'd say one day, he jumped up from his chair and wrapped his arms around me kissing my head, my cheek, and finally a long sensuous one on my lips. "There is no reason you can't keep working," he said. "I don't care what the norm is." He put quotation marks around the word norm with his fingers. "You studied hard for this. It's not something you throw away because some men think a woman should be in the kitchen. You're smart. A talented attorney. And I'm damn proud of you."

When I met Will, I knew right from the start that this man, who was five years older than me, was the total opposite of my father as far as women were concerned. Will told me how his mother took him with her when she marched down Fifth Avenue in 1917. He was two years old, in a carriage, carrying a sign demanding women be allowed to vote. My mother-in-law has a framed photo of that on the mantel over her fireplace. She has another of a group of women, some dressed in wild, colorful caftans, clothes I'd never wear in my own house much less a restaurant. She says back in the teens and twenties, they had lunch together every week in the Village. It was a special club they were in, and sometimes, she misses those meetings. I understand that. As much as I adore Will, girlfriend time is special. That's why, despite our age difference, I hope I'll see Crystal Alsop again. I felt we had a connection. Probably because we're both attorneys. A rare breed, though we are growing. Slowly.

Seated next to me on our sofa, my hand still folded in his, Will says, "Darling, we'll hire a nanny." With a wink, he adds, "Unless you think your mother would want the job." He laughs. "You should see the expression on your face."

I grab my hand back and slap my thighs. "There is no way my mother is taking care of my daughter. She'll fill her with all sorts of old-fashioned nonsense."

"What if it's a boy?" His eyes sparkle with mischief. "Can Florence watch him?"

"Oh, no. Whatever this child is, he or she will have a real nanny." Nanny or not, what I don't say and never have since I realized I was expecting is, *Do I really want to be a mother?* My chest tightens with the question I can't answer.

Will picks up his coffee. "So when will you tell your mother? She's going to flip her lid."

My husband quivers with excitement over this baby and he's right, my mother will be thrilled. Beyond thrilled, if that's possible. And me? I'm not sure.

"Tomorrow," I say and take a sip of my coffee. It's cooled, not the warm comforting brew I love and need now to help settle the confusion souring my belly.

"Well," Will says. "Don't forget to get your birth certificate. We need to get you a passport."

~

A misty rain greets me as I emerge from the depths of the subway onto Central Park West, wetting my face and sending chills through my body. A young girl hurries past, her high ponytail swinging side to side. Dog walkers tug on leashes, nudging their spaniels and poodles along. I bury myself in my jacket and hoof it down West Seventy-second Street. I know my mother's going to be thrilled with my baby news. It's how she'll react to my other plans that gave me a restless sleep last night. Will, on the other hand, fell asleep grinning like a little boy who won a stuffed animal at the fair.

"Hi, Thomas," I say to the Dakota's doorman standing beside the brass guard booth, the ever-present white gloves on his hands. I've known this man for years, before his full head of thick black hair thinned to salt and pepper. Unfortunately, the confusion sitting deep in my core prevents me from giving him my usual bright smile.

"Hello, Miss Brandt," he says in his familiar sing-song manner. "Oh, sorry. Old habit. I mean Mrs. Dodge. Your mother is expecting you."

I thank him as he opens the black iron gates leading to the courtyard. Making my way through and into the building, I think about how happy the staff here will be when they hear I'm having a baby. Many of them have known me since I was a little girl. We moved here when I was seven. They watched me playing jacks in the breezeway and jumping rope in the courtyard with my friends from the building. A few of the staff, including the super, came to some of the productions I was in at Barnard and all congratulated me when I passed the New York Bar and again last year when Will and I married. A few gave us gifts like the cordial glasses from the housekeeping staff we use for after-dinner drinks. What truly touched me was how many staff members hugged me when Grandmama died. They saw how devastated I was, crying in the hallways, my usual buoyancy gone. Thankfully, I got it back. It's what she would have wanted. Oh how I wish she was here with me now. She would understand why I want to keep my job. My grandmother knew I wanted a career, not to just be a housewife like my mother. She even encouraged me. Though, I still don't understand why she would say I'm more like my mother than I know. That she got wrong.

The elevator doors open on the sixth floor. I step out ready to have tea with my mother and deal with whatever else happens.

~

"Oh my goodness!" Mom says, clasping her hands on her heart. I just told her my news, leaving out the whole career part. She jumps up from the sofa and rushes across the living room, grabbing me in an enormous hug.

"You're crushing me," I say, trying to pull out of her arms, but she won't let go. She's rocking me side to side and I feel her wet cheek dampening my dry one.

"Oh, oh yes," she says and steps back. "The baby." Love glistens in her eyes as she gazes at me like I'm the most precious thing she's ever seen. She hasn't looked at me this way since I was a little girl, and everything in the room sparkles – even the art deco, black-lacquered coffee table I never liked, afraid I'd break the glass top. And the velvet swivel chair in that awful honeycomb color she bought when we moved here looks stunning today.

When my parents sold our townhouse to move uptown to this gigantic apartment building, my mother couldn't wait to get rid of every piece of furniture we had. "I will not bring that awful settee to our new apartment," I remember her telling Daddy. "The only piece of furniture that comes with us is Grandmama's writing desk. I know it means a great deal to her. The rest of the stuff you can dump for all I care."

I was heartbroken. Washington Square was my home. I didn't want to leave it with its winding paths where I ran, first chasing squirrels and later my friends when we played tag, and the fountain that sprayed us on hot summer days, and old men playing chess at stone tables, and carts selling chestnuts in winter and salty frankfurters in spring. I couldn't imagine living in a behemoth of stone and brick – though I didn't know that word back then – with so many other people in the same building. I was used to my own house. I laugh thinking of that now.

"What's so funny?" Mom says

"I'm just thinking how I didn't want to move here."

"Oh, you put up quite a fuss until we promised you Grandmama would come with us."

Looking at my mother, who is now holding my hands in hers, I feel a sad smile pull my cheeks. "I miss Grandmama, but I'm so glad my child will have her own who'll love her to bits."

My mother kisses my forehead. "Let's have a cup of tea," she says, "and talk about the baby. It'll be so much fun shopping for furniture and baby clothes. I never . . . " She waves her hands in the air. "I never thought I'd be a grandma. Come. I'll put the kettle on."

Opposite me at the kitchen table, my mother's eyes are wide open listening to my plans. "What do you mean you'll keep working?" she screeches. It resounds off the four walls. "You're going to be a *mother*. Your place is at home with your baby."

Rage ripples through my body. Knowing I'd never get anywhere if I holler back, I force myself to tamp it down. I knew she'd react this way, so why am I angry? Why does she do this to me? I love my mother, but she makes every muscle in my body quiver when she spews these asinine ideas. She said the same thing years ago when I told her I wanted to go to college. Then it wasn't about being a mother but about being a woman whose place is at home and I wouldn't need a college education for that. Loosening my grip on the teacup, I take a sip giving myself a moment to find the right words.

Keeping my voice soft, though my heart feels like it's beating louder than a bass drum, I begin. "Mom, I know how you feel." I hear my pleading tone and figure that's ok. She'll hear how important this is to me. "But I'm not like you," I add. "I can't be that woman. I've always wanted more. Being a housewife fulfills you. It's what you love and I appreciate that. You made a beautiful, loving home for me and Daddy."

"And your grandmother."

"Yes. And I realize it wasn't always easy. I wasn't easy." She rolls her eyes. "But, Mom, that's not the life *I* want. I need more to fulfill me."

"Oh, sweetheart," she says, letting out an enormous sigh. "I know you're not like me. You're one of those career women who think motherhood is not for them."

"That's not true," I say, shooting up straight and tall. "I'm happy I'm having a baby." Wow, that just came to me. I *am* happy about it. Yes, I am. I take another sip of tea, letting that realization seep in. My hand goes to my belly. I sense a little flutter. It's probably too early to be aware of my baby moving but, whatever, it feels like joy.

Mom and I talk a little more about how I'll make it work. How I'll combine a career and motherhood. "And still be a loving wife to William," she says. "He always comes first."

First, second, or third place, I have a feeling my baby, job, and husband will be swapping these positions from time to time. Unlike Mom, who always put my father first, I will have other responsibilities. Thankfully, Will understands. All I say though is, "I know. You're right." Then I add, "Oh, and I'm going to need my birth certificate."

Her fingers turn white squeezing the bone china cup in her hand. The tea sloshes over the rim. "Oh" she says, the words barely touch the air. She stares straight ahead, past me. "Your birth certificate. Why?"

"Because my wonderful husband is taking me to Paris."

"Paris." Now her eyes are on mine. "How lovely." She stands and gathers her half-filled teacup and saucer. Walking across the linoleum to the sink, she glances over her shoulder at me and says, "It's in the safe deposit box. At the bank."

I ask her to get it for me. With her back to me, she replies with a nod, but doesn't say a word.

"Mom, are you okay?"

"Yes. Suddenly, I'm very tired. Maybe you should go home."

I've never seen my mother like this. She's always present. Engaged. And she never wants me to leave. Part of me wants to stay, in case something is wrong with her. But I can't baby her, so I pick up my cup and saucer and bring it to the sink. After kissing her goodbye, I remind her to please get my birth certificate.

Silently, she nods and keeps squishing the soapy sponge on the fragile cup.

Chapter 39

Digging into my sewing kit, I find the safety pin I need. The waist on my gabardine slacks is just a bit too tight, as it should be for a woman in her fourth month. Thankfully, it's only an expanding waistline. So far no one can tell I'm expecting. And I've sworn my mother to secrecy, which wasn't easy, but I don't want anyone at work to have any way of finding out.

"Honey, can you give me a hand?" I say, sticking my head into the bathroom. Will is at the sink shaving, his face full of white foam, the aromas of vanilla, lemon, and lime infusing the air.

"Sure. What do you need?"

I feel a silly grin pull my cheeks and show him the safety pin.

"Ah," he says with that sexy glint in his eye and puts his razor on the edge of the sink. I stand sideways and lift my arm. His soft kiss on my bare waist titillates, but there's no time for playing around. I've got to meet my mother at Macy's to look at baby furniture.

"Mmm, delicious," he says. "And I don't mean the Old Spice." Then he grabs a tissue and wipes away the white clump from my skin. He slips the pin into the gabardine and closes the waistband, just a little looser than it would have been buttoned.

With a wink, he pats a dollop of shaving cream on the tip of my nose and kisses my lips, then turns serious.

"You know I want to choose the furniture with you," he says. "It's our baby, not hers."

I snatch the towel from his waist and wipe the foam from my nose. "Yeah, I know. I'm just placating her today. She's so excited. She needs to do something. You'd think she never had a baby of her own."

"Well, she's not paying for the crib. We are. And besides," he says, sliding the razor under his dimpled chin. "It's been two weeks since you told her. She better have your birth certificate today."

"If she doesn't, I'll make her go to the bank with me on Monday. I'll invite her to lunch, she'll like that, and tell her to have the safe deposit box key with her."

"Good, 'cause time's moving on, and we want to get this trip in before you're too big to wander Montmartre with all its ooh-la-la artistes and have café au lait on the Champs-Élysées."

Oh, I do love when my husband plays the romantic Frenchman. I blow him a kiss and go back to the bedroom to finish dressing.

After a cup of instant Maxwell House and dry rye toast – my usual these past several weeks and no comparison to buttery croissants on the picturesque Parisian avenue – I get up from the table and collect my dishes.

"I'll do that," Will says. "You go and meet your mom. Have a lovely day."

He stands and draws me into a hug. I wince. "Uh!" Stabbing pain shoots through my belly.

"What? What's wrong?"

"Ooh, wow. That was something."

Will tells me to sit. "Should I call the doctor? Is it the baby?"

"No. I'll be okay." I wave away his concern. "Sometimes this happens. It's that time of the month. If I wasn't pregnant, I'd be having my monthly cramps now. The nurse told me this could happen."

"Ah."

Will's face turns red. It's adorable how he can't handle any talk of "women's things" as he calls it. I thought he'd faint one day when I asked him if he'd pick up a box of sanitary napkins for me while he was at the drugstore.

"I'm okay now," I say, walking to the coat closet in the hall. The weather refuses to recognize that spring has arrived so I pull down my baby blue swing coat and slip my arm into the right sleeve. Nausea swoops through me. The coat drops off as I double over. Blue wool puddles on the floor. I hurry to the bathroom.

~

"The doctor said to rest," Will says, tenderly stroking my legs propped up on his thighs. I'm stretched out on the couch, totally spent from the ordeal. After upchucking breakfast and last night's dinner and I don't know what else, my mouth is dry and sour. Rubbing my sore belly with its tiny baby bump, I ignore the glass of water he brought me.

"Please, sweetheart, you have to drink. Doc said you need fluids." He lifts the glass from the coffee table and hands it to me. "Take a little, then I'll go get the prescription."

"I wish I could ask my father about this pill. The doctor says it's new?"

"Yeah. Thalidamy or mide . . . something like that. It's supposed to prevent miscarriages."

My head jerks back. "What? I just got sick. I'm not—"

"No, you're not." Will gives my foot a reassuring pat. "He's just being careful. Besides, he said it would help with the morning sickness you've been having. It's lasting too long."

Like a good girl, I drink some water. Will leaves for the drugstore and I close my eyes to rest, the hiss of the radiator warming the apartment, lulling me to sleep. Then I remember my mother and Macy's. Oh my gosh, I can't do anything about it. There's no way to get in touch with her. By now, she's left her apartment. She's on her way..

~

"Anna. Honey, where are you?"

I hear Will calling me. Hear his footsteps on the parquet floors, rushing from room to room. "In here," I squeak knowing he can't hear me through the closed bathroom door. The stabbing cramps are tearing my insides apart. I can't shout. I can barely speak. All I can do is sit on the toilet doubled over, moaning. Now he's knocking.

"Sweetheart, are you in there?"

I manage to croak out, "Yes."

"Are you okay? Should I come in?"

"No. Don't." I have a moment of reprieve and am able to tell him I'm okay, which is a lie. I've been in here for, I don't know, maybe ten minutes. Maybe more. All I know is what I saw in the bowl when I peeked through my legs, and I don't want Will to see it. To see the grape-sized, ruby-red clots that would have been our son or daughter. The child he's wanted with every ounce of his being. The baby that makes him wake up smiling every morning since we found out a tiny being was growing inside me.

Will keeps talking to me through the door, and I answer, telling him I'm fine. "Give me a minute." Finally, the dizziness passes. I straighten up and get my bearings, grab onto the edge of the sink, stand, and peer into the bowl. Tears stream down my face.

He opens the bathroom door and I fall into my husband's arms, sobbing. "I'm sorry. I'm so sorry." His strong arms hold me tight. I feel his chest against mine heaving up and down. Our tears soak each other's face.

When William and I were courting, I thought I knew how love felt. Even on the rainiest or snowiest days, when ice covered the sidewalk and cold stung my skin, everything was sunny because I was with him. Everything was a promise. It's still that way, yet now, I truly understand love. My insides squeeze in pain, not from losing the baby, but from taking this child from my sweet husband. From causing him torment. Agony.

The phone is ringing off the wall in the kitchen. I ignore it. It keeps ringing, six, seven, eight times.

"Oh, hell," Will cries. "I'll get it. You go lie down. I'll be right there."

We pull apart. He cups my face in his strong hands, kisses my lips, and goes to answer. I lean against the wall letting my head drop back. Sniffling, I wipe my wet face with the back of my hand, then follow him.

Will paces the linoleum, stretching the black coiled phone wire as far as it'll go. One hand holds the receiver against his ear, the other wipes his tear-stained face. I slide down onto the floor. Sitting, legs splayed, I listen to his side of the story.

"I know, Florence. You must have been very worried."

Even in his misery, my husband knows how to handle my mother. She's probably speaking a mile a minute saying she waited forever for me and we need to be careful of her heart and she's not getting any younger.

"I'm sorry," he says. "She wasn't feeling well and before we knew it, it was too late to call you. You were already on your way."

Pulling the wire to its full length, he comes over and tenderly strokes my head.

"No, there's no need for you to come," he says.

I look up at him. Please, no, I mouth. He waves away the fear he's got to be seeing in my eyes.

"It's just a cold and . . . right, a sore throat," he says. "Yes, I know. She used to get those a lot. She'll be fine."

He rolls his eyes. "Ah, okay." It sounds as if he doesn't know what to say, and William is never at a loss for words. Our eyes lock. He shrugs as if he doesn't know how to answer my mother. "Sure," he says. "Look at cribs and . . . bassinets? Why not?"

Whew! She bought it. Tears bubble in my eyes. My heart hurts for her too. She's going to be destroyed when I tell her the truth.

"Certainly, I'll tell Anna," he says, emphasizing my name, then he hangs up and turns to me.

"When will she ever stop calling you Rosy? Jeez, how many times have you told her?"

I sigh and surprise myself with my answer. "It's okay. I'm her little girl. Always will be, no matter how old I get. Besides, she's the only one left calling me Rosy.

Chapter 40

So many women. So many faces pressing against the barred windows, shouting down to passersby on the street. "Hey, send up some toilet paper, will ya?" "Got any smokes?" "Wanna party?" I scan the stone walls of the Women's House of Detention, all the way up to the eleventh floor, to see if my client, the woman I'm interviewing today, is one of them. She's incarcerated here, in this overcrowded, dank prison in Greenwich Village, awaiting trial on the charge of prostitution. To add to it, she has syphilis. Instead of being hospitalized in squeaky clean, antiseptic Beth Israel Hospital, as I was last week, she's locked up in the prison's hospital. I walk toward the entrance thinking how lucky I've been in life.

It's been one week since my D&C. Will called the doctor after he hung up from my mother and was told to get me to the hospital right away. Dr. Shea, who was a friend of my father, met us in the emergency room and in no time flat, I was in the O.R. under anesthesia. First thing Monday morning, when I was back in my own bed, my room perfumed with bouquets of roses and carnations from my wonderful husband rather than with hospital disinfectant, I'd called the firm, saying I was going to have a minor operation. No one in my office knows the type of surgery I had. They wished me a speedy recovery and told me to take as long as I need.

Need is an interesting word. If allowed, I would have been back in the office the next day. I need to work. Not for the money. We're very comfortable with Will's CPA practice. It's my own need, to get my mind on something other than the noise in my head, the thoughts banging back and forth like a tennis ball at Wimbledon. Do I want to try again? Not anytime soon. Do I even want a baby? Or is my career more important? And then there's William who wants a family, two maybe three kids, and a house in the suburbs with trees and grass, a backyard where he can play catch with his son. But I'm already thirty-one. Isn't it too late? Yet, I don't want to disappoint him . . .

"Anna!"

Hearing my name, I stop and look up at the prison windows. It's not coming from there. Again, I hear my name and turn around to see Crystal Alsop crossing Sixth Avenue, waving and shouting, "Wait up."

On the sidewalk, Miss Alsop clasps my gloved hands in hers. Her exuberance stuns me. Though it *is* flattering.

"I'm so glad to see you," she says, then dropping my hands, she takes me in, from my white silk blouse and apple-green jacket to its matching pencil skirt. "You look stunning, but . . ." She circles a pointed finger at my wide patent leather belt.

From the squint in her eyes, I know she's silently asking about my pregnancy. I shake my head in answer.

"Oh, my dear. I'm so sorry."

"Last week," I tell her and she draws me into a hug, which feels warm and wonderful. And odd. I barely know this woman. A moment later, unwrapping her arms, she tells me she was going to call me. "I wanted to know what happened, if you'd gone to the partners yet and how they took it. Seeing you here, at the prison, tells me you made a good case for yourself."

"Yes, I'm getting cases again. Your words, that day we had coffee, gave me encouragement. I'm back in court, where I want to be."

"You like the criminal work," she says, and I nod.

"It's a small part of my firm's work, but it's where I want to be. I like taking the pro bono cases. Indigent clients, both women and men, need free counsel.

"A bleeding heart, are you?"

"No, I don't think so. It's just something that should be. Not everyone can pay the big bucks. And I love the challenge of trial work. Always have."

With the sound of tires rolling by on the avenue, buses bellowing exhaust fumes crossing Tenth Street, and cars honking at pedestrians avoiding traffic lights, Crystal stands in front of me sucking in her cherry-red lips. She has a perplexed expression on her face. I wonder what she's considering. Then, with a smacking sound, her mouth opens and she asks, "Are you free for lunch today?"

Taken by surprise, I say "Sure. I've got to interview a client in there." I point to the prison adjacent to the Jefferson Market Courthouse on the corner with its intricate, gothic clock tower, a building so stunning I wish I could work in it. Sadly, it recently closed. "After that, I have some stuff to do back at the office. Are you free now? I mean, my client's not going anywhere. We could . . ."

"No. I've got to see a client too. And I'm meeting a friend at one. I'd love you to join us."

Surprised again, I take a step back. "But I don't want to . . ."

"No, no, no. I really would like you to join us. I've told her about you and she's looking forward to meeting you." She hesitates for a moment, then adds, "Helen's a journalist."

"Aha. So she wants to do a story on someone who was going to pull the wool over her boss's eyes and demand her rights as an attorney in his firm?"

She giggles. "Well, not quite that. She's interested in you."

"In me?"

"Yes." Crystal makes it sound as if there's nothing odd, that we're colleagues and she simply told her friend about me. Yet we're not. Sure, we're both attorneys, but we barely know each other.

"So how about it? Meet us at Tommy's at one?"

I've never heard of the place and tell her so.

"Thomas's Tea Room," she says. "The new place on Vesey Street."

"Oh, that's great. I've been meaning to get there. I love a tea house."

"Well, you're in for a big surprise. See you at one."

~

Crystal was right. This place certainly is a surprise. Everything about this tea room is a deception from the counter along the wall with men and women sitting on stools with seats of black vinyl, watching soda jerks whizzing up milk, chocolate syrup, and seltzer making egg creams, not a tea bag in site, to the vinyl tufted booths where heavy stoneware mugs sit on squiggly lined Formica tables. Where are the lace tablecloths and linen napkins, the Royal Doulton flowered teapots, cups and saucers, and the three-tiered cake stand presenting scones, cucumber sandwiches, and petit fours? This is not what I imagined.

The low hum of conversation filtering through the restaurant mixes with the raucous roar of the malted milk machine, and I switch my expectant tastebuds to a common BLT on white toast. Scouring the luncheonette for Crystal, I spot her waving from a booth in the back. I suppose they want privacy, if her journalist friend is going to pump me for a story.

"I'm so glad to meet you," Helen says after Crystal makes the introductions.

All the niceties that women say when first meeting are said, but I only have an hour and want to get to the real reason for this lunch.

"So," I say to Helen, "I imagine you want to do an article about me – or not just me but women who have lost their jobs these past few years since the men came home from the war."

Helen shoots a look at Crystal, as if she has no idea what I'm talking about, then back at me. "Possibly," she says. "I . . . I can't do anything right now but . . . maybe."

"Oh. I'm sorry. I misunderstood." Confusion must be written on my face because Helen and Crystal exchange another squinty-eyed look accompanied by Crystal's tiny shake of the head. Then Helen says she'd love to hear my story anyway.

"It would make a good feature, if I could get my editor to agree."

"What kind of pieces do you write?" I ask.

"Right now, I'm working on one about herbs for the home."

"Another fluff piece," Crystal adds with a bit of disgust in her voice. "See, Anna, Helen is experiencing similar issues to yours. Not being taken seriously as a woman who has studied her craft and is as good as any man. It infuriates me." She sucks a deep drag from her cigarette.

"That's not completely true," Helen says. "Don't forget Margaret Bourke-White, the first female war correspondent." Speaking over music coming from the juke box in the next booth – Teresa Brewer bellowing "Put another nickel in, in the nickelodeon . . ." – she tells me Bourke-White went to Czechoslovakia before the war to write about Hitler and Nazism. "So women do get big stories."

"Very few," Crystal says. "Henry Luce didn't let you write anything serious about the war, and you're a fantastic writer. You dig deep for every story you write, even if it's only herbs."

Helen laughs and looks my way. "Crystal is my champion, always has been, and I love her for it."

The waitress brings our sandwiches and tops off the tepid coffee in our mugs from a fresh hot pot. Helen continues telling me about her work at *Life* magazine.

"I've had to settle for writing fluff pieces, it's true. During the war, as close as I got to the action was writing copy for photos about a marine on his honeymoon and movie stars who went over to entertain the troops. Stuff like that. Anyway," she says, lifting her mug, "I'm not a photojournalist. I write the text that goes with their photos."

"Now that the war is over," I say, "and you're not sure a piece about women in the workplace would fly, what about writing something on the Women's House of Detention?" I look to Crystal whose wide-open eyes tell me she thinks it's a great idea. "I'd be glad to help with that," I say. "It's a funny story amid the horrors that go on there with women being subjected to enemas and cavity searches for contraband."

"And getting one small roll of toilet paper a day," Crystal adds. "If you need more at night you're plum out of luck. And—"

Helen cuts in. "I'm sure there's lots you two could tell me. But I want to hear Anna's funny story."

I finish chewing a piece of the savory combination of well-done bacon, crunchy lettuce, and tomato and sit back. "When the prison was being built," I say, "my mother and her friends thought the new art deco building was a luxury apartment house, not a prison."

"That's hysterical," Helen says. "Can you imagine?"

"Well, my mother did. One day she walked over and approached a gentleman standing in front of the half-finished structure and asked how she could get an apartment in the building. And," I chuckle, "he said, 'Kill your husband, lady. That'll get you in.'"

Belly laughs erupt around the table. "That's priceless," Crystal says, and Helen leans forward.

"Where did you live?" she asks. "You said she walked there."

"It was only a few blocks from our house. We lived in the Village, on the Square."

"Hmmm." Helen's eyes cut to Crystal sitting next to me, then, as if remembering she's talking to me, she quickly adds, "We lived in the Village too."

Crystal jumps in telling me about the rooming house on Thompson Street where they lived in the twenties. "But we've known each other longer than that. We grew up together in Gramercy Park."

"I've never been there," I say and catch Helen side-eying Crystal. I have no idea what's going on between them and don't ask. Though it's making me uncomfortable, I stay on the subject and keep talking. "I mean, I've walked around Gramercy Park but I've never been inside the gates or in any of the apartments. There're still some private homes too, right? Silently, they nod and I bring up the Village again, asking when they lived there.

"In the twenties," they say in unison and giggle. "We do that a lot," Helen says. "Sometimes we even finish each other's sentence."

It must be nice still having your best friend from childhood when you're as old as they are. I have no idea where my friends from Greenwich Village are. I haven't seen them in years, not since we moved uptown when I was almost seven.

"We lived in the Village around the same time," I say. "I wonder if you knew my mother."

"Maybe," Helen says with a shrug. "What's her name?"

"Florence. Florence Brandt." With questioning eyes, Helen looks to Crystal who shakes her head. "Yeah, I didn't think so. With all the people in the Village, it would have been something if you knew each other." I glance at my watch and see it's almost two. "This has been lovely," I say, "but I've got to get back to the office."

"Me too," they both say at the same time, giggling again, but it sounds more like a nervous laugh than a chuckle at something funny.

Crystal raises her arm, beckoning the waitress. I excuse myself to go to the ladies' room.

Coming back, I see them with their hands on the table, leaning in, deep in conversation. They sit back as I approach. I don't ask anything. Maybe Helen wanted to tell Crystal something she didn't want me to know. After all, she wasn't expecting me to be here. I'm kind of sorry I came. They're making me uncomfortable with their unsaid words. Yet they're both so lovely and, other than their weird glances at each other, they're very friendly and seem to like me. But I really don't understand why I was invited.

After paying the check, we go out to the street and walk toward Broadway together. Just before I turn left, Crystal says, "This was lovely. I'm so glad you joined us. Let's—"

"Yes," Helen cuts in. "Let's do it again. Soon."

I walk north toward my office thinking Helen must like my idea of a story about women losing their jobs to the returning GIs. Or maybe the Women's House of D. Why else would these two older women want to have lunch with me again?

Chapter 41

Two hours after saying goodbye to Crystal and Helen, the phone on my desk rings. My head is buried in *American Law and Procedure*. I put the book down and pick up the receiver.

"Anna Dodge," I say and hear Crystal's voice on the other end. She's inviting me to lunch on Saturday, at Helen's on the Upper West Side.

"So," I hear my voice turn up a notch. "She decided to do my story. Which one?" I bite down the smile climbing up my face, as if she could see me on the other end of the wire. I don't want to sound like a thrilled little kid, but the exhilaration that rushed through my veins when I flew in that airplane years ago is bubbling in me now. I've never been interviewed for an article for *Life* or any magazine. This'll be so much fun!

"Uh . . ." There's an odd hesitation in Crystal's voice. "Maybe. Not sure."

"Well, whichever story she's going to write, I'm happy to help. I guess we'll find out Saturday. Thanks for the invite. I'm looking forward to it."

We hang up after firming up the time and Helen's address. I sit back against the slats on my wooden desk chair looking at the gold-plated pen and pencil holder with its matching letter opener that friends gave me when I started this job and the stacks of yellow legal pads with notes scribbled on the pages and realize I have to be careful. Helen can't use my name, especially if she writes about women losing jobs to GIs. What if someone from my office reads the article? No, I have to remain anonymous, the unnamed source. A secret.

~

The uniformed doorman greets me and opens the imposing iron doors to Helen's apartment building on West End Avenue, and a plump faced elevator operator brings me to her floor. I ring the bell on 5G.

"I'm so glad you could make it," Helen says, inviting me into a large foyer and leading me to the sunken living room across a solid oak floor. The herringbone pattern evokes tender memories from my childhood, from floors I played on in friends' apartments on this same street, just a few blocks from where I lived.

"Let's sit here until Crystal comes," Helen says, taking a seat on the couch. "She's running late." Glancing at her gold wristwatch she lets me know Crystal should arrive around one thirty, a half hour from now. I sit next to Helen and admire the large windows with their intricate metalwork letting natural light flood the room. On this sunny May Saturday, there's no need for lamps.

"Your home is beautiful," I say. "There's a warmth in these buildings with their crown moldings and high ceilings." We chat about the craftsmanship, and Helen compares it to the much older townhouse where she grew up in Gramercy Park, all the while looking at me with inquiring eyes, which I don't understand. Maybe it's just her being a journalist, always questioning.

"I was living in the Village when I met my husband," she says. "Quite different from my parents' large home and tony neighborhood, but I loved it. The people were so much more interesting – artists, musicians, actors."

"Bohemians," I say.

Helen nods and I notice a new expression in her eyes. Pensive. "But my husband wanted to be uptown," she says. "I fell in love with this apartment the minute I saw it. It was a brand new building."

"When was that?"

She tells me it was 1925 and, recognizing our age difference again, I quietly say, "I was five years old then."

She nods, saying a soft "Yeah," but how does she know that? I never mentioned my age. Then she jumps up and invites me to see the rest of the apartment, pointing out her favorite nooks and crannies in the dining room and the window seat in her bedroom.

I admire everything, especially the black-and-white tiles in the bathroom with all the white fixtures – so much crisper than the green and ivory in my bathroom. "My husband wanted new and modern," I say, "but I prefer being wrapped up in the cozy blanket of yesteryear."

"It reminds you of your childhood on Washington Square?" she says as we walk back to the living room.

"Oh my gosh." My hands press my heart. "You remember that?"

"Well, you did tell us that's where you lived as a little girl." We sit on the couch again, angled toward each other. "But then you moved up to this neighborhood, to the Dakota."

"I guess I did mention it. No wonder you're a journalist, you remember everything that's said and, for the life of me, I don't remember if you told me where you lived." Helen cocks her head and runs her fingers over her Peter Pan collar as if she's waiting for my memory to kick in. "Oh, wait. You did!" I say, pointing a finger to the ceiling. "You were in the Village too, but you didn't know my mother." I feel my face flush. How embarrassing. She just told me a few minutes ago, and we even spoke about it at lunch earlier this week. And she remembers I lived on the Square! Yup. She's a journalist.

The doorbell rings and Helen gets up to let Crystal in, then the three of us move into the kitchen with the pink and green linoleum floor. I'm not a fan of the colors but it does match the pink cabinets.

"I thought it would be cozier in here," Helen says, opening the refrigerator while Crystal and I pull out our chairs at the table and sit.

"Kitchens are more intimate," Crystal says. "Remember all those times around your mother's table when we were kids? Even older." She looks at me and adds, "Oh, the stories we could tell about those days. Mrs. Stokes's kitchen always smelled like love."

I smile, imagining these two women as young girls eating cookies and milk at an old wooden table in a warm kitchen perfumed with flour and sugar.

"Did it have an ice box?" I ask. "My mother used to tell me about the ice man coming with his horse-drawn carriage delivering huge blocks of ice so she could keep the food cold. I don't remember that. In my mind, we always had a refrigerator, but I guess not."

The women chuckle yet it sounds more melancholy than cheerful. I have a feeling my question evoked a nice memory.

Conversations about ice boxes, old radios, and Victrolas keep us talking while we munch on Helen's tuna salad made with a chopped hard-boiled egg and sweet relish like Grandmama used to make.

"We had a radio in a gorgeous, polished-wood case in the shape of a cathedral," Crystal says. "It was about this big." She puts her hands up showing about a foot and a half distance between the top and bottom. "Some were bigger. Nothing like the smaller plastic ones they make today." She looks across at Helen. "Remember the concerts we used to listen to in the parlor on Thompson Street?"

"Of course. And my mother, Auntie Mabel she was called," Helen says, looking directly at me, "loved *The Goldbergs.*"

Not understanding her glare, and glad I can add something to this conversation about times gone by, I tell them, "My grandmother and I used to listen to *Burns and Allen.*"

Still focused on me but now with a faraway expression in her eyes, Helen whispers "Grandmama." It comes with a deep sigh. A split second later, her hand flies to her mouth.

My brow knits. The way she said Grandmama, the name quietly floating on air. Her suddenly wide-open eyes make the hair on the back of my neck stand up. I lean against the back of the chair and try to absorb the shock on Helen's face. Or is it embarrassment? Did she have a grandmama too? That she loved like I loved mine? It's not such an unusual name to use for a grandmother, is it? Yet silence covers the table like a shroud.

"Did you know my grandmother?" I ask, my voice barely above a whisper.

Crystal won't look me in the eye. She keeps shifting around her seat. The chairs may be made of wood, but they're comfortable. I can't fathom why she seems so uneasy. Is it because Helen called my grandmother Grandmama? She said it twice. Once in that breathy tone that made me twitch, the other, just now, when she answered my question. It is strange because Grandmama is the name the family used. Everyone else called her Mrs. Brandt.

I lift my coffee cup and try to make my statement sound casual, not like a cross-examination. "It sounds like you knew her very well."

"We did." Helen says, her voice soft and apologetic.

"You both did? Well, I guess I'm not surprised." I sip the coffee, put it down and sit back. "You lived near us in the Village." I shrug. "Grandmama used to take walks in Washington Square, so you could have met her there." What I don't ask is why she seems so melancholy saying the word Grandmama. Is it that she's sorry she died or something else? I plant a fake smile on my face and ask Helen to tell me more.

"There's lots more," Crystal says, using her courtroom voice.

Helen throws her a pill of a look, then, leaning across the kitchen table, she places a tender hand on mine. "There is a lot more," she says softly. "And . . ." she takes a deep breath then, looking at me with kindness in her eyes, says, "It's going to be hard to hear."

My skin prickles. I pull my hand away and sit ramrod straight. My eyes meet Helen's. Then I turn to Crystal who's fascinated by her thumb slowly circling the rim of the coffee cup. "Okay. Tell me."

With her elbows on the table, Helen steeples her fingers and brings them to her mouth. I can almost see thoughts running around her head. Then she lowers her hands and begins. "When Crystal and I grew up in Gramercy Park, there was another girl we were friends with. Lucy. The three of us were so close, we were like sisters."

Picking at my tuna salad, I listen to Helen telling me about this Lucy character who only wanted to be an actress. In my peripheral vision, I catch Crystal looking at me, a look that reminds me of myself questioning a witness. She's reading my face to see if there's anything I'm not saying, anything I know and am keeping to myself. It makes my stomach quiver.

"Lucy could have been a huge success," Helen says, "if it wasn't for her husband. You see, right after college, her parents made her get married."

"Made her?"

Helen nods. "That's the way it was for some girls back then. Lucy came from a wealthy family, though not a loving one. She got more love and affection from my parents than she ever got from her own. Anyway, that's neither here nor there—"

"No!" Crystal cuts in. "That's important. It's why Lucy couldn't—"

"Right. You're right," Helen says, putting up a hand, stopping Crystal from saying more. Then, eyes on me again, she continues. "As I was saying, Lucy's parents made her get married. She fought it, but they won in the end. Charles was a doctor . . ."

My breath stops. My eyes spring open. Just as quickly I scrunch up my face telling myself it's ridiculous. Lots of doctors could be named Charles.

Helen leans in, closer to me. "Yes. Your father is the man Lucy married."

An icy cold hits deep in my core. I can barely focus on what she's saying, something about Lucy and Charles's age difference.

"Even more," she says, "they differed on practically everything, especially after their baby was born. Charles forbade her to continue acting."

Crystal chimes in. "Basically, he kept her locked in a cage, as if she was a wild animal."

My eyes shoot wide open.

"Not a real cage," Helen says.

"It might as well have been one," Crystal adds with venom. "Locking her away at the lake house and—"

Helen cuts her off and reaches for my hand. I pull mine back and fist it on my lap. She keeps talking and talking about how Lucy tried to make my father understand how much she needed to perform, to be on stage, but he wouldn't hear any of it. My stomach clenches with every word uttered. I want to cut in, but don't want to stop her. Yet I'm afraid to hear anymore.

"Wait," I finally say. "What happened to Lucy? To the baby? Did they die? I mean . . ." I throw up my hands. "I don't understand. My parents . . . there wasn't another child. And . . ." My hands slap my thighs. "I don't get it. What are you saying?"

Their silence sits like a brick on my chest. Not a word is uttered. Realization slowly snakes itself around me. Bile fills my throat. Shoving my chair back, I race to the kitchen sink as the chair skids across the room, crashing to the floor with a bang. Hanging over the edge, I gag. Retch. Spit. Over and over. Helen rushes to my side. I elbow her away. I don't want to hear anymore. This is crazy. I struggle to settle. My pounding heart slows and I curl up, holding onto the cool white porceline rim of the sink.

"Are you all right now?" Helen says, circling her hand on my back.

"All right?" I growl, turning, our faces almost touching. "After what you told me?" Their story is outrageous. It can't be true. What kind of woman leaves her baby? This Lucy person is not my mother. I would have known. Dad would have told me. But then, why am I in a cold sweat, spewing spit and smelly tuna fish and who knows what in the sink? On wobbly legs, I go back and sit on my chair that someone graciously put back at the table. Helen joins me. We're alone.

"Where's Crystal?" I don't like that she's left. She's the one who brought us together. Who started all this. I guess her big friendship act was just that. An act. No wonder she's been so anxious to see me. It had nothing to do with my job. She couldn't even stick around to see how I'd react to this insane story. I get up and grab my purse.

Helen puts a hand up to stop me. "She went to get something from my bedroom. "Please don't go."

I shake my head. The teapot clock above the sink shows it's already 3:30. I've been here long enough. Too long.

"I know this is shocking for you," Helen says. "It was for Crystal when she realized who you were. And for me, when she told me. You're the Rosy we lost all those years ago. The Rosy we adored."

My head jerks back. How does she know that name?

"No," I shout and, with my bag under my arm, hurry to the front door. "I have to see my mother."

Chapter 42

The aroma of freshly baked bread from Rambach's Bakery drifts across Seventy-second Street as I hurry past, heading to the Dakota. The yeasty scent would normally have me yearning for the homey kitchen of my childhood. Now it makes me want to puke. If the earrings Crystal presented to me as I was about to leave Helen's apartment are truly one of the only three pair ever made and the other two belonged to Crystal and Lucy and Lucy is really my mother . . . well, uh, I can't even think about what that all means. I have to hear it from my mother's lips. And she damn well better be home.

"Hello, Mrs. Dodge," the doorman says. He's standing on the sidewalk in front of the entrance to Mom's building. "You just missed your mother. I got her a cab a second ago."

Gritting my teeth, I nod. It's not fair to take my frustration out on him so I swallow hard, say "Thank you. Tell her I was here," and stomp to the subway, tamping down my fury. Is it for my mother? Or should I call her Florence now? Or is it for Crystal and Helen ripping my gut apart? I didn't stay to talk to them. I could barely look at them, but, with one foot out the door, I did take the earrings from Crystal's hand. She and Helen stood in the foyer watching me as I studied the embossed image of a

Gibson girl on the gold disk with the three precious stones on her collar. I have to admit it looked the same as the pair Mom and I found in Grandmama's alligator handbag years ago shortly after she died. The pair I now wear. The pair I cherish, thinking it was my grandmother's. But I wasn't ready to tell them. Or to accept their story. I threw the earrings at Crystal and ran out the door.

The downtown train rumbles into the station, a realization rolling into my head along with it. That's why Crystal said she wanted to know more about my earrings, that they're not the usual ones we see in jewelry shops. No wonder! The subway speeds downtown, rattling on the tracks, mimicking the confounding thoughts flinging around my head and scenes from the day Mom and I found the earrings.

I remember it like it was yesterday. Daddy and I were sitting on the sofa in the living room, in Grandmama's spot. Not his. The overstuffed upholstered arm chair catty-corner to the couch was his usual place. But there we were, his arm around me while he read the newspaper with the scent of Grandmama's lavender dusting powder deep in the sofa's cushions. And I had to stay quiet, so different from when I sat there with my grandmother, cuddled in her arms, listening to *Burns and Allen* on the radio. I can almost here her now, mimicking George Burns saying "Goodnight, Gracie," the line he said at the end of every show. I remember wondering how my father could sit dry-eyed, reading the newspaper, when only a week ago we'd buried his mother. At the slightest little memory of her, I started crying. How come he didn't? She was his mother. I told myself he was probably thinking of her. After all, he'd never sat in that spot before.

Staring out the subway's dirty window into the dark nothingness of New York City's underground, I picture Daddy lowering the newspaper and turning his serious face toward me, suggesting I help my mother gather Grandmama's clothes to give to the church. I was sad we had to give all her things away but glad we were donating them. The Depression had been going on for so long, at least her fur coat would keep some poor lady warm that winter.

When I walked into my grandmother's bedroom, I found Mom buried deep in the closet. There were piles of shoes tossed on the floor, my grandmother's black or two-tone oxfords, and that one pair of red Mary Janes I loved. Even though they were way too big on me, I always wore them playing dress-up when I was little. Grandmama let my friends and me play with her things, all those shoes and hats, even her handbags and long strands of beads. I always had first choice because she was *my* grandma.

Mom pulled down a brown pocketbook from the shelf. She seemed surprised that it was shoved all the way in the back, as if Grandmama had forgotten all about it, and when she opened its tortoiseshell clasp, her mouth dropped open. I remember trying to grab the bag, to find out what was so shocking, but Mom kept a tight hold on it. Then she pulled out a little black velvet box and opened it. Her gasp could have sucked all the oxygen out of the room. She held out her hand to me and that's when I first laid eyes on the gold earrings. The pair that look exactly like the earrings Crystal showed me today. But how can they be? So what if they're round disks with a Gibson Girl embossed on it, with the same stones? A diamond, sapphire, and amethyst. The story is preposterous. Yet . . . My skin prickles. Cripes, I have to talk to Mom.

The subway stops at Fourteenth Street and I trudge up the stairs, emerging from the bowels of Manhattan to a bustling sidewalk. Instead of taking the bus across town, I walk the mile and a half to my apartment barely noticing the old buildings with relief carvings on their facades that usually catch my eye. I have no interest in what movie is playing at the Academy of Music across the street, though it makes me think of this Lucy person who they claim is my mother. Maybe I should go in and watch, see if Lucy Brandt is listed in the credits. Nah, that's poppycock. She probably changed her name. And why would I want to find her anyway? What kind of mother gives up her child, no matter what Crystal and Helen said in her defense? I kick up my pace, wipe the back of my sweaty neck, then rub my hand on my coat as if I can swipe away everything I heard this afternoon. Damn them! No, damn her! How could she?

Exhaust fumes from buses stink up the air. Cabbies honk and swerve around Chevys and Buicks. I pass Edelstein Bros. Pawn Shop and S. Klein's department store with women and men going in and out of their doors. Hearn's Jewelers pulls me like a magnet toward their large plate glass window. I fight the draw and keep going, realizing how ludicrous this is. Even if, as Helen claims, the earrings her father made for her, Crystal, and Lucy were the only three pairs ever created – one of a kind she claims – how does she know another jeweler didn't copy him? Grandmama might have bought them for herself, or maybe her husband gave them to her for Christmas or a birthday. Maybe she tucked them away in her handbag after he died because it hurt too much to ever wear them again. Didn't my mother tell me she never saw Grandmama wear them? I never did either. Anyway, if Lucy loved those earrings, as Helen insists, wouldn't she have taken them with her to California?

Oh my gosh, my head is pounding. I just want to get home and bury myself under the covers. Hurrying across Avenue A to the tall red-brick buildings of Stuyvesant Town, I dodge cars barrelling down the street. One nearly knocks me off my feet. "Watch where you're going!" I shout. Jeez, he missed me by an inch!

Safely on the other side, I enter my neighborhood. The green oasis in this busy city helps ease my hammering heart. I walk along the path, following the winding pavement to my building. The air is filled with children's happy voices coming from the nearby playground. I was a happy child. I had a wonderful life.

Why the hell did I have to meet Crystal Alsop? I could have handled the partners at Edward and Elm myself. Why'd I think I needed her help? Because she's a successful woman who had to fight the male-dominated field of law? Now look what it brought me. All this craziness about earrings and . . . and . . . Oh God! Maybe they're right. Swallowing the bile creeping up my throat again, I unlock my door. Will better be home. I need his arms around me.

~

"Way to go!" Will shouts from the living room. I'm in our little foyer, hanging my coat in the hall closet. His clapping is so loud, it could shake the door hinges loose. "Anna, come in here," he shouts when I slam the door shut. "This is some game!"

Sitting on the edge of the couch, his ear to the radio, my husband rocks back and forth ready to jump out of his seat and run the bases himself. Mel Allen's voice booms from the Philco. "A Ballentine Blast!" the Yankee's announcer shouts. "How about that? Mantle smacked it into the centerfield bullpen!"

Joining the roaring crowd in Comiskey Park, Will lifts his bottle of beer in the air calling out, "Yes! I told you this rookie, Mickey Mantle, is gonna be something." He scoots over making room for me. "Come on, sit," he says. "Listen to that crowd!"

My husband loves his Yankees. I, on the other hand, root for the New York Giants, ever since I was a kid. Every time Will listens to a game, I think of Dad and how much I wish he'd lived to know my husband. He would have loved arguing baseball with Will.

My jaw tightens with another wish. A more important one. I wish my father had lived to tell me the truth about my mother. Who she is. Who she isn't. I'm not only devasted he lied to me, I'm flabbergasted. How could he be so devious? And I can't believe my husband. Doesn't he sense I'm angry, aggravated, anxious? Hell, I don't know what word to use.

"That's great, dear," is all I say, without an ounce of excitement, and walk down the hall to our bedroom.

Chapter 43

Staring at the mirror hanging on the wall above my dresser, I sweep my fingers through my hair. The sandy-brown pageboy, no longer the blond of my childhood, is mine. So are the green eyes looking back at me and the lips that gave me my nickname, Rosy. *These are my ears*, I think, touching the tiny lobes and my long slender neck. *But who am I?* All my life I've been Florence and Charles's daughter, Grandmama's only grandchild. Like me, my mother was an only child. Her brother died very young, from tuberculosis, so I've never had any cousins, aunts, or uncles, and my maternal grandparents died when I was a baby. Or so I've been told. I have no memory of them though I do have a memory of my happy childhood. I lean closer to the mirror and narrow my eyes, searching for myself in the image looking back at me.

"Are you okay, honey?" Will says, coming up behind me, interrupting my examination. With his hands placed softly on my shoulders, he brings his face next to mine. Now both our reflections look out from the glass, and I shake my head no. He steps aside, turning to me and I fall into his arms. The tears I didn't realize I'd been holding inside erupt. "Sweetheart, please, what's wrong?" he says, stroking my back. I can't say a word.

All I can do is cry, sniff, and let him hold my shaking body. "Anna, you're scaring me." He pulls back and cups my wet face with his loving hands. My tears finally subside and I take several calming breaths.

"Come sit," I say, moving toward our bed. "I don't know where to start, what to say, how to . . ."

"Take your time." He sits next to me on top of our satin bedspread, his tender hand on my thigh. "Let's lie down. I'll hold you and you can tell me everything."

Will's voice is soft, even more comforting and patient than when I miscarried. I realize he's never seen me this distraught. *I've* never seen me this distraught, not even when Grandmama or Dad died, and now it feels like *I* died.

Encircled in his arms, his soft kisses planted on my head, I begin to tell Will the shocking story. His breathing quickens as the tale goes on. "Wait," he says, lifting his head. "They told you this Lucy woman is your mother?"

Still wrapped in his arms, I nod. He pulls back and sits up straight. I join him. We both sit cross-legged on the bed, and I continue relating what Crystal and Helen told me. My dear husband lets me finish before he utters a word. And that's a long time to keep quiet.

"Do you believe them?" he finally says. "Are we basing this story on a pair of earrings?"

"No." I look down at the embroidered design on our bedspread, my thumb tracing a gold fleur-de-lis. "But then again, they know too much about me. Where I lived. Where Grandmama lived before she moved in with us, stuff about my father and how he felt about mothers working outside the home and the charity work he was involved with, what hospital he worked at."

"That doesn't mean Lucy is your mother. It means they knew your father. That's not hard to believe."

As if they had a mind of their own, my shoulders lift and drop. Sliding down onto the cool bedspread, I curl into a fetal position, my back to Will. With my head on the pillow and my voice barely a whisper, I say what I've been thinking since I left Helen's apartment. "Why would they lie?"

Will spoons me, his breath warm on my neck. "We'll just have to ask your mother. Maybe that's why she never gave you your birth certificate."

"Hmm. Maybe." My eyelids grow heavy. I'm too exhausted to say anything more. Yet, he might be wrong. The day I was supposed to get it from her, I miscarried and it's only been two weeks. I haven't thought about my birth certificate and Will hasn't mentioned Paris. So maybe not. Drifting off to sleep, I want all of this to stop, yet I know it's only the start.

~

"Sweetheart," William says, his hand tenderly making circles on my back. "You've been sleeping for two hours. Come on, it's time to get up or else you won't sleep tonight."

With my face buried in the feather pillow, I mutter, "I'm up. Just thinking," then turn onto my back and smile up at him. "Who won the game?"

Will's smile is full of love and caring. "Yankees. Eight to three. But that's not what you were thinking about."

He's right. I don't care about the Yankees or the White Sox, but I want to put on a good face for him.

"Come in the kitchen," he says. "I'll make you some Campbell's tomato soup."

"With oyster crackers," I say, lifting my brows. How lucky I am. Will takes such good care of me and knows what'll soothe me, even if I can't imagine swallowing a spoonful right now. My stomach is jumbled up in knots, but I'll give it a try, for him.

~

Wrapped up in my husband's old comfy college sweater with the crimson H stitched on the front, I sit at the dinette table crunching the puffy crackers into the creamy soup. Then I dip my spoon into pure comfort, inhaling the scent of love. The warmth slides down my throat easily bringing me back to my childhood, to winter days with Grandmama striking a match, lighting the pilot on the stove to ignite the gas so she could warm up a can of Campbell's for me. I blink back tears. A sour feeling invades my belly again. I look up at my husband, seated across from me, his golden-brown eyes filled with concern.

"Not only did my father and mother lie to me," I say, putting down my spoon, "so did my grandmother. The one person I always trusted and counted on."

"Not your parents?"

I tilt my head one way, then another as if this is the first time I've considered this question. "No, not my parents. Grandmama always stood by me. She was my champion. Like the time when my father was insistent I not attend Barnard. He shut me down every time I spoke about it, saying he was okay with my going to college, unlike my mother who thought it a waste of time. But Barnard was not an option. Then one night, after Grandmama spoke to him, I don't know what she said, but he changed his mind.

"Didn't you say Lucy went to Barnard?"

"Of course!" I throw up my hands. "Now I get it, and I understand why he never came to see me in any shows I was in." I slump against the back of the chrome chair and blow out a huge sigh. "I guess that means Lucy really is my mother." Will nods, small up and down movements and, with my belly twisted in knots, I say, "It's time to talk to Florence."

Chapter 44

My mother hasn't changed a thing in my bedroom since I moved out last year. Other than my college dorm, I slept in this room, with its bold-colored floral carpet complimenting the canary-yellow walls, from the time I was six and a half years old until I turned thirty and changed my name to Mrs. William Dodge. A framed photo of me with my girlfriends on the carousel in Central Park when we were eight sits on my dresser in the same place I put it all those years ago. Dad took it with his Brownie. The sides of my lips curl upward a bit with the sweet memories of the fun we shared taking pictures and the days he took me to the post office with him to mail the camera, filled with the finished film, back to Eastman. We always went to the Lollipop Sweet Shoppe for ice cream afterward, me getting my favorite strawberry cone and Dad licking vanilla. And when the mail came a few weeks later, he'd wait for me to open the package with the new camera filled with a brand-new roll of film. Oh, Daddy, why did you have to lie to me and ruin my memories?

Swallowing sorrow, I lift another photo, one of me with Grandmama on the Boardwalk in Atlantic City, and run my finger over the smooth silver frame remembering that sunny day when I flew in an airplane over the ocean. Mom was petrified.

She didn't want me to go but that didn't stop me. It was exhilarating soaring over the water like a bird. I put the picture back on the dresser and, with misty eyes, gaze at the one next to it taken in front of our townhouse on Washington Square North. I'm two years old in it – at least that's what I've been told. My mother is holding me on her ample hip. Although everything pictured is either black, white, or some shading in between, I can tell her brown eyes are sparkling. That's how they look whenever she smiles. Sighing, I remember, as a little girl, how I loved that happy look on her face. It seemed like she was always grinning when I was little. As a teenager, that grin often turned to tight lips. We had our disagreements. Whatever I wanted or dreamed of disappointed her, until William came along. Now I understand why. If Helen and Crystal are right, I'm more like Lucy than Mom. In fact, I'm not like my mother at all! Not even physically, which always baffled me. She has a very ample chest. So did Grandmama. And she's short with big hips. Where did my tiny bust come from? My narrow waist and hips? My green eyes and tiny rosebud mouth, to use my father's description? Mom told me I took after her father's side of the family, though Crystal and Helen say I'm the spitting image of Lucy. Hmmm. More lies? It sickens me to think so.

Mom, with her wide, pink-lipsticked mouth, comes into the bedroom. A picture of me with Grandmama, planting flowers in the garden of our townhouse, is in my hand. "I remember that day," she says. "You two were so happy digging in the dirt, your knees all covered in brown."

I turn to look at her. "Why didn't you ever join us? We could have used your help."

My grandmother loved weeding and deadheading, but I remember, after we were living in the Dakota for a while, asking her if we could plant a garden. She said we weren't allowed, and that she never planted flowers in her life. I didn't understand and mentioned our townhouse's garden, and she said all the tulips, foxgloves, and baby-blue daisies and all the other colorful perennials were there when my parents moved in. I thought how lucky they were!

Damn it! How could I have been so stupid? All the lies twist me in knots. Yet, why would I have ever thought they were lies? My life was wonderful and, anyway, what kind of mother abandons her daughter? Every muscle in my body stiffens like a knight's armor protecting me from the battle inside my head. Inside my heart. Can anything really insulate me from the truth I damn well better learn, right now, from Florence? And from its fallout?

"You know me, sweetheart," Mom says with a laugh. "I was happier being in the kitchen making fresh lemonade for you and Grandmama, letting the two of you play in the soil, getting your hands filthy. Come on, I just made a batch."

Seated on the same sofa I sat on growing up, the velvet worn with time, looking out the window at the tall trees in Central Park, I lift the glass of lemonade to my lips. Unable to take a sip, to swallow anything, I put it back on the coffee table. It clunks on the ebony lacquer. I have to say something. I have to ask. I pick up a chocolate chip cookie and watch my fingernail scrape a sweet chip, the chocolate covering the tip of my thumbnail, a habit from childhood when I didn't want to hear what Daddy was saying when he was angry with me. Maybe I should have let Will come today. He'd know what to say. Then it would finally be out in the open and the heavy brick on my chest would be gone. *Oh, hell! Just do it.*

I plant a fake smile on my face and look at my mother, or rather the woman seated in the old red club chair across from me. But she is my mother. Even if I didn't grow inside her womb. Damn. My emotions keep flipping from anger to sadness to furious and back to heartsick, which I am.

"I'm so glad you called this morning," Mom says before I get to say a word. "I'm sorry I missed you yesterday when you stopped by."

Her eyes are full of compassion. She must think I need to talk about my miscarriage. As a little girl, even into my teens, I talked to her about everything. Once I was in college, it all became more superficial: classes, shows, clothes, that kind of stuff, nothing juicy.

"Are you okay?" she asks. "I mean, with the . . ."

"I'm fine." Heavy silence hangs over us.

"Sweetheart, it wouldn't be surprising if you and William are having some trouble. When couples go through something as tragic as you . . ."

"We're fine. In fact, we're perfect." What I don't say is "but you and I aren't." As angry and hurt as I am, I love my mother. I want to believe she has a good reason for never telling me. Erasing the curt tone I just used, I soften my voice and begin.

"Recently," I say, "I met two women, Crystal and Helen. They lived in the Village when we did."

"Lots of people did." Mom has always given me her full attention so I can't tell if hearing these names is what's making her sit up straighter or if she's simply interested in what I'm about to say.

"Crystal is an attorney, has been for thirty years or more. Pretty impressive. Not many women were lawyers back in the twenties, and Helen writes for *Life* magazine." As if inspecting a witness in the courtroom, I watch my mother's face. Her wide-open eyes and dropped mouth show me she suspects what I'm about to say. I steel myself for what's to come, then jump right in, enunciating each word slowly and clearly.

"They told me about Lucy."

"Lucy?"

"Yes, Lucy Brandt. Mom, please, I need the truth. And I need to know why you and Dad never told me."

My mother flops back against the worn leather chair, eyes focused on the floor. I watch her chest rise and fall with each quiet breath she takes. Her chin quivers.

"Mom, we have to do this."

She nods and, seeming to gather herself, lifts her head. Our eyes lock. She swallows hard then brings herself upright.

"I was afraid this would come out one day and you'd be terribly hurt. I told your father so many times, especially when you were a little girl, that we should be honest with you – that you had a right to know the truth. He vehemently disagreed. Grandmama also wanted you to know. We tried, but Daddy never wanted to hear that woman's name mentioned."

"That woman?" I shriek.

"It's what he called her. I'm so sorry, sweetheart. I loved your father but he was difficult. It was better to let him have his way. I couldn't change him and wasn't about to try. As I understand it, that was the problem with Lucy. She . . ."

Listening to my mother tell me about Lucy only wanting to be in the theater and trying to change my father's viewpoint, I see Crystal and Helen were right. Yet they gave me the low-down on my controlling father, and my mother is skirting the issue.

"Are you saying Lucy is completely at fault? That she's a horrible woman?"

"No no, not that."

"Really? It sounds like it. I agree, she is a horrible mother. But isn't marriage a compromise? Didn't you tell me that before I got married? Helen said Dad sent Lucy away, to a lake house or somewhere. He wouldn't let her see her friends or anyone, and he was making her give up theater completely. They said she loved me."

I have no idea why I'm taking this tactic. I don't want to hurt Mom, and I am not on Lucy's side. Not at all. She *left* me! Yet,

Helen says she did it because she loved me. If only I could understand that craziness.

Mom gets up and, with her lips pressed tightly together, walks to the window. Staring out, holding onto the pale-green painted sill, she tilts her head right as if she's contemplating something. Then suddenly she tilts it left. I wish I knew what she's debating. Instead of breaking in with my own questions – I have so many more – I sit quietly rubbing my hands on my thighs. Faint sounds of cars on Central Park West drift in from the open window.

"I have something for you," Mom says, turning to me, her shoulders slumped, arms dangling at her sides. "It's something I should have given you years ago. Come."

She slowly walks out of the living room then, in the hall, picks up her pace, her high heels clicking on the oak floor. I follow behind, curious.

Chapter 45

It's been almost sixteen years since my grandmother died. Why in the world is there still so much stuff on the shelves in her closet? Mom, her brown heels splayed out on the wall to wall carpeting, is standing in her stocking feet on the top of a metal step stool shoving old shoe boxes right and left.

"I know it's up here," she says, her face in the closet. "Give me a minute. I'll find it."

"What is? I'll look. You get down from there. You're going to fall." My five-foot mother is teetering on her tiptoes, determined to find whatever she claims she should have given me years ago.

She pushes aside a cardboard box picturing Buster Brown with his ubiquitous blond hair, red hat, and big blue bow with his dog, Tige, at his side. It probably still holds a pair of my little-girl shoes. Another box with a naked baby on the cover, lying on his tummy, a sprig of flowers under his bum, comes tumbling down. A pair of white baby shoes flies out.

"I can't believe you still have these," I say, picking one up.

"Lots of things up here are yours. School work, pictures you painted, programs from the shows you were in."

It looks like Mom made this closet a shrine to my childhood. Other than the few times in college when a girlfriend stayed with us during the Christmas holidays instead of traveling to her home miles away, I barely stepped in this room after Grandmama died. We'd cleaned out her closet and given the clothes away, so I'm not surprised there're only bare hangers now waiting for another overnight guest. I have the alligator bag and earrings we found. Oh, jeez, I want to smack myself. I was so focused on my questions about Lucy, I forgot to ask Mom about the earrings.

"Got it," she shouts. With an oblong, black-and-yellow cardboard box clutched to her side, she steps down backward from the stool.

I grab her elbow and help her off the last step saying, "Another thing Helen and Crystal told me . . ."

"Wait." She cuts me off, clasping the rectangular box, picturing a flapper in a yellow dress and matching heels, close to her chest.

The words "Full Fashioned Pure Silk Hosiery" stare out at me and I blink, wondering how silk stockings can hold any answers.

"You'll understand soon," she says, tapping the box. "It's all in here. Everything you should know."

My breath hitches. I reach for the box.

"One more thing," Mom says, not letting go of it. She sits on the edge of Grandmama's bed, the curious box resting on her lap. "I want you to know, I wasn't hiding this from you. I wanted to give it to you after your grandmother passed away but was worried what Daddy would say. He never knew about this box or what's inside. I'm embarrassed to admit, I obeyed his demands. You'll see Grandmama also didn't want to upset the happy home we'd made. I suppose you could say we were both a little afraid of him.

Holy cow. That's quite an admission. I lean against the oak dresser and meet my mother's eyes. They hold a mixture of sadness and relief, if that's possible.

"Take this," she says, presenting me with the box. "They were always meant for you."

Questions fill my mind and probably my face, though words don't come. I take the box from her extended hand and manage a whispered, "Thank you."

"Take your time," she says. "I'll be in the living room, if you have any questions." My mother walks out of the bedroom. Before closing the door, she turns to me and says, "Remember, no matter what you do or what you think, I'll always love you."

~

Sitting cross-legged on my grandmother's bed, holding the yellow-and-black hosiery box on my lap, I toss the top aside. The image of the flapper lands on the floor. Inside, I find a worn, reddish-brown leather journal stuffed with loose paper and envelopes and handwriting on the thin pages. My breathing slows and I slouch back realizing this is Grandmama's journal, the same one I saw her swiftly close the few times I walked into her room and found her at her desk. Just as I never wanted my mother to find my diary, which I threw away several years ago, embarrassed at what I wrote as a preteen about my crushes on boys and cringing at the thought of anyone ever reading it, I knew Grandmama's journal was also private. No matter how much I, as a young girl, was dying to know what my grandmother kept secret, I honored her privacy. I never snooped. And now, my mother is telling me to read it, that everything I need to know is inside. With trembling hands, I slip the journal from its box.

Gently, I unwrap the worn leather straps holding it closed. Unlike my diary, there's no key. The two leather flaps easily open and a light-blue piece of stationery falls out. I pick it up. The handwriting is not Grandmama's.

Reading the letter, I feel my pulse kick up. I fall back against the pillows, holding my chest, absorbing each word on the blue paper. Words I've been petrified to accept yet, in my heart, I knew were true. *"I want my daughter to have something of mine, something she can wear that'll connect us to each other."*

My daughter! Oh my God. And the signature is Lucy's.

Staring into space, with the journal open on my lap and all the other loose papers strewn over the bedspread, I remember the day Mom and I found the gold earrings with the diamond, sapphire, and amethyst chips. Mom said since I was turning sixteen soon, I should have them. An image of my mother, standing in Grandmama's bedroom, stuffing a blue piece of paper into her apron pocket comes to me, and I remember thinking she was lying. It was a strange feeling because my mother never lied. She always taught me not to fib, saying she'd ultimately find out the truth, and she did! It was when I was thirteen and told my parents I was going to a party at my friend's house and yes, her parents would be home. She lived in another building so I never imagined them finding out the truth. Mom and Dad sat me down in the living room and gave me a stern lecture about never lying to them again. Well, Mom, should I give you a lecture now?

My jaw clenches. I push aside the rage creeping its way in again. Calm down, I tell myself and re-read Lucy's words asking Grandmama to, "please give these earrings to Rosy on her sixteenth birthday." This is what Mom shoved in her pocket that day. Yes, I remember. But why didn't she throw it out? Ha! She said it was a shopping list and I thought that was nuts. Who writes a shopping list and keeps it in their handbag shoved in the back of a closet? Plus, Grandmama didn't go grocery shopping. Why would she have a list? And how about Mom telling me the next morning that Dad says I can't wear the earrings – that they're too expensive, or precious, or whatever he said – for a girl my age. What horseshit!

That evening, after Mom and I finished gathering Grandmama's clothes to donate to the church – the day we found the earrings – my parents had a huge row. Daddy's voice bellowed from his study, reaching me in my bedroom down the hall. All I heard were a few angry words, something about not wanting her to know or do something. Then it got quiet. Either he stopped talking or he was whispering to my mother. Who else would it have been? We were the only ones in the apartment. I remember wondering who "her" was, thinking it was probably me, and I couldn't figure out what Mom said to him to make him shout so loudly. He hardly ever raised his voice with her, which is probably why that evening has stayed with me all these years. Plus, she was in his study. The Inner Sanctum. I was the only one he let in there, so it was all even more puzzling.

Curious me went into the hall, closer to the study door. I kicked off my shoes so they wouldn't click on the wood-planked floor. I heard Mom yell "Don't you shush me," which stunned me. I couldn't believe she had opened her mouth to him. She was always docile with Daddy, letting him rule the house. Something big must have been bothering her, enough to have knocked on his door. I didn't know what, but now it's starting to make some sense. And I don't like it.

Six more open, light-blue envelopes glare up at me. I'm twitching to tear into each one. Instead, I take a breath and sort them by the postmark date. The first is from 1922, from California. Carefully, I extract the letter and, with my spine ramrod straight as if tight muscles could guard me from what's to come, I read. "To my dear daughter, It's been eight days since I left you with Grandmama who loves you very much."

My body folds into itself. Three simple words – my dear daughter. If I had even a smidgen of doubt left, it's gone now. Lucy is my mother. Collapsing against the headboard, cushioned by my grandmother's feather pillows, I go on. Tears bubble in the corners of my eyes reading the words, "I can imagine how hurt you've been living with that lie, and I realize it'll be very hard for you to get past it."

Whoa! Lucy assumed my father told me lies about her. If only! At least I would have known something. With my fingertips squeezing the edge of the letter, I read to the end, sucking back tears. Unable to hold it together for one more second, I drop the paper, grab a pillow and bury my head in it. I don't want Mom to hear me keening, to hear the cries erupting from the depths of my belly. How could she keep this from me? Jeez, it's been seven years since Dad died. She could have told me! Is she still so afraid of him? Afraid he'll come back from the grave and . . . and . . . do what? Cripes! I always knew she was weak. But Grandmama? I thought she had more backbone. She spoke up for me so many times, especially when I wanted to go to college. I guess Lucy's the only one who could stand up to him. With the back of my hand, I swipe snot from my nose and mouth, almost laughing to myself. Hell, even she couldn't. She had to sneak out and steal away in the night.

My blubbering settles to sniffles. I wipe my eyes on the pillowcase and bring myself upright. Shoving the pillow behind me against the headboard, I settle back and pick up the letter again. I realize Lucy is correct. I'm hurt. Devastated is more like it. She wrote, ". . . there are always two sides to every story and you need to hear mine."

Okay, I heard hers. She laid it out nicely in this letter which she wrote eight days after she abandoned me. And she's right, I did deserve a mother who would put me first. Lucky for me, I have one. Oh my God, I'm so twisted in knots. I'm furious with Mom, but I love her. I understand Lucy's reasons, yet she left me. I can't get past that, no matter how right she was that I was better off with Grandmama and Dad. He's the biggest culprit here. If he wasn't so controlling, she would have stayed. But then what would my life have been? She obviously didn't love Dad, and Mom absolutely did. Would it have been better living in a house without love? With parents arguing? With a mother who'd rather be on stage playing a role than performing the real role of mother?

I slip the letter back into its envelope and find a piece of paper I'd inadvertently left inside in my anxious rush. It's also in Lucy's handwriting, a note to Grandmama to "Please give this to Anna, when the time is right." She called me Anna. The room is still, like the moment before a storm when the sky darkens and the birds cease their song. Nothing moves, not even an eyelash, as I begin to comprehend more about my father. He never called me Anna, not even when my teachers and everyone in school did, and not later when I practically begged him to, saying I was an adult. He insisted I would always be his Rosy Posy. Thank goodness he dropped the Posy but . . . Oh my God, I'll bet he insisted Mom and Grandmama call me Rosy. Another way he controlled them.

After tucking the paper back in the folds of the journal, along with all the other papers and cards that fell out, I tie the leather straps around it. As much as I want to read every word on every page, I need to get home and climb into my own bed. But first, I have to find out a few more things.

Chapter 46

The elevator doors open with a ding. I step off clutching the cardboard box to my chest and walk down the rubber tiled floor in the corridor, where kids love to roller skate. Heading to my own apartment, I'm greeted by the sweet aroma of chocolate drifting out from apartment D. My neighbor is always baking something scrumptious. The young mother in F must be preparing another Italian meal. Basil and garlic infuse the hall. No matter how well made this four-year-old building is, it's still an apartment house and, often, we sense what each other is having for supper. My stomach is so twisted up, I can't even imagine swallowing a dry saltine.

Opening my door, I find Will standing there waiting. "I heard the key in the lock," he says. "How'd it go with your mother?"

"My mother? Which one?"

"Oh my God. Anna, sweetheart." He folds me into his arms. I burrow into his chest, the precious cardboard box pressed against my belly. The tears I held back my whole way home – on the subway and the bus, running on the sidewalk and standing in the elevator – erupt. They soak his cotton shirt. I cry it out with Will's arms around me.

My tears finally subside and I lift my head. Will kisses the wetness from my cheeks. Our lips meet in a tender kiss. Then I step back and look into his compassionate eyes.

"What's that?" he says, pointing at the box in my hands.

"The truth."

"Oh?" He looks perplexed.

"Yeah. Let's go sit."

With a strong, supportive arm around my shoulders, he leads me to the living room. I place the yellow-and-black box on the coffee table. He picks up his unlit pipe. A stale woodsy scent of tobacco lingers. The smell reminds me of my father, making my stomach turn.

Sitting together on the couch, we angle toward each other. Will chews on the pipe stem while I tell him everything, from the moment I walked into my mother's apartment until she handed me the box holding Grandmama's journal.

"And that's it," he says, looking at the oblong box on the table. "She saved it all these years? And your father didn't know?" I never heard Will so stunned. "Honey," he says, "This is insane. Who does that?"

I explain that my mother was afraid of what my father would say. "Reading Lucy's letter, I get it. My father was so controlling."

"Wait. What letter?"

Realizing, in all I related, I hadn't mentioned the letter Lucy wrote eight days after abandoning me. I tell Will all about it. "It's in here," I say, reaching over to the coffee table.

Will watches me open the box. "You sure you want me to read it?" he says after I hand him the letter written on blue stationery.

I nod and sit back quietly, watching the expression on his face change from stunned to anger to shocked as he reads Lucy's words. The same emotions roil inside me.

"She calls you Anna," he says, lowering the thin paper to his lap.

"Before I left her apartment, I told my mother I had only one question now, though I'm sure there will be more, and she'd better answer honestly."

With the unlit pipe in his hand, my husband listens to me explaining exactly why my father wouldn't call me Anna. I finish and can't help smiling when he throws up his arms, astonished.

"Just because Lucy gave you the name? Holy cow! Your father was something. I'm sorry sweetheart but . . ."

"I know." I pound the air. "I'm, I'm, so, oh God, I'm so angry! Why is he dead? I want to shake him and have him look me in the eye and explain why. Why he lied to me. Why he was so horrible that my mother had to run away and leave me."

Will takes my fists and wraps his warm hands around them. "I know you're angry. I can only imagine what's going through your mind, but let's calm down and discuss this."

"I can't talk anymore." I pull away, barely able to breathe. "I'm sorry." I suck in a deep breath, then another. "I gotta lie down. I . . . I've gotta forget this for a while."

"Sweetheart, please, calm down," he says, pressing his hands on my shaking arms. "You're frightening me."

My breathing slows and I tell him I'll be okay.

"All right, then. Let's get you into bed and I'll bring you a cup of tea."

~

Tucked under our soft cotton blanket, the bedspread crumpled on the floor and a steaming cup of Tetley at my side, I stack Lucy's letters by the postmark date on the envelopes. I don't understand why there are only six, starting in 1922 and ending in 1926. Other than the first one, they were all sent in September, the month I was born. I peer inside one envelope and see what looks like a birthday card along with a piece of thin blue stationery. Quickly, I check the others. All cards, a few with what looks like letters enclosed. Why'd she stop sending them? Did she forget about me after a few short years? Or maybe she remarried and had other kids and didn't need me anymore. Hell, she didn't need me when she had me! No. I pick up my tea cup. That's not fair. If Lucy meant what she wrote, she would have stuck around if my father wasn't such a bastard. The hot tea burns my throat almost as much as those words. I can't believe I'm calling my father a bastard – my daddy who I worshipped, who tucked me in at night and took me to baseball games – who pretty much gave me whatever I wanted. I take another sip of the strong brew and place the cup on the saucer on my night table, then lift the first delicate card from its envelope.

As if holding a precious antique, my fingers lightly touch the edges. I imagine my mother standing in a notions shop somewhere in Los Angeles, since that's what's on the postmark, choosing this card with a teddy bear pictured on top. It's pink bow matches the number two printed in the top right corner. At least she remembered my age.

Reading the letter she wrote to my grandmother, folded inside the card, I learn that Lucy got a part in a play. My chest squeezes thinking that must have made her feel like she'd made the right decision.

I put the card and letter back in the envelope and lay it face down on the quilt, then pick up the next from 1923, then 1924 when it hits me. We moved to the Dakota in 1927 shortly before I turned seven. Unless Grandmama gave Lucy our new address, there was no way for her to know we were no longer in the Village. The address she had for us on Washington Square North wouldn't have worked anymore. I wonder if the post office returned mail back then. Yet none of her envelopes have a return address on them so it wouldn't matter anyway. She'd have had no idea where we were. That's why her cards and letters stopped in '26. She hadn't forgotten me. Tears threaten to pour down my face. I blink and sniff and push the envelopes away, destroying the neat pile I'd formed, and grab my pillow. Hugging it close to my breast, my knees tucked up, I burrow under the covers, hemorrhaging tears. Are they from anger or sorrow? I have no idea. All I know is this queasy, rotten feeling twisting my gut, turning it upside down and inside out, has got to stop. But can it ever?

~

When I stare into the mirror above the bathroom sink, puffy eyes look back at me. Where did I get these eyes? Not the puffiness, I know that came from crying myself to sleep, but the green color now rimmed in red? Dad's eyes were gray. Mom's are chocolate brown. I lean in closer. *Who are you?* I wonder. *Where did you come from?*

Scooping up cold water in my hands, I splash it on my face. That doesn't do anything except wake me up, which is good, so I press a cool, wet washcloth directly on my eyes. It might help the puffiness, but it's not going to erase the thousands of questions in my mind or fool my husband who I'm going to join now, wherever he is in this modest apartment I love and where we're building an honest life together.

Will is seated at our dinette table reading the *New York Post*, an empty soup bowl coated in red next to him, strains of violins and violas coming from the record player. He looks up at me, his face filled with compassion. "Did you have a good sleep?"

"Yeah, I can't believe it's already seven. I slept for three hours."

"You needed it, and I didn't want to wake you so I opened a can of soup. Want some?"

Shaking my head, I tell him, "Just some toast. I'll make it."

"No, sit. I'll take care of it." He gets up, plants a kiss on my head, and goes into the kitchen. Through the open archway, he sings, "And cut it into four triangles."

With all that's going on, my husband can still make me giggle. He always teases me about the way I eat toast – well-done, with sweet butter and strawberry jam, never the grape jelly he likes. Heaven forbid there's seeds!

"I brought Grandmama's journal," I say, leaning into the kitchen to smell the warm scent of perfectly toasted Wonder Bread. Will cuts it diagonally from each corner, making four triangles. "I want to read it with you."

Hopefully, reading her words with Will at my side, I won't break down again. I can't imagine there are any more tears inside me. Only anger. My father was such a hypocrite! And Mom – I never want to be so weak I can't stand up to my husband, especially for something I strongly believe.

I take the plate with the perfectly made toast from my husband and bring it to the table. He follows with two cups of tea and we sit next to each other, Vivaldi's *The Four Seasons* playing softly in the background.

"Delicious," I say, licking the sweet strawberry jam from my lips. Before taking another bite, I add the thought that's been running around my head since I woke up. "Maybe the reason my mother agreed never to tell me about Lucy isn't because she was afraid of my father's wrath. Maybe it's because she was petrified of me finding out, that I wouldn't think of her as my mother anymore."

"Makes sense." Will sits back, arms folded across his midriff. "Her telling you she forgot about the journal after he died isn't plausible. At some point, something would have triggered a memory, like when you were pregnant. If she really wanted you to have it, she might have given it then. Or . . . maybe not. She probably wouldn't want to share grandmahood."

"What about when I asked for my birth certificate?"

He springs up straight. "Of course. That's why she never wanted to give it to you. Holy smokes!"

I tell him I'm going to ask her point blank why, then pull the journal closer. "Now, let's read this. See what else we find." My heart kicks up a beat as I untie the leather straps.

With the journal open between us, we both lean over and read Grandmama's first entry dated May 1922. Will looks at me when he finishes.

"She seems to admire Lucy," he says. "That she has backbone."

"I wonder where the letter is," I say, referring to the one my grandmother mentioned. The one Lucy sent my father telling him why she left. "I didn't find it when I went through the box."

"Forget it," Will says. "He would have thrown it out. The great surgeon would not want anyone knowing his wife left him."

I consider that and agree. Dad was too proud a man. "I wonder what he *did* tell people. After all, his colleagues would wonder where she was. Or their friends."

"He must have lied, said he divorced her which, obviously, he eventually did."

"Yep. The lies keep piling up." My glib tone is a cover-up to the devastation I feel. My whole life, everything I believed, has been erased. Wiped out.

We continue reading my grandmother's journal entries. Seeing her use Anna instead of Rosy in her writing, my eyes mist. "It's odd she never mailed a letter to Lucy, just wrote to her in here," I say, tapping an ink stained page.

"You said there was no return address on the cards Lucy sent."

"You're right. But I haven't read them all. After only two or three, I fell asleep."

I grab the batch from the box. Flipping through the envelopes, as if dealing a deck of cards, I find the one dated 1925, where I think I left off. "No address here, but why's the envelope thicker than the others? Oh my gosh," I say, finding a plain sheet of blue paper plus another envelope folded inside. I tear it open.

"Look at this. It's a letter to Helen and Crystal, from Lucy. How'd my grandmother get it?"

Will grabs the other lone piece of blue paper and scans it. "Lucy wrote a note to your grandmother asking her to give this letter to Helen and Crystal," he says. "Seems she didn't know where they lived."

"Huh. That's odd."

Will shrugs, as if what I said doesn't hold much importance, although best friends would know where each other lived, wouldn't they? Damn it. I don't know what to think. Are the women lying to me too? My skin prickles with that thought, but no, it can't be. They seem to know everything about Lucy, even about her parents, her nanny, where she grew up. They told me so much, it has to be true.

"We struck gold, sweetheart!" Will says, waving a piece of paper in the air, sounding like he finally found the missing piece in a scavenger hunt.

I snatch it from his hand and scan the words written on the page. A sense of relief snakes over me.

"Don't get your hopes up, honey." Will places a loving hand on my shoulder. "It's almost thirty years. She might not live there anymore."

"But it's a start. With an address, I can get a phone number." I spring up from the dinette chair. "I'm going to call Information right now."

The sorrow in my husband's eyes follows me to the black phone sitting on the kitchen counter. "Be prepared, sweetheart. If she doesn't live there anymore, we're at a dead end."

He's wrong. Lucy wrote her address in the letter. She wanted Grandmama to find her. If she doesn't live there anymore, they'll have another number for Lucy Brandt. Or they'll give me the phone number for the address in her letter and I'll call. Someone there might know where she is now.

Chapter 47

The gray dawn peeks through the window shades. According to the clock on Will's night table, it's only 6 a.m.. Too early to be up on a Sunday morning, but my chest doesn't know that. It's pounding harder than Gene Krupa on his bass drum. In reality, my dream probably only took five or ten minutes, but it felt like I was running through a house, opening and closing doors for hours, upstairs and down, then running through a maze of bushes in a park. I couldn't find my way home. I got on the street but didn't know which building was mine.

"What's the matter?" Will says, looking up from his pillow, his hair flopping over his brow. "Can't sleep?"

With my hand on my heart trying to slow it down, I tell him about my dream.

"Come here," he says, drawing me down into his arms. He smells from sleep, all warm and musky. "It doesn't take Freud to figure out you were searching for your mother, especially when there's no Lucy Brandt listed anywhere in California."

Will is right. Information didn't have anything for me last night. It's as if Lucy doesn't exist.

Will fondles the lace straps on my nightgown, then strokes his fingers along my décolletage, his soft touch the balm I so desperately need. We lay together listening to the soothing patter of raindrops on the window. His lips kiss the soft spot behind my ear, then slowly travel down my neck and between my breasts, his tongue sliding lower and lower. Dreams and letters fade away.

~

After a morning of scrumptious lovemaking followed by an hour of deep, luscious sleep, the quilt and sheets tumbled together at the foot of the bed, Will props himself on his elbow. "Let's get away from journals and letters today," he says when I stir. "You need a day off."

"What about my mother? I need to speak to her."

"Do it tomorrow. I want you to relax today. Come on, I'll take you out for breakfast, then we'll spend some time with Renoir and Degas at the Met. Who knows? Maybe we'll splurge and have dinner at the Russian Tea Room."

Runny eggs and biscuits, an art museum and Chicken Kiev for dinner sounds marvelous. I'll call my mother tomorrow and set a date with Crystal and Helen.

~

Framed paintings in palettes of cobalt blue, emerald green, shades of yellow, and vermillion fill the walls of the Impressionist gallery in the museum. When I was a child, my parents often took me here on a Sunday morning. All we had to do was walk across Central Park to lose ourselves in The Metropolitan Museum of Art with its paintings and sculptures, ancient pottery and so much more. We could even see the top of our apartment building over the tree line from the roof. But I don't want to think of those days now.

I join William who's viewing Renoir's "Girl with a Watering Can" across the floor. My eyes go straight to her blond hair with the red bow, so like mine when I was little, then to the green watering can in her hand. Mine was red. A banged-up metal one. I remember a day watering flowers in the garden. I must have been five, maybe six – we were still at the townhouse. I told my grandmother I needed a new watering can. She said mine was special, I'd had it since I was a baby and should treasure it. I threw it away when we moved. My chest tightens thinking Lucy might have given it to me. It may have been the last thing she ever did. Except for the earrings.

The room spins. Vivid colors swirl in my eyes. I hear voices but see nothing else. Feeling myself sink to the floor, I grab William's arm, dragging him down with me.

"Whoa, honey." He pulls me back up and, with his other arm strong around my back, leads me to a stone bench in the middle of the floor.

Slumped forward, my head hanging down, Will's hand pressed on my back, I manage to breathe out, "I don't feel good."

"Breathe," he says. "Just breathe."

We sit a few minutes with me bent over inhaling and exhaling, wishing I could lie down on the cold floor. I hear a woman asking Will if she can help, if we need an ambulance. I shake my head and mumble, "Oh, God. I gotta go to the bathroom."

"Can you stand?" Will says

"Give me a minute." I lift my head. Too weak to keep it up, I drop it on his shoulder. The woman offers to get me a cool compress and Will thanks her. I stay like this with my husband stroking my hair, asking if I feel any better. People walk past us. Some ask if they can help, others say nothing though I feel their stare. I'm mortified. This is so embarrassing.

Finally, I have the strength to stand though I'm still a little woozy. Will helps me to the ladies' room, which is all the way down the wide corridor. The museum is so damn big, it takes forever.

Almost there, I spot the nice woman hurrying toward us. "I'm sorry it took so long," she says. Will takes the cold cloth from her and holds it to the back of my neck. The three of us walk together past several galleries and the wide staircase leading down to the main level. "I'll help you in, honey" the woman says as we approach the rest room. "I'm a nurse."

After about ten minutes in the bathroom, though depleted, I feel better. Will is at the door waiting for me when I come out, and we decide to skip viewing the Egyptian mummies and antique musical instruments and our romantic dinner at the Russian Tea Room. After thanking the lovely nurse, who waited in the bathroom making sure I was all right, we walk out of the museum onto Fifth Avenue. "No subway and bus for you," my husband says, his arm high in the air, waving down a taxi.

The cab drives south along the avenue, the trees and paths of Central Park to my right. Mom is in the Dakota, only a short ride across. But where is my mother?

~

Will and I step into our apartment, the loud brring of the telephone greeting us. "I'll get it," he says, hurrying to the kitchen. "You should lie down."

Even though I'm sure it's Mom – she's probably been waiting for my call all day – I let my husband answer. After that anxiety attack – which is what the nurse called it – in the museum leaving me totally spent, I'm afraid I couldn't have a sane conversation with her right now.

In the bedroom, I kick off my espadrilles, grab the bedspread and toss it on the floor where it should be. Or in a closet. Or the garbage! Dad got me into this absurd habit of making my bed first thing every morning.That's stopping right now!

Will's voice, coming from the kitchen, is as angry as I feel. "Florence," he's saying, "What did you expect? Of course, she's—"

Now he's not saying anything. Mom must have cut him off, defending herself or saying she never meant to hurt me or some other garbage. My eyes go to the telephone on my night table. Should I? I can't stand not knowing. Then I hear my husband's voice again traveling from the kitchen, across the hall, to our room.

"Yes, all of them," he says, then he's quiet again. She must have a lot to say. After a short while he says, "Don't, Florence. If anyone should be crying, it's Anna. She has a hell of a lot more—"

I grab the receiver and stick it to my ear. "Mom, I'm here."

"Oh, Rosy, sweetheart, I'm so sorry." She's sniffling, apologizing for being so weak. "I should have given—"

"Yes, you should have." I soften my tone. She's hurting enough so I tell her the truth. "I get it. Right now, I'm too exhausted to talk. Just know I'm angry and disappointed and confused. But no matter what I decide to do, you'll always be my mom."

Chapter 48

Part One, the local watering hole where attorneys gather after a day in court, is buzzing. Men in groups of threes and fours stand in front of the large, marble-topped bar sipping their bourbons and vodkas, talking shop or last night's ball game.

"Did you see that catch Hodges made?" one says as I pass by. He turns and looks me over, a swift head-to-toe scan. I ignore him and keep walking, my heels clicking on the wood-planked floor. Maybe some women find leers and wolf whistles a compliment, but I cringe feeling several pair of eyes following me to the back, to a wooden table tucked against a red brick wall. Women are a rare occurrence in this pub, but it's where Crystal suggested we meet when I called her this morning. It was the first thing I did after arriving at my office, before taking off my hat.

"We're so glad to see you again," Helen says as I pull out a chair and sit. "I was afraid we scared you away."

"No, you didn't. At the time, well . . . it was scary hearing everything, all the stuff you told me, it was . . ." I stumble trying to find the right words, yet all I can get out is an apology for how I reacted.

"There's nothing to be sorry about," Crystal says. "We know it had to be shocking to learn your family lied to you all your life."

The waitress comes to the table asking for our drink order. I could use a stiff one but order a sloe gin fizz instead. Helen asks for a gimlet, and Crystal says, "Vodka straight up, two olives." Even her drinks are tough, nothing sweet or fizzy for this woman who doesn't mince words. Even though they're the truth – my family did lie to me – it pierces, hearing it.

"It still is a shock," I say. "And I believe everything you told me, though it was hard to swallow at first." I continue telling them about confronting Mom and her giving me my grandmother's journals and Lucy's letters and cards. Then I slide the lock on my leather briefcase and pull out a piece of thin paper.

"I found this letter tucked away in my grandmother's journal. It's to both of you. From Lucy. It seems you never received it."

Helen gasps. Crystal's mouth falls open.

With a dazed look on her face, Helen reaches across the table and takes the paper from my hand. Crystal scoots closer to her and together, each with fingers holding an edge, they bury their faces in the letter. I stay silent, giving them time to absorb the words.

Eyes wet, Helen looks up. "Thank you," she whispers. "We thought she dropped us, that she didn't care, all that mattered was her new life and it tore us apart. And now, with this," she points to the letter in Crystal's hands, then presses hers to her heart. "Oh my gosh. You have no idea what a gift this is. What a gift *you* are. It wasn't only losing Lucy that ripped us apart, it was losing you too. We adored you. And now, we have you back."

I don't know how to react, what to say. Here's a woman I barely know whose overcome with the truth about a dear friend she thought she lost years ago. And that friend is my real mother? Seems like many truths are swirling around, binding us together, all because of a pair of earrings I wore one day. My fingers stroke my earlobe, as if I can feel the gold disk with the three gems.

The waitress arrives with our drinks. Ice clinking in my highball glass is the only sound I hear. Crystal blinks back tears, staring at Lucy's words. I nurse my cocktail, watching them both reread the letter.

Wiping the wetness from her cheeks, Crystal sits back and takes a long pull on her bourbon, then places the glass back on the table. As if she's trying to work out a puzzle in her mind, her words drift in the air. "I've been so angry with her," she says. "For so many years." She turns to Helen with the saddest expression on her face. Helen clasps her hand and nods. So many unsaid words, so much understanding seems to pass between them. I feel like a voyeur at a very poignant moment.

The quiet sound of muffled conversation from the tables and bar drifts through the smoke-filled air. Helen folds the letter and slips it into the original envelope from so many years ago.

"Can we keep this?" she asks in a tear-filled voice.

I feel like I want to cry too. "Absolutely," I say. "It's yours. I'm only sorry you never received it."

"I can't imagine what Lucy thought when we didn't answer," Helen says, looking at Crystal. "How hurt she must have been."

"How about how hurt we were?"

I bristle at Crystal's irritated tone. But with a big blow from her lips, her shoulders slump and she moans, "Oh, what a waste of time." With sympathetic eyes, she looks directly at me. "What are you going to do?"

I hear honest concern in her query. My thumb runs over the rim of my glass. I watch it circle, two, three times then quietly say, "I don't know." I tell them about getting nowhere with my call to Information.

"You asked for Lucy Brandt," Crystal says. "Try Lucy Perkins. She might be using her maiden name."

Of course! Why didn't I think of that? Other than not knowing her maiden name, or that she even existed. I have to force myself to stay in my seat when all I want is to rush out and get home and call the operator.

Crystal lifts her wallet from her purse and hands me a nickel. "Call Information right now," she says, pointing to the pay phone in the narrow hall behind me.

~

"Holy cow, how long can this woman talk?" I slam the heavy black receiver down on its base and look over at Will leaning against our bedroom's door frame, his arms crossed. I'm on the edge of the bed, trying to call the operator, again, but my neighbor won't get off the phone. I scored zero with the call to Information from the pub. No Lucy Perkins in Culver City or anywhere in Los Angeles. Now I'm going to ask for Standing Ovation's number, the acting school where she worked, if this woman ever gets off the phone. "I hate these party lines," I grumble. "I wish we had our own phone line."

From Will's pinched face, I can tell he's as frustrated as I am. "Not happening," my husband says in his lay-it-on-the-line manner. "Tell her you have to make a call. Ask her to hang up."

I lift the receiver again and follow his advice.

"Oh sure, honey," my saccharine-sweet neighbor says. "I'm just gabbing to a friend across town. Give me a minute and I'll be off."

I'm glad she has money to waste gabbing. In this city, the more minutes you talk, the higher your bill, and that's for local calls. Thankfully, my wonderful husband says I can talk as long as I want when I get Lucy on the phone, though what will I say? "Hi, this is your daughter, Anna." She'll probably faint. Or maybe she'll deny it. Not want to see me. Tell me I had a good life so leave it be. Or maybe she'll cry and tell me how much she misses me. My gut twists with all these thoughts battling around my head. Steeling myself against them, I lift the receiver again. The dial tone is the best music right now. With my index finger in the "0" on the rotary dial, I turn it one full circle. The operator answers and I ask to be connected to Information.

It only takes a minute or two to get my answer. Dazed, I lower my hand, clunking the heavy receiver on its base. I fall back across the bed, my legs hanging off.

Will comes over and sits. "Good news?"

I look up at his hopeful eyes and shake my head. I stare back up at the white ceiling as the words slowly leave my lips. I can barely hear them. "The school's not listed either. It doesn't exist."

Will sucks in a breath and lets it out with a deep sigh. "Oh, sweetheart, I'm so sorry." He lies down and I cuddle into his warm embrace. The open window brings the whoosh of cars on the avenue, the rustle of trees in the evening breeze. With my eyes closed, breathing in my husband's freshly laundered scent, I feel myself give way to the reality. I'm never going to find my mother.

"My mother," I repeat, whispering to myself, needing to feel the syllables on my lips. Do they taste sweet? Or sour? Bitter? Or bland? My head rattles, unable to decide. Then, quick as a finger snap, I sit up. I look at my husband who has the most confused expression on his face and I announce, "I'm going to California.

Chapter 49

Standing under a jacaranda tree bursting with purple blossoms, its honey scent perfuming the air, Will gives my hand a gentle squeeze. Our eyes are on a slim woman across the street. She's watering orange and red flowers bookending the slate walk to her front door. For her, it's an ordinary overcast June day here in Culver City. There's a red tricycle parked on the small lawn, a doll carriage left against the wrought-iron fence, and a jump rope lying across the front step. It looks like a happy home with children's toys strewn about, freshly painted sky blue shutters, and window boxes with red geraniums draping over the edge. The street is quiet. A car passes now and then, birds twitter in the trees, though there's no sound of children. They're all in school, I imagine, this being a Tuesday morning. Though there's probably a little girl napping inside. Seems possible with the types of toys I see.

"That can't be her," I say, my eyes still on the woman in pedal pushers and short-sleeved blouse, her hair streaked with gray. "She'd be too old to have little kids."

"Maybe she's the grandmother," Will says, his eyes also on the woman.

I look down and study the cracks in the sidewalk. If she's the grandmother, that means she remarried and had kids and forgot all about me.

"Or maybe that's not Lucy." Will squeezes my hand again, pressing it with love and hope. "Come on. Let's find out." He leads me across the road to the fenced yard. We stand on the sidewalk in front of the black gate.

Holding a big metal watering can, the woman looks up from her flowers. "Can I help you?" she asks, eyeing us both head to toe. She shoots a look up and down the street though I don't know why. Maybe to see if we parked in a wrong spot, but we took a bus from the hotel.

Just as she eyed me, I'm taking her in, top to bottom. She's a bit hippy. Not as much as Mom but more than me. Her lips are similar to mine, but so what? If she *is* my mother, wouldn't I feel something? Thankfully, William breaks the awkward silence.

"We're looking for someone who lived here back in the1920s and '30s," he says. "Lucy Brandt."

The woman straightens, her grip on the watering can tightens. From the look in her eyes, I'd swear she's nervous. My skin prickles. Maybe I should have worn the earrings as Will suggested this morning when I was getting dressed. Then I think we'd know for sure if she's Lucy. But I was afraid when she saw them she'd know it was me and might lie. She might not want to meet me and admit I'm her daughter, especially if she has a new family, and it sure looks like she does.

Before she has a chance to answer, Will adds, "But she might have gone by Lucy Perkins. Perhaps you know where we could find her." Without asking permission, he opens the gate, takes my hand, and we step through.

She takes a step back. Sounding like a curious little girl, she asks "Why?" though her eyes never leave my face.

"Because my wife here, Anna, would like to meet her."

The watering can slips from her fingers, hitting the ground with a clang. I never believed the phrase "she turned white as a sheet" but this woman definitely lost all the color in her cheeks. She sucks in a lungful of air and sways. Will grabs her elbow, steadying her. I quiver.

"I think we need to sit," he says and leads her to the front step. I follow, unable to utter a sound, my heart pummeling my chest.

We sit on the hard stone. She turns to me and cups my face in her silky hands. The most delicate, loving touch I've ever felt.

"Is it really you?"

Feeling my eyes water, I nod.

She sinks back, drawing her hands to her chest. "Oh my." Her words float on a slow, soft breath, then she swallows hard and I can't help it, I let out a nervous giggle, shoulder shake and all.

"My gosh," she cries. "You still have the same infectious giggle. How did you find me? Why did it . . .? What?" Unfinished questions tumble from her mouth.

William, who's been standing off to the side, leaning against the house watching us, squeezes in next to me. With moist eyes, he says, "I think you both have lots of questions. Is there somewhere else we can talk?"

Lucy jumps up. "Oh, yes, yes. Of course."

We follow her around the house to the backyard where eye-catching flowers in reds, purples, and yellow fill the four corners of the charming yard. A young woman with flaming red hair sits on the grass playing patty-cake with a baby. Seeing us, she sucks in a breath and scoops the little one onto her lap, as if we're kidnappers about to grab her child. Keeping her furrowed brow on us, she side-eyes Lucy.

"Nothing to worry about," Lucy says. "Everything's all right. These are friends of mine. We haven't seen each other for ages."

"Nice to meet you," the redhead says. She hoists the baby up and stands. Though we haven't been introduced, William and I murmur the same platitude.

"We're going to sit here," Lucy tells the young mother, pointing to the round picnic table on a cement patio. Her eye lift accompanied by a dip of the chin must be sending the woman a message because she immediately wishes us a lovely time catching up and walks to the back door. Lucy watches her go inside, then invites us to sit.

Throwing a quick glance at my husband, I see he's as confused as I am. If this is her daughter or daughter-in-law and grandchild, wouldn't she introduce us? She might not say who I actually am, but she'd at least give our names. What's with all the secrecy? And why was this young mother so frightened?

Always able to read my body language, my husband taps my hand, letting me know he understands how awkward and nervous I feel. I'm never at a loss for words, so my muteness now is deafening.

"Lucy," he says, leaning in. "I'm sure you're confused and stunned by all this. How about Anna starts at the beginning with how she learned about you? Just a few weeks ago."

Her back arches and William repeats his last phrase adding a "yes." I love him for opening this dialogue because I had no idea how to begin, and Lucy was so tongue-tied her questions tumbled over each other. I can imagine how she feels and wish I understood my own emotions better. I'm angry she abandoned me yet understand why and, in some ways, don't blame her, but how could she leave me? I was a baby! Anyway, I begin my story with meeting Crystal and her fascination with my earrings.

"The gold disks embossed with the Gibson Girl?" Lucy says.

"Yes, the ones Helen's father made for the three of you, with each of your birthstones." I think every ounce of air just escaped her lungs.

Balanced on the edge of the chair, she listens as I explain everything, all the way to reading the cards she sent me and the letters to Grandmama, but I leave out the journal.

"You can't imagine how much it hurt never getting a reply from my mother-in-law. It took me so long to get the guts to send her my address. Then not hearing a word back. Nothing. It tore me apart."

I give her an understanding smile and dig into my shoulder bag lying on my lap. "These are all Grandmama's journals, in a sense they're letters to you," I say, pulling out the old leather journal. Lucy's hand shakes taking it from me. "Read them later, when you're alone. You'll understand why she never wrote. And how much she wished she could. I was stunned reading about my father's control over her."

"Ha!" Lucy laughs, then shakes her head. She looks like the world and all its problems are pressing down on her. From her pinched lips, I can't tell if she's going to complain about my father, which I don't need to hear, or apologize for leaving me. Thankfully, it's neither. She only asks if my father knows I'm here.

The moment I say, "He's gone. So is Grandmama," the backdoor clicks shut. We all turn to the sound. A tall girl, maybe twenty, stands there, her face frozen in fear.

The sorrow on Lucy's face instantly morphs to a friendly grin. "Hi sweetie," she says. "How'd it go?"

She certainly is an actress. One minute she's consumed with the past, her heart seeming to ache for what she wrought, and the next she's all sunny and light, like any ole day of the week and I'm a casual acquaintance who stopped in for tea. I don't know which part is real.

The girl, standing stiff, not moving an inch, tells Lucy she got the part. Lucy seems genuinely pleased and congratulates her. "Tell me all about it later," she says. "I'm here with some friends now." I watch the girl, whose muscles suddenly relax, turn and go back into the house.

Again, Lucy doesn't introduce us? We're just 'some friends?' Hiding my annoyance, I unclench my jaw, slip on a friendly smile and ask if that's her daughter.

"Oh no." Here's the sorrowful look again. "You're my only daughter. My only child."

"Then who are these women? And who was that baby?"

Lucy adjusts herself on the cushioned seat and with her hands folded on the table top, says, "I really shouldn't tell you."

"Then don't," I say even though I'm dying to know. And furious that she won't. Damn, she's really good at secrecy too. What the hell is going on?

"But you don't live around here," she says as if she's considering each word. "And . . . with all we have between us, I think I can trust you." She looks to me and William and we assure her she can. "Without going into all my reasons, when I inherited this house from Mrs. D—"

"Who's Mrs. D?" I can't help cutting her off. Who the hell is this Mrs. D? Another relative I don't know about?

Lucy explains about the boarding house and her relationship with the owner. "Until I met Mrs. D, I never felt a mother's love. My nanny loved me, I think, and your grandmother cared for me, but my mother . . ." Her eyes hood over. There's no need to finish the sentence. The utter sadness in her unsaid words hovers like a heavy morning fog.

My husband looks at me, his face filled with compassion. I think we both understand Lucy better now. Even so, am I supposed to forgive her? Watching a cardinal fly from his perch on the orange tree, I wonder if the desire to nurture is in one's genes. Can it be passed through blood? Did it skip Lucy? Is that why I've chosen a career over motherhood?

Lucy's face brightens. She sits up taller. "I was stunned when the lawyer called and said Mrs. D left the house to me. I wasn't sure what I was going to do with it. I didn't want to run a boarding house though it's too big for one person. Then, after hearing stories from a few actresses I work with, it hit me. I'd create a safe house for abused women."

"Physically abused?" I say. "I've dealt with cases like that. It's so hard to prove and so horrendous for the woman. It's a wonderful thing you're doing."

"Thank you, but they're not all physically abused. Some are like me. They've been controlled, caged in by jealous or insecure men – or who knows why. There's nowhere for them to go. To be free."

My shoulders stiffen. It's hard to hear her comparing herself to abused women, yet that's how she felt and I have to accept it. And accept the truth of it. My father kept her locked away from the career she wanted. From the life she wanted.

"What about acting?" I ask. "After all, that's why you left."

"Yes. It is. I'm so sorry."

"Stop. I don't want apologies. Just tell me, are you still acting? I looked up the school you wrote about and it's not listed." I'm sure my squinty eyes tell her I'm wondering if she lied.

"It closed a few years ago. After her son died in the war, the woman who owned it didn't have the stomach to teach children anymore. Soon after, I was offered a position with an acting school in Hollywood. MGM sends us their ingenues, and I do take the occasional role in a play."

"Did you ever come back to New York for a play? Wouldn't that be every actress's dream?" I can't help the accusatory tone in my voice. An attorney should never attack a witness on the stand. But this is not a court of law. It's my life. I want to know if she ever came back to New York. And why she didn't look me up.

The gloomy overcast sky darkens, mirroring the look in Lucy's eyes. Her fingers play with her bare earlobe then, dropping them on her lap, she begins. "Years ago, I had the opportunity. It was a difficult decision for me."

She sounds like she wants my understanding. I'll listen but this better be good. "Ultimately," she says. "I was too scared to go back. Too afraid that everyone I loved – my friends, your grandmother, Helen's parents – no one would want to see me. You were only thirteen at the time, and I would have loved to see you, but I didn't know if you knew about me, or would want anything to do with me." Sucking in her lips, gazing down, she shakes her head, blinks several times, then raises her head to meet my gaze. "It would have hurt too deeply being back in the City and having my worries confirmed. It was easier staying here, not knowing for sure that they erased me from their lives. I hurt them deeply, and had to accept that."

More air than I ever imagined I had blows from my lips.

"Please," Lucy says, "Tell me about you now." Touching her chest, then reaching across and placing a hand over mine, she tells me how she's imagined meeting me one day. "You have no idea how glad, how happy, how delighted – I can't come up with the right word – Oh my gosh, just having you sitting here with me, seeing you so grown-up, so beautiful." She sits back and folds her hands together, right over left, then left over right, then back again like she doesn't know what to do with them. With a bright smile, she stands. "Come inside. I'll make us some tea."

Will and I sit at the kitchen table covered with a brightly flowered tablecloth, watching Lucy fill the kettle. While the water flows, she glances over her shoulder. "How about some toast and jam? I don't have any cookies, other than the children's animal crackers."

"Oh, I love those," my husband says, "but toast will be lovely." He lifts his brow to me and I give him a little shoulder shrug. Maybe with all this today, her stomach is also in a jumble and, like me, toast and tea are her go-to for settling.

Lucy drops the white bread into the toaster and busies herself with the tea preparation. A warm comforting scent wafts through the kitchen as questions fly about my growing up. She brightens when I tell her I graduated from Barnard and went to NYU School of Law. The toaster pops and two well-done pieces spring up. She places them on plates, then spreads creamy sweet butter and strawberry jam from corner to corner. I watch her cutting the toast diagonally, once from the right, once from the left. My eyes lock with Will's seeing her cut them into four triangles. She brings the plates to the table and hands me mine.

Blinking back tears, I look up at her glistening eyes and simply say, "Thank you."

Epilogue

After Anna called last night, I hung up the phone and broke down in tears. In a straight forward yet tender voice, she said, "Hi, Mom. Will and I just walked in from the airport and I want to tell you about my meeting Lucy. Let's have breakfast tomorrow." Like rain on a parched desert, relief poured over me simply hearing her use the woman's name, not saying "my mother."

The entire week Anna was away I barely ate, worried sick about our relationship and asking myself so many questions. Am I losing my daughter? Will she now call me Florence instead of Mom? What if she couldn't find Lucy? Did I want that? We'd never have closure on this, yet if that were the case, I wouldn't have to fear losing her to that woman. And what if she *did* find her and Lucy didn't want anything to do with Anna? Oh, how my heart broke worrying about that, how hurt my baby would be. She'd been hurt enough. By me.

There were so many what ifs running around my head all week imagining her laughing and crying with Lucy, drinking freshly squeezed orange juice from the plump fruit they'd pick together in Lucy's backyard, or . . . oh so many images played before my eyes, whether I was awake or asleep. Now, having her sitting across the kitchen table drinking coffee, the three stones in her earrings glistening in the morning sun streaming through the window, these thoughts are quieted as she tells me about Lucy.

"It's incredible," she says. "We're both caring for abused women. Me defending them in court, Lucy using her house as a safe haven."

Petrified she's going to point out all the similarities between them and how different she and I are, all I can do is sip my coffee and nod. I learn Lucy is still acting, occasionally, and teaching at an acting school. I'm glad about that. Otherwise, it would be worse for Anna, not that it's easy for a child to accept being left for any reason.

"And Mom, Lucy's never married," she says, then giggles. "Well, never remarried."

My heart drops to my stomach realizing this means Lucy doesn't have children, other than my daughter. What if she wants her now? Can I share my precious Anna?

I watch my daughter, her fingers wrapped around the handle of her coffee cup, contemplating the white paint on the ceiling. With my teeth, I scrape the lipstick from my mouth, wondering what's going on in that pretty head of hers. Is she thinking of a way to tell me she wants Lucy in her life? Or, oh my gosh, is she thinking of moving to California? To be closer to her? I grab a cigarette from its case, slip it between my lips and light up. After a long deep drag, I lean forward toward my daughter, who's grown into a beautiful, accomplished woman. Taking her soft hand in mine, I say, "How about we send Lucy a plane ticket to come to New York? We'll invite Crystal and Helen and have lunch here. All of us together.

THE END

Author's Notes

I first learned of the Heterodoxy Club in *The Lions of Fifth Avenue*, the wonderful novel by Fiona Davis. This secret club with its unorthodox women intrigued me and, immediately, I knew I wanted to include them in a future book. So down the research rabbit hole I went. I discovered the non-fiction book, *Hotbed,* by Joanna Scutts, which became my bible for *Abandoning the Script.* Although many members of the actual Heterodoxy Club deserve a book of their own, I wasn't comfortable fictionalizing any of their lives. Instead, I used some of their stories to create my characters and even mixed up some of their first and last names, along with names of a few Suffragists, to give my women their identities. For example, Anna Dodge, Rosy's grown up, married name in my novel, took her first name from Anna Strunsky, a Heterodite, and her last from Mabel Dodge, also a member of the club. Lucy is named for the prominent suffragist Lucy Stone and the Heterodite Charlotte Perkins Gilman. The real Gilman shows up in the novel in reference to her novella, *The Yellow Wallpaper*, which is still available. I also read it as part of my research and for my own curiosity. Her shocking story set Lucy's in motion.

In addition to my fictional characters, there are some historical people mentioned in my book. You can Google any name and find out who I've created and who is real, and if I've piqued your interest about the Heterodoxy Club, get a copy of *Hotbed* or watch an interview with Joanna Scutts here: https://kpfa.org/episode/letters-and-politics-september-1-2022/

As historical fiction writers often do, I've played with some dates for the sake of the story. For those of you who might do further research, you'll learn that Polly's Restaurant, where the Heterodoxy Club met, was no longer on MacDougal Street at the time of my story. It actually moved around the block in 1919. I was so taken with descriptions of the original Polly's, I kept it on MacDougal Street, which is no longer scruffy, as it is in Chapter 1. Also, in Chapter 40, I have the Women's House of Detention being built while Anna, Florence, and Charles lived in the Village, a short walk from the site of the prison. In reality, the House of D was built in the early 1930s, opening in 1932, when Anna's family would have been living uptown in the Dakota. History buffs, please excuse me.

In *Hotbed*, Scutts writes, "Because of lack of records, we don't know what was discussed at any particular meeting, nor who attended . . ." Therefore, I had to create the scenes in Polly's from my own imagination, though from my research I know that topics such as the ones my characters discuss, as well as the guest speakers I've mentioned, were actually at Polly's. In fact, the words Elsie Clewes Parsons speaks in Chapter 8 come directly from research, not my imagination.

Also, in Chapter 8 we learn about Etta Caulfield, a woman who, if not for it being Halloween, would have been arrested for wearing slacks. That probably sounds ridiculous to you, as it was to so many women back in the 1920s, but there actually was a law, though disregarded by most, against women wearing trousers. When you read that scene, you may have thought I'd made it up. I didn't! It wasn't until 1923 that the US Attorney General declared it was okay for women to wear slacks in public.

As a warning, the Pyrex percolator Lucy uses to make coffee, and which brings back lovely memories to me, is the only Pyrex that is meant to be used on top of the stove. More modern Pyrex appliances are not stove-top safe.

Recently, I've read on social media that women were not allowed to have their own bank accounts until 1970. I personally know that isn't true, but for the sake of my novel, I did some extra research on the subject because Lucy, in the 1920s, has her own bank account. Here's an interesting article busting the myth:

https://femmefrugality.com/myth-busting-womens-banking/

Although The American Plan, mentioned in chapter 27, is not widely known, and shocking for many readers who might think I made it up, here is a quote from Scott W. Stern's book, *The Trials of Nina McCall*, which he quoted from another source and can be found in the "notes to pages" in his book –

for much of the twentieth century, tens, probably hundreds of thousands of American women were detained and subjected to invasive examinations for sexually transmitted infections . . . These women were imprisoned in jails, "detention houses," or "reformatories" – often with due process – and there treated with painful and ineffective remedies, such as injections of mercury . . .

All references to the Plan come from Stern's book as well as these websites:

https://www.mcgill.ca/oss/article/history/american-plan-win-world-war-ii-incarcerate-promiscuous-women#:~:text=The%20American%20Plan%20was%20a,targeting%20and%20persecuting%20innocent%20women.and

https://www.history.com/news/chamberlain-kahn-act-std-venereal-disease-imprisonment-women

https://daily.jstor.org/when-america-incarcerated-promiscuous-women/

https://newrepublic.com/article/148493/forgotten-war-women

Now for some baseball facts that I played with. In Chapter 42, I have Will listening to the Yankee game on the radio when rookie Mickey Mantle hit his first home run in the Major Leagues. That game was actually played on Tuesday, May 1, 1951, but Anna was working that day so, for this story, I had to make it a Saturday. Since I always have baseball in my books and this is a historical event for Yankee fans – especially Mickey Mantle fans – I wanted you all to know that it's not a mistake, it's for the sake of the story. I hope Yankee fans will excuse me.

Art museum aficionados might question my having Renoir's "Girl with a Watering Can" in the Metropolitan Museum of Art in Chapter 47. At the time of this writing, the painting is in the National Gallery of Art in Washington, DC. It may always have been there yet I have a memory of seeing it in New York at the Met with my mother when I was a young teen. We bought a print of the painting in the gift shop and it hung on my bedroom wall for years. I wish I knew where it was now.

Again for the sake of the story, and something I hope you appreciate, we learn in Chapter 57 that Lucy opened her home as a shelter for abused women. In actuality, shelters were not opened until 1964. The first shelter for battered women in Pasadena, California, known as Haven House, was sponsored by Al-Anon. As a grassroots movement these efforts spread quickly across the country, growing to over 250 shelters by 1979. Some 700 shelters were serving 91,000 women and 131,000 children by 1983. Although not a battered woman, Lucy felt she was abused, and I imagined her creating a safe space for other women. Book clubs might have some great discussions on why she did.

Thanks so much for reading *Abandoning the Script*.

Acknowledgments

Now it's time for me to publicly thank all the people who helped make this story into the book you're holding in your hands. I've never been a fan of the term "it takes a village," yet the wording is spot on. From my defunct Florida writers group who, early on, helped me make Lucy into, I hope, a sympathetic character, to my writing partners and beta readers Jane Loeb Rubin, Wendy Rossi, and Grace Sammon – you've each helped make this a better book. Grace deserves a special thanks for riding shotgun with me on *Abandoning the Script* from the first nugget to the first typed word all the way to The End and beyond.

There are many people who, in confidence, shared their stories with me helping to genuinely create Lucy and Anna. I appreciate your honesty and honor your anonymity.

Several others also helped with my research on so many topics that found their way into my story and characters. A huge thanks goes to Nancy Fagan, Dr. Carol Peyser, Fiona Davis, Susan Bob, Ellie Weisholtz, Bunni Mendelsohn, and Dan Schlossberg for spending time with me sharing your experiences and expertise. Judy Zell and Lisa Montenarro, thank you for creating the plays, including their titles, that Lucy performs in. It was tons of fun using your ideas and naming you as the playwriters. Thanks also goes out to Marsha Thaler for, over tea one afternoon, showing me her earrings that became the jewelry in this story. I changed the stones but the Gibson Girl remains the same. It's very special having my readers involved in my story making.

Pamela Taylor, my editor extraordinaire, who never seems to tire of me asking questions, deserves an enormous thank you. It's been wonderful traveling this writing journey with you on four books. I look forward to working together on more.

To Reagan Rothe and the entire Black Rose Writing team, thank you so much for having faith in my stories and making my dream come true.

And to my husband, Sam Rosen, thanks for understanding the quiet I need when I'm "in my room" and for being my biggest cheerleader – and for all the help you gave me on the courtroom scenes in the book. Any mistakes are all mine.

A book isn't a book without readers. I hold you all in my heart. You're the reason I write. Thank you!

Book Club Discussion Questions

I adore meeting with book clubs, whether virtually or in-person, and I'd love to be invited to yours. We'll have fun chatting about everything that drew me to writing Abandoning the Script, why I gave the characters their names and, especially, how I chose the earrings so prominent in the story. Whether we're together or you're sitting sipping tea or wine with longtime friends, here are some questions I've created for you to discuss with your book club. Have fun digging in.

Lucy makes the heartbreaking decision to leave her child behind. Do you believe she acted out of selfishness, courage, or both?

Lucy believes her daughter is better off without her. How do you interpret that belief? Does it change your perception of motherhood and sacrifice?

Anna's entire identity is shaken when she discovers the truth about her mother. In what ways does her journey parallel her mother's?

Rather than judging Charles, can you justify his actions in relation to his past and the culture of the times?

Mama Brandt begins as a woman rooted in convention and ends as someone full of empathy. How does she embody both traditional and progressive ideals of womanhood?

Was the family's decision to keep the truth from Anna justifiable?

Florence is a quiet character in the novel until the epilogue. Why do you think the author added her voice to the mix? If you were in Florence's place, would you offer the same invitation?

Although we don't see Helen or Crystal wearing the unique earrings Helen's father made for the girls 'sixteenth birthdays, Lucy wears her pair for many years. Do you think the earrings mean more to Lucy? Why, and does the meaning of the earrings change from the beginning of the novel to the end?

The theme "blood is not all that makes a family" runs through this story. Do nurturing and truth outweigh biological ties? How is this reflected in the relationships between the women in the book?

The novel distinguishes between secrets and lies. Mama Brandt keeps secrets, but does she lie? Lucy does both. Think of all the characters with their secrets and/or lies. In your opinion, which is more damaging in this story – and in life?

The early 20th century placed strict expectations on women's roles as wives and mothers. How do the actions of the women in the novel reflect the pressures and possibilities of their era?

Thinking specifically of the years covered in the novel, how did societal limitations influence decisions women made about love, career, and motherhood? Do you see any parallels in today's world?

For fun, pretend you are the author writing a sequel to this novel. What kind of closure or healing do you imagine for each woman?

If you could ask any character one question, who would it be, and what question would you ask?

Which woman's journey resonates with you the most? Why?

About the Author

Fitness professional turned novelist Linda Rosen, after living most of her life in New Jersey, now lives with her husband in sunny Florida happily wearing sandals all year long. She is a member of the Women's Fiction Writers Association and co-founder of the South Florida chapter of the Women's National Book Association where she holds the position of VP of Programming. In addition, Linda is on the board of Trails of Delray, her local chapter of the Brandeis National Committee, and an administrator of the 5K+ member Facebook Group Bookish Road Trip and editor of their newsletter, *Wanderlust.* When she's not writing you'll find Linda playing pickleball, swimming, or reading with her feet in the sand. Follow her at www.linda-rosen.com.

Other Titles by Linda Rosen

Note from Linda Rosen

Word-of-mouth is crucial for any author to succeed. If you enjoyed *Abandoning the Script*, please leave a review online—anywhere you are able. Even if it's just a sentence or two. It would make all the difference and would be very much appreciated.

Thanks!
Linda Rosen

We hope you enjoyed reading this title from:

www.blackrosewriting.com

Subscribe to our mailing list – *The Rosevine* – and receive **FREE** books, daily deals, and stay current with news about upcoming releases and our hottest authors.
Scan the QR code below to sign up.

Already a subscriber? Please accept a sincere thank you for being a fan of Black Rose Writing authors.

View other Black Rose Writing titles at
www.blackrosewriting.com/books and use promo code
PRINT to receive a **20% discount** when purchasing.